KILLING GAME

RISHI'S WISH: PARTS I-III

C.M. MARTENS

MORE FROM C.M. MARTENS

Rishi's Wish:

Book 1; Parts I-III: Killing Game

Book 2; Parts IV-VII: We Are Forever

Book 3; Parts VIII-IX: Wish's Curse

Book .5: TEN-ZERO-NINE

Book 4; Parts X-XI: Born to Die

Book 5; Part XII: The End of Dying

MAGIC FADE

-a YA-NA crossover fantasy adventure

with hints of romance-

In the Fade (out now)

Undone (coming soon)

GET TEN-ZERO-NINE FREE

DOWNLOAD THE TERRIFYING PREQUEL TODAY

Some things you can't take back.

All Steve wanted was to find the balls to tell the girl of his dreams how he felt.
And he finally had.
Today was that day. A day engineered with no distractions. A day for just the two of them. No roommates. No cowardice. No second-guessing the friendship they'd built over the last year wasn't more.
Today was the day his hellish existence would move into the light.

Snatched away by four simple words, Steve's day turns dark. From one second to the next, the future he meant to take into his hands turns into a speeding train bearing down on him. Unable to change the fate that forces him to betray his love, he succumbs to the circumstances that long ensnared him.

No longer his friend, simply subject 10-0-9, he watches her suffer the procedure none has survived.

When she wakes, when she finally comes to, the first to survive, Steve wants to take it all back. The nightmare of hoping she survived was nothing compared to this.

To all those unsure:
Keep at it.

PART 1

She imagined it was like getting hit by a freight train. In that nano-second before thoughts vanished, as pain flared, she wondered just how strong she'd become that a train hadn't killed her on impact.

But there were no trains here. No tracks, used or abandoned, that ran through this part of town.

Of course, that piece of trivia occurred to her later. In the moment that pain shot through her and her head throbbed in tandem with a racing heart that threatened to render her unconscious, there was no room for thought. If not for the snarling of some crazed animal on the periphery of her senses, she might have considered the damp earth of the ditch the perfect spot for a rehabilitating nap.

There was as much sense for the snarls as there was for a train, so the observation of a predatory animal so close, and highly annoyed, seemed important. This thing, this sound, this train-that-could-not-be-a-train was significant to what was happening, and even more so to what would happen.

This future problem, the *would* and *could* of it all, pushed her to her knees. The sting of the brush bit her palms, enflamed the hurts of the initial tumble. It was dark, though a full moon was kind enough to reach silvery fingers out to illuminate the confusion that surrounded her.

Not a train, but some version of a boy that could only have come from some *B*-movie production set. Dirt-caked skin, tattered clothes torn, and eyes set into a sunken skull was not easier to interpret than a train or a large animal. No one looked like that, just like there were no train lines here or large predators that hunted full-grown humans.

The spitting rage of the boy pulled adrenaline from her in a rush that washed away her pain, her confusion, and her mounting terror. There was no time for any of it. There was only survival as a second attack mimicked the first, and explained everything. There was never a train. There was only this rabid humanoid finding a lone traveler on the back roads of a nowhere town. At this time of night, only Dee was still awake, drawn to the night in a way she could never explain.

-Guess we should have made good on our promise not to go out so late.-

Her inner voice, the nagging vocalization that nettled every problem, large or small, burned through her adrenalized focus. Another part of her mind cursed at it, shut it down as she braced, rolling and falling away when the creature leaped once more.

The miss of its second attack exhilarated Dee, but her celebration was short-lived when no pause preempted a third attack. She had only enough time to throw her arms in front of her face in a vain attempt to defend herself. Like offering up a bone to a mad dog, the creature drove fangs too unreal to be human, too real to be some movie set cast-off, into her forearm.

Agony washed over her, yet some layer of primal instinct held, kept her struggling until she kicked it away. The sound of forearm bones shattering, of flesh-tearing, would add music to already layered nightmares. But at that moment, it was the motivation that kept her from death.

Her strike sent it away. It landed with a grunt of expelled air, and this time, it did not come back for more. Instead, it took off in a blur of speed. A quarter-second hesitation was all the time Dee needed to figure she was the one who should take this thing out before it hurt someone else.

Miles later, she rounded the bend, flashed through the parking lot, and slowed just a half-step at what loomed ahead. Stretched before her, the epithets of the dead glistened like lanterns from the reflected moonlight. The serenity of the view coaxed her past the locked gate which she leaped in a feat that barely scraped the ability of her heightened dexterity.

It was when her feet hit the graveled drive over the threshold that she paused to consider just what the hell she was doing.

The cliché of the cemetery was another detail she would consider later. Now, the pain of her arm threatened to overwhelm her senses, her knees weakening under her full-body ache. Now that she'd stopped running the pain in her swelled.

-*What are you doing?*-

Centered in her right arm, the throbbing of her injuries pulled at her, her weight multiplied under fading adrenaline and the image of a boy-that-was-not-a-boy flashing fangs and violence.

What *was* she doing there? Did she really think she should be the one ridding the world of—whatever *it* was?

Expression set against the pain, she squared her shoulders, gasping when the small movement sent shocks of torture through her arm. She clutched it to her, wrapping the battered appendage over her stomach, keeping it there with her less-pained arm while blood that had slipped from her for the past few miles cascaded in a steadier stream.

It was a lot of blood. Even as she tried to focus on what lay ahead, on the mission she'd assigned herself before she could go home and sleep for days, she couldn't keep this thought from tugging at her.

So much blood.

This voice was not the naggy, pushy one. Much less annoying

and more logical, this voice she should consider paying attention to.

Except for the thing that could hurt someone else. The thing she was the only one in a position to do anything about.

Resigned, she stepped forward. First aid could wait. It had to wait.

-Why does your position mean you are the one to deal with this?-

There was the snark she couldn't seem to lock away.

Sucking her lips, she contained her frustrated answer that would have been something like: *And who* would *the right person be?* But an argument with herself wouldn't draw helpful conclusions. A conversation with herself might not even be healthy for her deteriorating state of mind.

Still, the annoyance the question raised pierced the veil of surrealism surrounding her while drowning out the terror that built in the back of her mind, threatening to bring her to her knees.

Staring into the hills of flowing graves, she allowed consideration for her decision to be here take center in her mind. Chasing the creature had stalled the need to think. Even in this quiet wake of the chase, she struggled with the reality of what had happened —what *was* happening. It had been unimportant in the attack and during the pursuit. Now, it might just save her life to reflect on what it was she'd given chase.

She had no name for it. At least, no name she was willing to say out loud. Saying it out loud meant forcing herself to consider that she really might be crazy. Or, that reality was much different than she believed.

Neither seemed like the better alternative.

Regardless, here she stood, at the threshold of a graveyard, in the middle of the night, short hair tossed like some mad scientist as she bled from a gash that ran from wrist to elbow, body aching like she'd wrestled a speeding train.

-Not to sound like a broken record, but if we'd kept our promise and just stayed in——-

The panic of what lay in front of her overrode the guilt this idea sparked.

Still, as bizarre as this all was, something about it tugged at hidden memories. Something about the thing she chased. Something about the night and blood and pain and—she just couldn't quite put it all together.

A year ago, she'd been attacked, forced to crawl home after years of running. She couldn't be sure this *boy* hidden among the tombstones was the same thing. She couldn't be sure that night hadn't been some insane nightmare, but in the face of the present, the chances seemed great that it all had been real.

-How many creatures of the night do you think there are?-

She ignored the question, understanding the absurdity in thinking there was more than one kind of scary, yet on the same train of logic if there was one, why couldn't there be many?

-Unless there are none, and you really are insane.-

Triggered by these words, her blue eyes no longer saw the cemetery stretched before her. Instead, she saw the inferno that had taken the house in the woods she had no memory of going to; only the vague memory of leaving, knowing she'd somehow escaped the death that had taken her friends. The sharp smell of chemicals, the brightness of the blaze surrounded by an overwhelming confusion wrapped her senses in the recall.

With considerable effort, she shook the images from her mind to force leaden feet forward. First this, then handle her fading sanity.

After a handful of steps, she stopped. With one arm useless, and no experience with fighting, she wasn't sure what her next move should be. Maybe lure the thing home so she could show Mike?

-What? Trap it in the basement?-

It was a stupid idea, but how could she prove it was real? Proving she was not out of her mind seemed as crucial to her as surviving. Maybe more.

-Take a picture?-

She stifled a burst of laughter at the simplicity of it.

An ironic chuckle followed when she realized her phone was missing. Likely back where she'd been tackled, her mind conjured an image of it lost forever in the thick brush. Another image, this one of a sweatshirt with pockets that zipped things like phones safely away laying uselessly on her bed brought her teeth together in a frustrated clench.

-I'm sure fitness clothing designers had assault-and-battery in mind as key design points.-

Annoyed by her bad luck, she found no humor in her head's wit.

More bad luck brought on by ineptitude triggered the creature to attack at that moment.

Driven by instinct, she ducked and rolled. The creature flew over her while she writhed in pain, never taking her eyes from the thing that remembered its desire to kill her. It landed in a graceful coil that brought it back to its feet while she flopped and struggled to find her footing. Searing pain from incurred injuries brought spots across her vision.

-You are so going to die.-

Teeth clenched against the silent announcement, she forced her legs to push her from the ground. Committed to engaging it, she squared towards it, but it ran off. A zig-zagging gait made attempts to trace its path impossible in the shadows of the tall hills. Instead of wanting to fight her, it seemed more eager to play.

-A game? Cat and Mouse? Who's who?-

She ignored the voice's implication. *She* was the one chasing here, making *her* the cat.

-Making this game cat and cat? Or cat and bigger cat?-

She ignored her self-mocking, eyes studying the lay of the land as if something in the topography would give her some insight into what to do. Unable to maintain a visual of the creature, she was wary of moving forward. Turning to exit seemed an equally bad idea. It had snuck up on her while she was looking for it. Turning away seemed a sure way to get dead.

Staring ahead, frozen with indecision, she tried to remember the reason she thought this chase was a good idea to begin with. This thing could kill her, and she had no skill to ensure it didn't succeed.

Pure instinct had compelled her to follow it. At a dead sprint, she'd pursued without thought. Reason hadn't returned until she'd stopped inside the cemetery.

-What? Don't think your heightened strength and speed is enough to take it head-to-head?-

More to run from the voice in her head than that she had formulated a plan, she took a step forward, then another, eyes frantic to penetrate the too-shadowed area.

Each unhindered step instilled a layer of confidence. As a blanket of surrealism wrapped her thoughts, pushing thoughts of pain and death to darkness, she allowed the reminder of what she'd become to strengthen her resolve. Holding on to this, she let this moment of empowerment take a turn at manipulating reality.

Maybe she *could* take this thing.

Movement farther in the cemetery, ahead and to the left, caught her attention. The arms of a concrete angel beckoned her forward, welcoming her towards victory. Believing this a sign that her chase was motivated by some redeeming cause rather than misguided instinct, she focused her attention on that spot.

She crept through the shadows, intent on surprising her prey, but when she arrived, there was nothing to find. She stared stupidly at the neatly tended plot, grass inked black by night.

Continuing to crouch, maintaining silence, she listened as she'd never listened before.

-You're not very good at this.-

A car at the far entrance distracted her attention, the crunch of tires telling of its turn onto the unpaved paths that curved through the cemetery.

Her attention was taken from this new problem when the old's rushing force met her in another surprise strike. The creature's enjoyment of tackling her was pissing her off. Whatever this game was, it needed to end.

Its body slamming into hers brought an exclamation of air from her lungs. Hissing growls sent panicked chills across her skin even as she fought to get her arms free from an iron-like hug.

Attempting to rip her arms from their trap only served to instill more carnage on her already battered body. The shredded skin of her damaged arm pulled away, so she wasn't sure what might be left to hold it together.

The sharpness of the pain overrode all thought, and she tightened her muscles in a body-sized cringe before going limp in defeat.

-Really? Just go fetal and hope it gets bored?-

Adrenaline surge overrode the pain of her many injuries, and she was suddenly free, tossing the creature away with a push of legs. Something wet ran down her face. Shutting off the part of her brain that wondered if the beast had managed to take a bite out of her for after she survived, she focused on completing her getaway.

Rolling to its feet in a display of agility that left her jealous, the two squared off, both panting as they stared each other down.

She noted the layer of grime covering it, hiding any clue to what its original skin color had been. Its similarly filth-dyed hair was matted so tightly to its scalp, only thin wisps protruding from the knot allowed her to tell there was hair there at all. But mostly, it was in the eyes, something just off about its facial structure that defined the thing as not human. Did its eyes bulge just too much? Was its brow-line retracted just so that the forehead sloped too sharply? Were its limbs elongated beyond their normal reach?

Whether one of these or all of them, it was too subtle to pin down in her current distress.

The creature pounced.

Rather than get out of its way, her great idea was to take it on.

-So much for your getaway.-

Insides jarred by the clash of bodies, she found the air she'd regained pushed back out of her. They were motionless, pushing against each other in a test of wills.

The distraction of keeping her skin from its jaws was enough of a disadvantage that she lost her forward momentum. She fell backward, forearms crossed against the creature's chest to keep it from making a meal of her face.

More pain exploded through her as her body slammed into the grass. Whether this pain was from a fresh wound, or old, she hoped to survive to find out.

-*This seems familiar.*-

Hoping another kick would save her, she leveraged her legs beneath her, managing to get one in a position to push out at the thing snapping at her face. Her arms burned with the effort to keep its mouth from fastening on her, while pain threatened to send her into unconsciousness.

She threw all her will behind that one-legged kick.

Free, she scrambled onto her stomach, pulling herself through the damp grounds of the graveyard in a half-crawl, half face-shimmy. She didn't make it far before the boy-that-was-no-longer-a-boy caught her leg.

Groping in desperation, her hand settled on a piece of broken tombstone. It was all she had to fend off the snarling vestige intent on ending her life. With a secure grip, it dragged her towards it. She swung...

-*You really are going to die.*-

...feeling the bone of its head cave under the mass of the stone. The snapping sound of the impact echoed in her stomach, sending her senses to war. Willing herself not to throw-up, she maintained a tight grip on the makeshift weapon, swinging for a second blow.

Another snap, this time from a facial crack, and she was free. Scrambling on a hand and knees until she could get to her feet, she tripped on steps that propelled her faster than her balance could maintain.

Stumbling, she sensed the creature line up for another leap. In the recesses of her brain, she wondered how she could still be conscious after so much blood-loss, while a more primal part of her maintained control of her physical movements. This instinct paid more attention to the wrought-iron fencing buried in a season of overgrowth than on her encroaching death. This instinct allowed her to grab the new weapon, rise, and spin to meet the next assault.

As if choreographed, the two met, becoming one as the metal post pierced through the creature's body. Its face shrieked in surprised defeat while its fangs clamped open and closed mere inches from her face. Letting go, she kicked it away before she, too, dropped to the ground.

Out of danger, the emotional torrent adrenaline had kept at bay flooded over her, manifesting as silent tears. Already on her knees, she heaved the contents of her stomach into the damp grass.

Gasping from both physical and mental trauma, she rolled away. With cheek pressed to the damp earth, her eyes fluttered closed.

Darkness took her.

Hamal had had no trouble finding her and even less tailing her over the last few days; his job made simple since the girl rarely left the house.

Whoever she was, she was clueless that anyone had any interest in her. No security other than a lock on her door. No awareness of her surroundings as she left each night to trek her jogging path through town. He didn't worry that anyone would catch him snooping around, especially the girl he watched.

Possibly the most boring person he'd ever seen, he still had no information to suggest she was worth this much trouble to anyone, especially to one as powerful as the one who'd sent him.

Desiree Galen. Small-town girl, living in a degraded upstate town, complete with the small-town life.

As far as Hamal was concerned, Adam's Center, New York, was the center of Hell. If Hell was the most mundane place one could think of, anyway.

Her only friend, a Mike Nolan, hung around for reasons Hamal had yet discerned. Mike's work took him out of town more than he was ever there, but he'd never officially relocated. A romantic relationship between the two would have explained things, but Hamal had found no evidence they were anything but good friends.

Hamal smirked. *Idiot.* He couldn't understand the use of a female friend, especially not one who kept him living in a place like this. Hanging around a place like this for *anyone* was senseless.

The only information he had managed to collect was that Mike called Desiree, Dee. Hamal had made a notation of this, the words close to slicing through the paper from his fervent tracing of the note in an outlet for his obsessive boredom. That, and a detailed map of both her house and Mike's, along with their surrounding properties, was all he'd been able to add to her file.

He laughed to himself at the ridiculousness of the assignment. Didn't they have drones and satellites for surveillance jobs like this? Way below his pay-grade, Hamal had only agreed to take it because Zi had personally asked.

As Dee came jogging around the corner of the night darkened street, a fact about her flashed through his mind. A fact that could be interesting. A fact that could be nothing. A fact that ate at his pride so he couldn't just forget it.

He drummed his fingers against the leather steering wheel of his luxury SUV, annoyance at her outperformance of him coming through in this tick of motion. Nothing in her file suggested she was anything other than some random girl, but the fact that her endurance far outreached his own ate at him. Finding this out on his first night when he'd failed to tail her festered in his mind.

He sighed, a huff of air that expressed his annoyance at a

mission barely started. Not that anyone was monitoring his mood, or would care if they were, but it made him feel just a little better.

To circumvent this problem of tracking her through town, he'd set up cameras along the girl's jogging route, tuned to give him live-feed of her progress from her front door, through her journey, and back again. His gamble that she traveled the same path each night had paid in full, which helped heal his wounded ego.

Parked in the center of this course, between the sparsely placed streetlights, he waited. In a town like this, everyone was sure to know everyone else, so his SUV would look suspicious. Proactively, he had stopped by a few of the local haunts to drop hints that he was in town doing some work. If anyone noticed him, he'd sown the seeds of explanation. Not that she would hear any town gossip. As far as he could tell, she had no contact with anyone other than Mike.

He'd noted this with more heavily traced marks in her file.

As she moved closer to his position, he relaxed into the bucket seat, ensuring his obscurity in shadow. As unlikely as it was, there was always the chance she would notice him sitting there. Whether or not she recognized his truck as out of place, someone hanging out in the middle of the night in their vehicle would draw attention.

The portable screen he used to view the camera's video sat in the seat next to him. Tented by a thick, dark cloth to keep the viewer's light from reflecting to the exterior of the vehicle was something else that might garner a look.

He held his breath.

When his presence went unnoticed, he let out the held air, then glanced at the screen to watch her turn the corner behind him.

Anticipating another eventless night, he picked up her file from the center console to keep his hands busy. As many times as he'd been through it, he still hoped some nuance of information would clue him into what he was doing there. These late-night jogs were weird, but they were nothing that required the level of attention his presence indicated. Especially nothing that explained the secrecy stressed around him being there.

Flipping the folder open, he stared at her picture. Short, dark hair framed a nice face. Pretty even. Her cerulean eyes held sadness as she looked away from the photographer to some faraway point.

Eyes flickering from her file to the monitor, he noted nothing of interest. Settling more comfortably, he dragged the file onto his lap.

Five-foot six. One hundred forty-five pounds. Athletic. Hair cut in a sort of naturally tousled look, though it had grown out a bit since the picture was taken. Dropped out of college after her father died at the end of her sophomore year. An only child, she'd inherited everything. However, she had turned the operation of her father's company over to Mike, who'd expanded the very profitable construction firm into consulting as well.

Mike's head for finance was the reason for Desiree's growing accounts. She was worth over one-hundred million dollars. From what her file told Hamal, she didn't use much of it. The house was paid off. She had no extra-curricular activities and rarely traveled. The occasional night out with Mike, which he usually paid for, was the only time she spent money on anything outside utility bills and groceries. Running shoes seemed to be the only thing she splurged on with any consistency.

What was more strange, though accountable to grief, was that as soon as the papers were signed that gave up responsibility for her property to Mike, she'd dropped off the grid. For four years, she seemed to vanish, never touching her father's money.

Hamal knew it was in this unaccounted history that he'd find the answers to why he was here. If only he were allowed to approach her, Hamal was sure he'd get all the answers he needed. He had no doubt she would be putty in his hands. If not for the parameters that forbade him from making contact, he'd be talking with her right now. Possibly between the sheets of her king-sized bed.

He shook that thought away. If the assignment had come from anyone else, Hamal would have ignored the decree and reached out to her. As hard as his curiosity pulled at him to figure out the mystery, he wouldn't cross that one. Not even for this.

Instead, he was left to watch, wondering who this girl was and how she might have garnered the attention of one who pulled so many strings.

His eyes moved back to track her progress on the monitor while he leaned over to change the infrared view to night-vision. The red, blue, and green of the screen turned to a green-tinged world where her form shone brightly against the background of the night.

He'd noted the wireless earbuds in her ears as she'd passed and couldn't help but wonder, from a strictly professional point-of-view, how she could deal with running at night after cutting off her strongest working sense. What if something came at her? There was no way she could see that well in the night that she should risk blunting her sense of hearing.

Maybe the girl had a death-wish.

He straightened in his seat.

If she did have a death-wish and something happened to grant that wish was he supposed to stand by and document what happened? His directives were clear; he was here merely to observe. But should he interfere in this case?

Not for the first time since arriving, he fumbled with his phone. Another parameter had been not to make contact with home-base under any circumstances.

He'd never been on such a troubling case. How could such a dull girl be the focus of such a confusing mission?

These were questions above his pay-grade. If he was here merely to observe, then observe was all he would do. If the girl wanted to die, then maybe that was all he was supposed to find out.

Slapping the thin file closed, he tossed it aside and nestled back into the seat, wishing he hadn't already finished his coffee.

Lids heavy with boredom, he almost missed the blur of movement that cut across the screen. He jolted forward to manipulate the video to rewatch what happened.

Had she just been attacked?

He watched the video in slo-mo to be sure.

Completely unprepared, the second hit to his ego since arriving, he leaped from the vehicle. Sprinting, shotgun in one-hand, night-vision goggles in the other, he made his way to where his mark was most assuredly dead.

He hated being right, especially when he hadn't expected to be *this* right.

The thing that had ambushed his mark was the last thing he'd thought to see turn up as a player. If he'd had more time to wonder about the nature of its appearance, he might have re-thought his forward pace. There were things he was good at, and there were things above the ability of his DNA to accommodate. What had attacked Dee was one of those things he wasn't sure he'd be able to help with.

Accustomed to looking for the barest of clues, Hamal saw the phone lying in the ditch, right alongside the scuff marks and battered grass that told of the struggle the pair had shared before racing off into the night.

He gazed down the path the two had taken, curiosity peaked that she had chased it. He allowed the fact that she lived through the attack to filter quietly in the back of his head as other questions raised by the event took precedent, the most critical being: if Zi had known the players involved, would he have sent Hamal? This was a job for someone much more durable than Zi's favorite human pet.

More questions raced through Hamal's head as he followed the trail of blood, knowing he'd arrive too late to be of any use. There was too much blood for her to last long.

He knew the speed of the thing that had attacked, but struggled to correlate her speed with that inhuman pace, despite every clue pointing to that fact. If she'd been a Soldier, Zi would have known. If she were another form of Castoff, someone would have been aware of her. They wouldn't have left her to her own devices. She wouldn't be living this benign existence watched by someone like him.

Right?

Forgetting the questions he couldn't answer, he focused on the sign ahead: *King's Quarry Cemetery*. Laughing to himself, he couldn't help look around to see if someone was setting him up for some elaborate joke. A cemetery was where the fight ended? C'mon!

The sound of bodies colliding brought his attention from his possible candid camera debut. She was alive *and* fighting it?

Hiding in the shadows of the sparse groupings of trees, he watched, helpless, as Dee fell to her knees while the creature lined up for a final attack behind her. A part of him wanted to move forward, but he knew there was no way he'd arrive in time to save her, even if he thought the intercession might help or be allowed. When she pulled a shaft of metal fencing from the brush, turning in time to impale the creature's final attempt at taking her life, his mouth fell to his knees.

All he'd seen over the last few miles suggested she was capable of this. That he hadn't found her dead body along the way was telling enough, but his brain struggled to align the dull girl he'd been tailing on previous nights with this new persona more akin to the creature who'd attacked her. Whatever the answers, why he'd been sent to watch her was finally clear.

This new perspective on the mission sparked an excitement he hadn't felt in a long time. As he continued to watch, his mind whirled with possibilities and what they meant for the true nature of his mark.

This excitement tempered when the girl fell to her knees, followed by her throwing up violently. When the sounds of retching faded, Dee seemed to think about pushing herself to her feet; instead collapsing to her side. Finding something to be excited about, only to lose it so soon was enough to send him forward.

"Shit. Shit. Shit." The word was his mantra as he made his way to her. Bypassing the gate took little concentration. Finding cover under a full-moon was more difficult.

He knelt next to her, eyes scanning the Revenant that would not be getting up. Its skin was already shrinking in on itself, showing a glimpse of the husk it would become that always reminded him of a mummy he'd seen in a museum when he was a boy. He noted the head wounds that told the story of their fight, impressed she'd bludgeoned the thing as she had. Not near the power of the ones he worked for, these Revenants were still nothing to laugh at. He wasn't sure he could have wounded one in such a manner and he definitely wouldn't have survived the initial ambush.

His ego survived these observations. Matched against any human, he was the best, but when compared to the things that were more, he never tried to compete. He'd seen too many lives end from that kind of pride.

He processed this in a scan of eyes while he knelt next to the one he couldn't lose like this. Not now that he knew more about what she was.

Fingers searched for a pulse at her neck while his eyes scanned the damage done to her body. Her wounds were severe. He'd never guess she could be alive if shown them in another context.

As he continued to check her over, he noticed the blood, moments ago flowing liberally from multiple lacerations, slowing. Her heart-rate, thready and irregular only seconds ago, was a steadier, stronger pulse against his touch.

He took off the night-vision goggles to look at her with his own eyes.

Athletic muscularity was highlighted through tight running pants. A tank top, mostly torn away, showed the athletic bra underneath still intact. Blood seeped at her knees, and there were tears in her thigh, ribs, and most notably, the arm he worried she would never use again, mangled in a way that suggested she should have bled out from the wound long before she made it here.

He winced at the dichotomy of her clean bicep and untouched hand book-casing her forearm. It made the injury seem more traumatic, seeming detached from the rest of her.

She moaned, pulling his attention from cataloging her injuries, eyes wide that she would recover consciousness already.

Who was this girl?

2

Dee was sure she'd heard a voice curse; felt fingers on her neck. When she managed to pull her eyelids apart, there was no one, only the shriveled face that had been her attacker staring at the sky, metal fence-post sticking from its chest.

-What's with that thing looking like a mummy?-

She giggled with delirium at the observation.

Her weight shifted, flooding pain through her, and there was no more laughter. There was no more anything as moving took all her focus.

She managed to get herself to a kneeling position without using her arms. Head hanging to her chest, she paused to gather her will, body fighting her desire to stand. She was one giant hurt. As one fought for attention over the others, another she hadn't even known about rose to take top place. Her right arm was held close to her stomach by the left, and she vaguely remembered the creature using the appendage as a chew toy. The bleeding had stopped, though a fresh current now leaked out of her, spawned by her movements.

It was only through masterful compartmentalization that she

didn't pass out. That and her inner-voice making light of the severe wounds tethered her sanity.

This tether was too thin.

The reality of her staring at her own shattered bone through her own shredded skin slammed into her, bursting through those things that had sheltered her. Her world narrowed to a four-inch space between her hands filling with the contents of her stomach until there was nothing left.

As she continued to dry heave, she remembered the light touch that had brought her back to consciousness, focusing on the sensation to better determine the truth of it. Someone checking her pulse? Had that same someone cursed, thinking they'd found a dead body in the cemetery? What did they think of a mummy lying next to her? Who would even be out at this time of night, and where had they gone?

-Maybe a ghost checking who was disturbing its territory?-

She might have rolled her eyes if she had any control over her movements. Dry heaves continued to wrack her body.

When she regained control of her actions, she leaned back on battered knees, cradling her arm as she panned her surroundings. Seeing nothing out of place, she slowly, gingerly, rose on unsteady legs.

Thoughts of nameless strangers and ghosts left her head when she stepped on a phone lying in the grass—her phone.

Picking it up, she looked at it as if something on its surface might reveal its appearance, too late to be of any use.

Another shaky step forward had her kicking the body of the thing she shouldn't have forgotten. Ignoring its withered form, forbidding questions of the *hows* and *whys* of its posthumous physiological changes, she pondered what to do with it. She couldn't just leave it here, could she? Would someone be able to trace it to her if they found it? And what would they find if they ran tests on it?

Did she even care?

-I'm pretty sure you'd be a lab rat if anyone ever figured out anything about you. Don't leave this body here.-

The idea of someone learning how much of a freak she was brought her attention from the shriveled husk at her feet to the question of how she would get home. Exhaustion pulled at her. So much she was tempted to lay back down in the damp grass. She was miles from Mike's, which was miles closer than her place.

Her head hurt, pounding from blood loss. Chilled to the bone, sure she was using the last of her energy to concentrate on the strangest of problems, she wiped absently at her battered arm. This brought her attention to the fact that it was still trickling blood, and the hand of that arm was numb in a way that even staring at it brought her no sense that it was part of her.

Fighting hysteria, she returned her attention to the corpse at her feet. Her battle with fatigue made it impossible to hold onto more than one thought at a time, so she'd forgotten this issue that needed a solution before she could work on getting home.

Her eyes glanced into the dark landscape again, remembering the lingering touch that had fluttered over her neck, searching for the someone she knew had been here. Had that someone been watching over her? Had this same someone saved her last year from a similar fate?

-No one saved you from this thing. You killed it all by yourself.-

That was true, but it didn't mean no one had helped her before or hadn't been here tonight.

-Like a guardian angel or something?-

The ridicule in her head was thick as she panned the cemetery, tired eyes losing focus among the silvery stones reflecting the moon's light. What should have taken mere seconds kept her standing there far longer. Still, she was sure she'd be able to see if anyone was out there.

E ven knowing there was no way she could find him nestled in the shadows, Hamal slid more securely into darkness. The way her eyes probed the area shouted at his subconscious to be less visible. Her movements were too precise, even in her dazed state, for someone who couldn't see well in the night.

Putting back on the night-vision goggles in preparation to follow her through a canopy of trees to her house, he monitored her movements, barely breathing. He stared wide-eyed when she grabbed a leg of the husk and dragged it the hundred feet to the far side of the grounds where a steep hill dropped to a thicket perfect for hiding a husk no one would come looking for. At her level of blood loss, exhaustion, and simple lack of mass, she shouldn't have been able to drag that much dead weight so casually.

His brain raced through possibilities, both practical and unlikely, that might explain all he'd seen this night from the girl who, less than an hour ago, he hadn't believed was worth his time.

Forcing himself to pay attention, he watched her stare after the fallen corpse, her expressionless face motionless for several minutes. The fact that she was conscious said much about her mental fortitude. He reiterated to himself that she should be dead. The ulnar artery in her wrist was severed in multiple places. It was her blood that had laid such a clear path for him to follow. That she was staring off in a daze shouldn't worry him since she was fatally wounded.

When she lifted her phone from a pocket, he knew it could only be Mike she would call. There was no one else, as far as he'd seen, she could call this late. There was no one else she could call, period.

He couldn't hear her conversation from his position but watched with studious appraisal. When she began her journey out of the graveyard, pace plodding, he followed at a distance.

3

"This better be good." Mike's voice cracked from the hangover of sleep.

She almost laughed, but a lack of energy stopped it fast. "I got a little banged up."

She heard him come fully awake. "A little banged up?"

His tone was accusatory, and she might have flinched if her body had the energy.

"Yeah. I just need a little help." Her tone was apologetic.

She sensed his nodding, so continued, "I'll meet you out back in twenty minutes."

She wasn't sure if he spoke after that. She hung up, not trying to be rude, just forgetting, in her dazed state, to see if he had anything to add. She headed towards Mike's, forcing her pace beyond that of a walk, ready for a bed in a way she'd never known.

When they'd traveled far enough that he was sure there wasn't some location he didn't know about, Hamal advanced to settle into a position he would be able to overhear any conversation. Risking the extra time to pick up his bag from his truck, he was glad he took the chance. The only place for him to spy was from the cover of the treelined property, too far away to hear anything without aid.

Positioning his night vision gear more comfortably over his face, he slid the small shotgun microphone from his pack, eyes scanning the moon-tinted landscape for signs of the injured girl. The fuzzy black material surrounding the four-inch, tube-like device, screwed into a collapsible pole was the perfect color and shape to blend with the shadowed trees surrounding him. Connected to a pair of high-end headphones, he would be able to hear whatever was said more clearly than if he was standing right next to him.

The metallic rattle from a doorknob drew Hamal's attention to the back of the house that juxtaposed the surrounding country with modern urban style. He watched Mike step outside, his thin frame hunched with the vestiges of sleep. Hamal noted the thick towel the man held just as genuine concern replaced his look of sleepy annoyance.

Hamal's gaze followed Mike's as he moved down the few steps of the raised deck to meet Desiree in the grass, wrapping the thick towel he'd brought around her. "Dee, what the hell. You said *a little banged up.*"

She leaned into Mike, allowing a second of connection before stepping out of his grasp to move towards the house. "Guess I'm not crazy."

What did that mean?

From Mike's expression, Hamal knew he understood their meaning too well.

Then they were in the house, cutting Hamal off from any information their conversation might give.

Annoyed he never bugged Mike's place as he had Desiree's, he weighed the risk versus reward of creeping towards the house. As long as they stayed in a room near a window, he'd be able to pick up their conversation without difficulty.

G *uess I'm not crazy.*

She knew the words would hit him like a slap to the face. This entire event would conjure memories from another night, just over a year ago, when she'd curled herself against his front door, blood, whether her own or another's, splattered across her. Mike's expression of unbridled fear from that night was forever etched into her memory.

He hadn't let her out of his sight for weeks.

"No doctors." She'd quickly read what he was thinking from the set of his eyes.

Her statement broke his seething silence. "No doctors? I don't know how you haven't bled out already! I'm taking you to the hospital!"

"Exactly, I haven't bled out. I'm fine. Doctors will only ask questions I can't answer."

Her voice was impassive. She watched Mike's face crease as his mind raced to find an argument to contradict her.

She knew he'd given up when he guided her into the kitchen. He pulled out a chair for her to sit in before moving to the bathroom where he collected towels and hot water, antiseptic cream, and bandages. She trusted her unexplainable healing factor while he pretended it wasn't real.

Dee listened to his rummaging, knowing she'd be able to sleep once he finished mothering her. She knew she needed to give him this time so he would feel better about not taking her to see a doctor. He needed to see she was alright.

Making his way back to the kitchen with a collection of meager first aid tools, Dee sat up, stifling a groan.

She forced a smile, kept her voice even. "Relax. I really am fine. Super exhausted, but fine." A yawn slipped out, before a glance at her arms hanging loosely in her lap brought attention back to the obvious. "Considering."

"Considering it looks like you were mauled by a pack of wolves."

"Yes, considering that." Voice thick with sarcasm, she sat straighter in the chair as Mike went to work on her.

"Always with the jokes. Even like this. Never listen to anybody—"

Desiree let him have his muttering, closing her eyes to lay her head on the back of the chair while Mike patched her up. Neither of them had any experience with first aid that made them adequate to handle cuts and bruises, let alone wounds that would make a trauma surgeon cringe. Still, Mike had seen enough that he wouldn't push the doctor issue. Even if he wouldn't acknowledge it, he wasn't stupid enough to ignore it.

She was *changed*. Even if they wouldn't talk about it, it was real.

A year ago, when she'd come home, propping herself on his front porch half-dead, she'd allowed him to convince her she'd been the victim of a mugging, not the victim of an attack from a creature that only existed in fiction. But he'd seen the injuries she'd sustained. He'd seen the recovery that defied explanation. And now this.

Would he finally allow himself to wake up to the idea that what she claimed was true? Would he finally accept the idea that a *vampire* had attacked her?

She winced from the word, wishing she had another label. But the more she tried to squelch the expression from echoing through her head, the louder it became. It's what she had called it then, though she couldn't remember why. Over time, her memory of what had happened to bring her home had gotten cloudy.

Still, it's what she was calling the thing she'd seen tonight, though, as the strange evening made its thousandth re-run through her head, she wasn't sure if it was an accurate enough description of what had attacked her. Had it tried to drink her blood?

-Was it going for your neck when you put your arm in its mouth?-

Maybe.

H amal lay against the pillows. In the background of the tiny motel room, the television played re-runs of some sitcom. It didn't matter. He wasn't paying attention. His thoughts rushed over what he'd seen in the cemetery and what he'd overheard at Mike's.

Not even he could guarantee coming out alive against the creature she'd run down. He wouldn't have tried to run it down. He wasn't an idiot.

There were so many layers to what the encounter suggested, yet he focused on the surface of it. For now, replaying the image of her pushing the creature away after impaling it on her makeshift weapon was enough. No mere girl could have taken the force of that attack, let alone stabbed it by pulling a piece of wrought iron fencing from the earth.

His mind trailed to all he'd heard, and the little he'd been told directly about Revenants. He'd never heard any roamed free, unaccounted for. That they were allowed to live was a point he didn't understand but was never stupid enough to ask. That one would be so close to a settled population was unheard of, and he was sure he'd never heard of one used as an assassin. Even so, it was the only way he could explain the coincidence of this one running across his mark's path.

Maybe not an assassin. Maybe a test? A creature of supernatural strength without skill was the perfect probe to see just what surprises lay under the surface of the supposed normal girl.

Both scenarios suggested that someone knew about her strange similarities to a very private group. That someone wasn't Zi. Hamal wouldn't be here if he believed she had any of the skills he'd seen from her tonight.

Whoever it was, Hamal would have to be more careful. If another party was watching her, they'd see his interference, and he was too quickly linked to Zibanitu's House. Though his humanity kept him separate, everyone would know what his being here meant. That they couldn't use his presence to issue a formal complaint was what made him such an asset.

Sitting up, he grinned at his reflection, the mystery of why he'd been sent clear.

More at ease from his deductions, Hamal replayed the girl's romp in the graveyard. He conceded that luck had played a large part in her success, but despite trying, he couldn't deny what her success meant. His excitement continued to escalate. He moved to his feet, pacing across the small space, wanting to call in what he'd seen, but knowing it was too early to break his order of no communication.

Another parameter of the mission answered. Communication was an easy thing to intercept, and Zi didn't want any link to this girl getting out.

The next question was whether she was some odd, naturally occurring anomaly, or someone's misplaced creation.

Whatever her origins, she was strong-willed enough to chase down the thing that had ambushed her. That, added to her being a natural fighter, had Hamal itching to begin her training.

4

Fire beckoned her closer even as flames licked painfully over her skin, singeing hair from her face and arms. Still, she continued forward, drawn by a compulsion so strong the fire's sting wasn't enough to turn her away.

Then, a crash; a loud crack of wood splintering before burying her in smoldering fire...

Dee sat up fast, clutching the sweat-soaked sheet to her. As her brain released the last of the dream, she fell back to the pillows.

When Mike left the house that morning, she'd crawled from his guest room, limping gracelessly through the trees like some prison escapee to her own home to settle into her own bed.

Now, late morning, she had every intention of sleeping for a week.

As she was drifting back off, her phone rang, startling her.

Mike's voice was in her ear before she'd found her voice, "You're not here."

It must be lunchtime. Of course, he would waste the break in his day to check on her. She squeezed her eyes shut. She could have at least let him know she'd gone back to her place.

"Yeah. I just wanted my own bed." Her voice, laced with shame, was a pathetic apology.

There was silence on the line for a few seconds, and Dee held her breath, waiting for Mike's hurtful, yet justified, response.

"I don't know how you can stay there." His voice was quiet, distracted.

It was a running conversation that Mike thought Dee should sell the house. He couldn't understand why she surrounded herself with a shrine to the man whose absence continued to shape her life.

"I just like it here."

Mike grunted, a response that said both nothing and everything.

Silence stretched again. Dee closed her eyes, falling back to lay against the pillows, sadness replacing the gladness that her friend wasn't mad at her. He might not be angry but the chasm that existed between them was real. And that was all her fault.

"I'll swing by with dinner, okay? It'll be late, though."

-Why he doesn't just write you off, I'll never understand.-

She made a mental note to make more of an effort to be a better friend. The *best* friend.

-Will you? You're going to give up your nightly jogs? The thing you actually promised you'd stop doing, but kept doing anyway?-

"I'll be here."

Unspoken sentiment kept the line open. Dee held her breath, silently urging him to voice his concerns. Just as the silence grew heavy enough to reach awkward, he hung up after a quick goodbye.

Dee flung her phone down, watching it bounce forward on the bed like a skipping stone before resting near her feet, its silver exterior a shining mark against the charcoal of the bedding.

Her first instinct was to ask how things had gotten so bad between them, but she already knew. She was the reason. Her leaving, taking off for so many years with barely a whisper of where she was or how she was doing, ruined any relationship between them. He'd been like a brother to her. A best friend. And she'd abandoned him, too caught up in her own existential dilemma to worry about anyone else.

She took a deep breath, then another, forcing her mind to a place where getting out of bed possible.

Her naked form moved slowly across the room to the window whose heavy curtains, colored the same charcoal as her comforter, kept the daylight locked away. Blinking at the onslaught of sun, she stared across the front lawn that ran thirty meters to the tree line.

Fall. Last night, she'd been thinking of fall. How the humidity of these last days of summer would thin out into perfect nights. Then, she'd been hit from the side by a creature no amount of wishing could make just a dream. Closing her eyes, she traced the night's events, focusing on details she'd lost as they were happening.

She'd been lucky.

She should be dead.

-You should be dead.-

She didn't like that her inner-voice agreed with her.

Shoving the thought into one of many compartments in her mind, she pushed past the frightening idea and on to another.

Vampire.

-Does vampire really explain what that thing was?-

What should we call it, then?

Great, now she was having full-blown conversations with herself.

She sighed, moving to the connecting bathroom to start a shower, thoughts continuing to repeat last night's adventure.

Were there more of those—whatever they were—nearby? Should she go after them? Protect the town?

-Now chasing after them is a good idea?-

She couldn't ignore the point. On the other hand, if someone got hurt by one of those things, it would be her fault. Did she want that sitting on her conscience?

-It's not your responsibility.-

Letting the spraying mist gather heat, Dee took a seat on the pillow top chest that housed the thick, long towels she loved. She was still so tired, though the throb of her injuries had faded to a dull background pain. Had she healed so much overnight?

Her eyes moved to the gauze on her arm. Having prolonged the moment when she'd have to acknowledge the limb that would never be the same, she now unwound the thick layer of porous material. As the binding slowly came loose, she wasn't sure if she was more worried the last of her wounds would be healed, or wouldn't be. If she were healed, it would mean her powers had increased. But if the wounds weren't healed, could she admit she was in trouble?

Unwrapping the last layer, she flung the tangled material away. Smooth, clean scars zigged and zagged, intersecting around the skin from elbow to wrist. The marks were all that remained of an injury that should have crippled her permanently. Less than a full day for her body to repair shattered bone, torn muscle, and build new skin.

Clenching and unclenching her hand to loosen the tightness she knew should be much worse, then rotating her arm to probe how the muscles reacted, she was ecstatic, and frightened, by her recovery.

Closing her eyes, she took in a shaking breath.

-Let's not get overdramatic. This is a good thing.-

Sure, this was a good thing. Too good. What the hell was she?

-Who cares. You're like a super-hero.-

She'd known about her superior strength, heightened speed, and fantastic agility, but her self-testing had never involved severe injury recovery. She knew she'd heal. She'd gotten other scrapes and sprains before, but never had she thought one night of sleep would knit bone, muscle, and skin back to almost new.

A spike of adrenaline surged through her, so she forgot her exhaustion and the running shower. She sprinted down the stairs and ripped open the front door. Once on the wrap-around porch, she stopped short. Where was she going? There was no one to tell. No one to ask about what was going on. Nowhere to run.

-And you're naked.-

Lifting her face, eyes closed, she allowed the humid rays of the sun to bask her in their nurturing light.

Thankfully, the voice in her head allowed her this quiet moment.

5

D ee picked up her pace as if running from the truth of her thoughts was a real thing.

She'd been running the darkened, vacant streets of this town every night for the past year and until two nights ago she'd never had a problem. It seemed paranoid to stop doing the thing that made her happy after one bad experience.

-Even though it goes directly against your promise to Mike?-

Her speed intensified as the thought proclaimed itself, arguments why her broken word was valid warring against her guilt.

If there were more of those things out here, she needed to know. She needed to stop them before any innocents got hurt.

Of course, this was not a point she mentioned to Mike. Rather than debate her refreshed pledge to him, she'd quickly agreed. She knew he'd chain her up if he had the slightest inkling she might go out to purposefully risk her neck, even if her reasons were altruistic. He still didn't quite believe her, but he couldn't avoid the fact that an attack had happened. While the attack didn't prove the existence of a supernatural world, her amazing healing attributes forced questions she knew he'd rather avoid. They were questions she'd rather avoid.

She'd spent the day after the attack sitting around, debating this single thing, trying to find the argument that would let her make good on her promise. But she kept coming back to the same conclusion: if someone got hurt, the guilt of it would be more than she could bear.

So, here she was. Running through the darkened, wooded landscape despite having said it was something she'd cease.

Distracted by a tingling in the back of her skull that had slowly grown over the last few minutes, she slowed her pace. Like a word on the tip of her tongue, the semi-familiar feeling was just outside memory. Had she felt this the other night just before she hit the ground?

-*There!*-

There.

She dropped just in time for the attacker to sail over her. She stared stupidly as the creature refocused on its mark, launching itself back at her. Bracing herself, Dee managed to use its momentum against it, throwing it past her into the woods that surrounded the country road.

As if detached from herself, not sure what to do, Dee followed its path with her eyes, then peered into the dark in anticipation of a third attack. Feral hissing pinpointed the creature's location, and her eyes snapped to its face.

Despite the shadows, the night whose moon was shrouded in clouds, she noted its hateful stare. Its ferocity spiked the fear riding her body, freezing her movements. When the thing spoke, the hair on her body stood on end.

"He thinks it is you, but all I see is a girl. He wastes his time."

Shocked by the words, too surprised to hear their meaning, Dee stood transfixed as the creature prepared to launch itself again.

Quietly, as if locked in some backroom in her mind, Dee was aware of a voice suggesting she pay attention to what was coming, but her brain was processing everything in a detached slow-motion, even as the rest of the world continued at its break-neck speed.

He? What he? Who?

Could she convince the creature to have a conversation with her? Would it tell her what was going on?

Crunching footsteps from the road brought her attention back to her surroundings. Her turn to see what else had shown up halted when the creature used its moment of distraction to rush. The sound of steps stopped, closely followed by a loud blast that pushed her attacker to the side. Whipping her head towards the sound, Dee saw that the explosion had come from some guy's shotgun.

-What the hell?-

Dee turned her full attention to the newcomer, eyes flashing upward as movement in the trees gave away the position of a second creature dropping behind him.

The man turned quickly and fired another loud blast that echoed through the woods as this second body found its head scattered among the leaves.

The gore of the exploding face set off her gag reflex. Before she could give in to the instinct to throw-up, the first assailant's mad rush drew her back to the fight. Injured, but not out, the creature dove for the newcomer whose focus remained on the second attacker.

Dee lunged, tackling it before it could reach him, rolling in the earthy bramble to find herself straddled by the thing that, it was clear now, had once been a woman. Her long, thinning hair was a strangle of wispy threads that only emphasized the minor changes in her face. Her pupils dilated to take over her irises and her teeth reached too far from her gums, pushing out her lips. Her fingers seemed just too long. And most notably, the look on her face that spoke of something more base than any human mind could reach. All this created a scary picture of violence.

-Was this your plan?-

Struggling to keep the snarling mouth away, Dee agreed with her inner-voice that this seemed, again, all too familiar. Maybe she had no business being out here with these things. Sure, she was as strong as them, but strength had nothing to do with fighting skills. Her last encounter had said much about her luck, not her ability to battle. It seemed her luck was all used up.

"Don't move."

His words were unnecessary. Dee couldn't move, locked in perfect balance with the strength of the creature whose snarling face pushed towards her, fangs suggesting that maybe it had never been human; that maybe vampires *were* real.

Another boom from the shotgun blasted all thoughts from her mind, forcing eyes closed against first, the shot, then the warm wetness of pieces of the creature's face raining down on her.

The warm goop was the straw. Her psyche caved.

Hysterical, Dee crab-walked out from under the dead pressure of the body, continuing away from what was left of it until her movement stopped against the pressing inertia of a tree. The thing's head was sprayed into the brush, though its body continued to twitch.

Eyes blinking too fast, brain trying desperately to see anything but the gore in front of her, she rolled to her hands and knees, retching an empty stomach into the bramble of the forest floor, hoping the man with the shotgun wasn't there for her as well. There was nothing she could do until the bile finished its release from her stomach.

Energy sapped, eyes blurry with tears, she pulled her attention to the man who waited for her to regain control of herself.

She hadn't noticed his calm acceptance of her reaction to having blood and gore rain down on her or his quick check of the bodies to make sure they wouldn't rise again, despite their lack of brain matter. When she finally glanced up, rolling slowly away from the puddle she'd made, he was checking his weapon.

Satisfied with whatever he'd checked on his gun, he turned to Dee, offering a hand to help her up.

She ignored his offer garnering an amused smile from him as she rose to her feet.

-*Kill this guy!*-

The thought was earnest, though she pushed it from her mind without trouble. Rather than kill him, or run as her panic insisted, she studied the man who was the only reason she still lived.

Deep-seated arrogance wound tightly around his medium build. The tight, long-sleeved shirt he wore showed off a muscular frame that was functional rather than bulky. His over-six-foot height was too close, so she took a step back, eyes following the scar that ran down the left side of his face from his temple, skirting the edge of his eye socket before jutting out slightly to follow his cheekbone to end at the corner of his mouth. The scar hid an attractive face behind a sense of menace, and the short haircut screamed military, enunciated by the black tactical clothing he wore.

His eyes scanned the gore littering the ground before returning an expression of amused contempt to her. "Interesting choice."

Dee raised her eyebrows in question, his comment drawing her into a defensive stance. To hide her reaction, she used the edge of her shirt to wipe her face as best she could, holding her breath against the smell, refusing to throw-up again. Using the dark to trick her eye, she repeated to herself that it was mud. It was only mud.

-Mud despite the fact we haven't had rain for weeks?-

The man was pointing to the wooden stake Dee had shoved into the pocket of her sweatshirt. She'd forgotten it and it now lay on the ground, useless. Telling herself she'd lost it before she could have used it allowed her to meet the stranger's humored gaze with a challenging frown. "Yeah? Guess I figured blasting the whole state into alert with a shotgun seemed overkill."

The stranger swept his eyes over the two bodies that would have been gnawing at Dee's bones right then, if not for his interference. "You think this was overkill?"

She shrugged, a wave of exhaustion sapping her energy for more banter. Dropping her hands from the failed attempt at cleaning her face, she looked around. She just wanted to get home, climb into bed, and claw these images from her mind.

-Kill him. Take his weapons. He can't know about you.-

What could he possibly know? And why was her inner-nag so intent on killing this guy? It wasn't like she'd done anything to pique his curiosity except get her ass kicked.

-I think the fact that you're out here at all is curious.-

That might be true, but he was out here too.

-If you kill him, there will be no worrying.-

I'm not killing him.

She ignored his amused expression while he waited for her to sort through her thoughts.

Refusing to feel self-conscious under his gaze, Dee stood tall, meeting his arrogant expression for the first time, almost daring him to laugh at her, frowning when amusement filled his eyes. She wasn't sure what she would have done if he'd chuckled out loud.

Then it hit her, the obviousness that his presence meant he knew what these things were.

She softened her expression, floating her eyes away from his to survey the carnage again. Taking a deep breath, she asked, "What are these things?"

The bloody mess scattered before her triggered another gag response. Afraid she might throw-up her actual stomach if she let her brain focus on it, she brought her attention back to his face. A tremor had started in her hands and she needed something to think about that wasn't the image of brains spread over the forest floor, some of which was drying to her face.

"Is this the first time you've seen these things?"

Did it matter if she told him about her? Maybe she should. Perhaps, it would be a good idea to let someone know. Someone who knew more than she did about these things.

-No! No! No!-

She closed her eyes against the raging in her head, allowing the paranoia to grip her so she wouldn't start blabbing her life story to this guy. The weariness settling over her wasn't helping her senses. Trusting her inner-voice, knowing she wasn't in her best mind, she shrugged, opting for a non-answer.

He walked to one of the bodies and kicked its leg. "They're called Revenants. I've never heard of them being so close to human populations." Mumbling to himself, he said, "First time for everything, I guess."

He turned back to her. "Guess you were just lucky enough to run into them."

She stared blindly, remembering the night in the cemetery. "I saw one the other night."

"Yeah? Where?"

Dee stepped closer. "Two nights ago, actually. Tackled me out on the road near here."

His surprise seemed genuine. "Really? That's hard to imagine. What happened to that one?"

Dee looked down, wondering how much she should say. It seemed prudent to lie, but she wanted, *needed*, more information.

She didn't catch the smile playing at his lips as she said, "It's dead."

A different smile came over him. An expression Dee couldn't read. "I see. As are these two. You think there are more around?"

-Don't start trusting this guy.-

The voice in her head was ignored while she watched the man, his athletic body pressing against his shirt. He obviously knew how to handle himself. A part of her wanted to invite him home to pick his brain, while another part agreed with the voice's suggestion that she kill him to resolve any future problems. Yet, she sort of owed him her life.

She shuddered at the thought that her life really had been in danger.

"You're lucky. Not many come within their reach and live to tell about it."

"You seem to be alright," she said, turning away from him.

"My life is not like most."

These words brought her attention back to his face, her smile matching his. "Neither is mine."

"That's obvious." His eyes roved over her again.

She frowned, the crickets and frogs creating a wall of sound around them.

"Do you actively—hunt—these things?" She wasn't sure the word to use, gesturing with her hands as she searched for vocabulary. If she'd thought chasing some creature from a bad horror movie through a cemetery was surreal, having this conversation in the woods with some mysterious stranger needed its own adjective.

"Not so much. I'm as surprised as you to see them here."

Her eyes widened at this before squinting in distrust. "So, then, what are you doing here?"

A mischievous glint highlighted dark eyes. "I could ask the same of you."

-Kill him!-

He hadn't stepped forward, but the look on his face and the tone of his voice gave the illusion he was suddenly closer, a looming presence pushing against her. She stepped away, eyes scanning the darkness for the most localized path of retreat.

He spoke again before she figured out how to respond. "They're not so many of these things to warrant actively hunting. I've never even heard of them being this close to where they might hurt anyone."

She nodded, eyes distrustful, not looking at him as she scanned the darkness.

-If you're not going to kill him, at least get out of here.-

Ignoring the voice in her head, she mulled the strangers words over. "You said that."

The cocky expression on his face was hard to interpret. She was annoyed with herself when she couldn't meet his heavy gaze.

"Why are you here, then?" She insisted on an answer though her attention remained on the trees.

"I'm not sure you'd believe me."

She frowned, head-turning so her eyes could come back to his face, her expression clearly saying, *don't screw with me.* "Try me."

He shrugged apologetically, glancing down at his fingers. "I don't know you well enough to tell such secrets."

Her eyebrows rose in disbelief at his brazen attitude, and she was reminded of a friend lost to the fire. He'd also been obnoxious in an arrogantly joyous way that had grown on her. She almost smiled, but wouldn't give him the satisfaction.

Still, the annoyance flashing in her eyes was real. "Fine."

She turned, walking away from him into the woods, in the opposite direction from where she needed to go. She didn't know him, and getting near enough to him that he might pull something would have been stupid.

"What's your name?" he called after her, halting her steps before the darkness swallowed her from his vision.

Her head tilted, but she didn't turn around. "Dee."

"Dee, glad I was here to save your ass. I'm Hamal."

She spun, eyes flashing anger, simmering to annoyed humor when she saw the smile on his face. "Hamal? I think we're even."

He called after her retreating shadow, voice laughing, "How you figure?"

She waved a hand in a gesture that could have meant anything, this time not stopping to answer.

6

Hours later, Dee paced, thoughts wandering from the idea of tracking Hamal down to kill him to wishing she'd invited him back to her place. Even if he wasn't right for information, it'd been a long time since she'd spent the night with anyone.

-Really? The guy blows two bodies to pieces, and you want to get naked with him?-

She admitted it was an absurd leap, but who better to intertwine her life with than someone who was already aware of the creepy-scarys wandering the night?

-Or who better to murder than someone who could bring trouble to your doorstep?-

She sighed, throwing herself back on the bed, hair still wet from her shower.

She ran fingers down the scars on her arm, the only sign of her injuries days old. Opening and closing her fist a few times to marvel at the miracle of it, she let it fall back to her side, thinking back on all the things she'd found she was able to do.

Her thoughts focused on the most recent event and the creature whose words suggested they'd come just for her, despite what this Hamal implied about them rarely bothering human populations. The fact that they were here was proof that he didn't know everything about them.

-Maybe he doesn't know anything. Or maybe, he brought them here.-

He brought them here? She couldn't ignore that they'd both shown up at the same time.

She closed her eyes. If he was here on some mission to harm her, what should she do? Should she leave town? Where would she go? How long before he found her again? And why would he have saved her from her most recent encounter with the strange and unreal?

-You should have killed him.-

At least Mike would be safe if she skipped town.

Alarm shot through her at the idea that this newcomer might use Mike to get to her. Would leaving help Mike or merely force Hamal to go to him when he might have otherwise left him alone?

Her head ached, spinning with too many questions. As risky as it was, maybe her best play was to find this Hamal and see what information he had.

S he hadn't realized she'd fallen asleep until she woke. Chilled and uncomfortable, she was still at the edge of the bed, feet on the floor, naked form bare to the room. Riddled with goosebumps, she crawled up the mattress. Digging under the covers until warmth stole over her, she gladly succumbed sleep, even as the sun attempted to breach the thick curtains. But unconsciousness didn't come. Something kept her from falling over the edge.

Focusing on her senses, she scanned to see what it might be keeping her awake. There were no sounds but had a sound woken her?

A rattle from downstairs brought her fully awake.

When the smells of coffee and the sweetness of French toast wafted over her, she remembered Mike had promised breakfast. It was a thing he'd started a couple of months ago. He'd come by and force-convince her to leave the house in an attempt to get her to connect with the real world.

-Real world?-

Her inner-voice scoffed at the idea, and she agreed, but it made Mike feel better to think she was trying to make something of herself, whatever that might mean.

She rolled over, searching for the time.

Ten am.

Forcing herself from the warmth she'd just found, she stumbled, eyes half-closed, to her closet. She pulled on yoga pants, sports bra, and a tank top before allowing her feet to propel her to the kitchen and the tantalizing smells that drew rumbles from her stomach.

"Morning 'Case!" His voice was chipper, and she resisted the urge to wince. Instead, she managed a laugh from behind her foggy-brained stupor. He hadn't called her that in a long time. *Headcase*, or just *'Case*, had been his nickname for her back during her teenage years when she'd been stupid enough to think she knew everything, arguing her opinion on every topic. So heated would she get during these conversations, swearing she wasn't mad though her every gesture and volume suggested otherwise, that the nickname had been born.

He handed over a mug of black coffee as she headed for the table set near the double sliding glass doors that were often open to let in the sounds of the woods. Now bathed in morning sunshine, she squinted as the rays washed over her skin.

"Late night?" His voice was light, but she knew he was fishing to see if she'd been behaving herself.

"Not so late." She blew into her mug to distract her face from his studious stare.

She was glad she'd gotten rid of the clothes she'd come home in. Covered in blood and brains and vomit, they were buried in a bag within a bag in the trashcan in the garage beneath other garbage. Even in the throes of exhaustion, she hadn't wanted Mike ever to see them.

His voice portrayed disbelief. "Glad to hear it. I thought we could go out today."

He turned, holding two plates piled high with delicious breakfast carbs. She stood to grab the real maple syrup from the fridge, wishing it had been warmed, but not wanting to let the French toast cool to make it so.

"Go out, where?" She forced her voice to remain bland.

He dove into his breakfast without pouring syrup over the toast. "Just out." His mouth was full, but she understood him fine.

She poured syrup over one side of the stack in front of her, setting it down slowly as she considered her options. After what she'd put him through earlier in the week, she wasn't sure she could come up with a good enough excuse to say no. There wasn't much to do in their small town, and she was a little curious about what he had in mind.

"What's the weather doing today? We could go for a hike." She smiled as she said it, watching Mike's face.

Her obsession with the outdoors, with physical activity in general, was new. Mike didn't exactly share in her enthusiasm, especially now that her endurance so outmatched his. The only time they'd tried it, it'd been a day full of him yelling for her to wait up while she swallowed her annoyance at his slow progress.

Keeping his expression neutral, he grunted noncommittally.

Ultimately, they decided to drive the hour and a half to the nearest town large enough to be labeled a city and see what they could find to do. Dee appreciated that Mike worried enough to take one of his rare days off to entertain her. He didn't like that she just sat around all day, living off what her father had left. She didn't like that he worried, but she couldn't blame him for it, either.

Last year, when she'd returned home after being away for over four years, she'd taken all the steps necessary to get back into school, but never pulled the trigger. She was currently missing the second semester she would have been attending classes. School was a good idea, something that might help her figure out where her life should go, but something in her just couldn't follow through. Part of her thought it was a waste to go when she didn't know what it was for. Another part simply stalled on restarting her life. Avoiding reality worked for her.

While all these points often came up on outings such as this, today was not one of them. Mike held his lectures in check and Dee allowed herself to relax from the pressures of hiding. It was nice to reconnect with him, to remember they had been friends before he became a guardian, always fretting and fussing.

A pang of guilt settled in her stomach. Maybe she should have stayed away and let him live his life, rather than force him to stay and watch over her. If she'd never returned here, would he have eventually moved on?

There'd been a girlfriend when he was in college, then another he'd been with when her father died. She didn't know what happened to that one. It never came up, and she never felt right asking, too afraid she had been the reason for his life halting in the town her father had always expected them to move on from.

Digging for the information she was too afraid to ask directly, she commented, "So, I haven't seen any girls around."

Mike stared out the windshield. "Nothing serious. Not a whole lot of eligible bachelorettes matriculating to no-wheres-ville."

She laughed. It had been one of the things she and her father had planned for; that she move to a city with more people and opportunities. Staying here was never in the cards, yet here they both were, one trapped by the memory of the very man who'd wanted more for both of them, the other caught by those trappings.

"You're traveling a lot, though."

"Sure. Busy schedule. Not much time to take a breath and look at the sights, let alone date."

She felt worse. "Maybe it's time we relocate."

She was staring out the passenger window, not sure what her face would betray, not sure how she even felt about the suggestion that popped out of her mouth. Could she leave her father's house?

"You think you're ready for that?" His voice was quiet, tone proving he'd stayed only for her.

Her eyes closed. A tear fell down her cheek. "I can't wallow here forever."

"Where should we go?" Mike's voice was more cheerful, less guarded than his initial question. She tasted the excitement in his words. Her stomach dropped further.

She shrugged, taking a deep breath to wash the sadness from her voice, forcing a smile to reach her eyes as she turned to him. "Dad always pushed for New York or San Fransisco."

Eyes on the road, Mike said, "You were at NYU."

"Yeah, California is so far."

She remembered Mike's involvement in the conversations with her father. Her father had been instrumental in guiding both of them towards their futures, knowing the small town was great for a quiet, protected childhood, but not so great when establishing oneself in a competitive job market. Dee had been a rare adolescent in absorbing her father's every suggestion, never seeming to mind his guiding hand, never rebelling for fun's sake.

After he'd passed, she'd struggled to find her way. She'd held on for a few months, always planning to return to school. In the end, she'd given in to the dismay that swarmed her. Running off to tour the country, she'd maintained just enough contact with Mike that he knew she was alive.

She knew it'd been hard for him, especially when her weeks-long trip turned into months that turned into years. What she heard in his voice whenever she called to check in had her calling less and less. She'd been a coward.

-You're still a coward.-

She refused to imagine what it had been like for him when she'd disappeared. An entire year she'd vanished. No trace. Through all that time, he had stayed in the hopes that she'd one day reappear.

-Good thing he did.-

"Maybe California is the right answer this time around." His words brought her attention back to the conversation.

She nodded, thinking of Hamal, and whether he would find her on the opposite side of the country.

Pushing her fear of things unknown aside, she forced herself to remain engaged with Mike. "Let's schedule a house-hunting trip."

A smile filled his face so bright Dee couldn't help but match it.

H amal watched the house all day. Nestled into the brush beneath the trees in Desiree's front yard, he arrived just in time to see her leave with Mike. When they hadn't returned after a few hours, he got cranky, wondering if she had it in her to flee. He hadn't read that in last night's body language, but she'd never left for such an extended period. She'd barely left the house, aside from her midnight jogs, so a day trip right after their meeting had him fidgeting with anxiety.

When Mike's car pulled into the driveway that evening, Desiree nestled in the passenger seat, his pinched muscles finally relaxed.

He dropped lower in the shadows as Dee perked around, eyes scanning the darkness in a way that was more perceptive than normal. Her eyes moved over where he hid, and his heart skipped a beat.

If she had, she didn't indicate it, calmly turning to follow Mike into the house.

Still isolated from his superiors about what he should do with her, he was sticking to his plan. He was sure the presence of Revenants-as-assassins was proof enough that one of the other Houses was after her. How Zibanitu and Porrima weren't all over this, he couldn't know, but he knew enough about their protocols to know that if they hadn't reached out, it was for a good reason.

Wondering for the zillionth time who this girl was kept him excited rather than fearful.

7

Excited to have something to stimulate him after torturously waiting around with nothing to do for days, Hamal had to wonder if maybe she really did have a death wish. Would any other sane person be out, running through the night after being attacked, twice? Anyone else would have barred themselves inside to ensure the monsters couldn't break through the door to find them hiding under their beds.

It was another reason he was excited to engage her, not only to succeed in his mission but to figure out what made her tick. Her reaction on both nights to her attacks told of how afraid she'd been, but she'd faced both situations head-on and was still out for more. That was the most telling of anything he'd seen so far.

His truck sat half on the road, half in the grass near her first attack. As he had every other evening, he watched her jog her standard route through the camera feeds, looking up to watch her move past the truck when she drew close. But, instead of keeping her usual path through the town streets, she turned into the trees.

This change in pattern was a development he hadn't been ready for. He scrambled out of his truck, grabbing his pack before hiking off into the brush, hoping he'd be able to track her even as he knew he'd never be able to keep up, cursing the lazy relaxation he'd fallen into.

As he pushed through the trees, a flare of nervousness poked at him. If she could see where she was going in this environment well enough to sprint through it, she would have easily seen him lurking in the shadows of her front yard. Was she leading him into a trap?

He ignored the unfamiliar feeling of nervousness that threatened his senses. While the idea that she'd seen him skulking about her front yard made him nervous, excitement overrode it. His blood thrilled at the possibility of a trap ahead. It had been so long since a situation had pushed his limits. He'd seen a glimmer of her speed. He'd seen her survive wrestling, not one, but two, Revenants. Knowing she had no fight experience, he was eager to see if he could take her. His exceptional training versus her brute strength could be an exciting match.

As he crept through the woods, he pulled his NVG's from his pack. Their use illuminated the dark world to a monotoned white hue. This augmented sight allowed him to pick up his pace, though he continued to focus on not snapping every branch underfoot to announce his presence to everything within fifty meters.

His attention snapped to the side when his ears picked up sounds other than the cacophony of frogs and crickets. There weren't any large night creatures he needed to worry about in this part of the country, so he wasn't concerned it was some terrifying predator out for its nightly kill, though if other Revenants were about, he might have a worse problem. He moved at a quicker pace, taking the risk that what he was hearing was Dee and not something he knew he couldn't handle on his own.

The trees ahead erupted in loud thrashings as something humanoid darted by, followed closely by a second thing, their size not nearly as massive as the noise of their passing suggested. Based on the size and gait of the second form, he was sure he'd found Dee, glad she seemed to be chasing, rather than being chased.

No longer worried about how much noise he was making, he followed the pair. When the sound of their passage changed, he stopped fast, waiting for their changed direction to return them to him.

M oving into the trees was like slipping through a portal to a peculiar world where she had *purpose*.

She let the feeling wrap around her, refreshed by the empowerment that was a long-lost friend. So long she'd been harboring a self full of doubt, pushing questions behind shields of avoidance, that this odd sense of confidence was as welcome as it was strange.

If she'd given herself time to reflect, she might have realized much of this facade was brought on by the previous night's battle, her adrenaline high tricking her memory into viewing the event as an exciting adventure rather than a terrifying near-death encounter. But instead of contemplating this sudden shift in reality, she ran.

What should have been evident from the start slowly filtered to the forefront of her mind: her eyesight was astonishing. Until meeting Hamal, she hadn't clued into it. Even on the brightest of nights, the trees sucked light to inky blackness. In the last moments of their conversation, she'd been able to see him fine as day.

Then, a couple of nights ago, he'd hovered just behind the treeline in front of her house, crouched in darkness that should have been enough to hide him from any searching eyes. His confident posture, portraying his full belief that there was no way she could see him, had made that fact clear.

She was still deciding what to make of catching him spying on her.

Oddly, it didn't incite dread, but rather a strange calm. Despite her subconscious still suggesting she kill him, she couldn't find it in herself to be afraid of him.

-Just kill him.-

But what if he had answers? If she got rid of him, she had no way of tracing his path to find what he knew.

She let these thoughts pass to nothing as she succumbed to the thrill of the wilds around her. She pumped her legs harder, the snapping of leaves on her face a steady discomfort worth dealing with for the exhilaration of her power.

Stopping fast, she studied the strange tingling in the base of her spine, wondering at its cause. Was it the same feeling she'd had the other night?

It was too subtle for her to be confident in its similarity. Still, she didn't ignore the warning. When realization struck her, she was ready.

The creatures. She could sense when they were near.

Unlike the other night, when the idea had still been a question, tonight, it was so evident as to challenge how she hadn't been sure before.

-Just highlights how special you are.-

Spinning, she caught the action of the thing before it launched at her. Dee pinned it in place with a weighted glare. Staring into its eyes, having ruined its surprise attack, she felt the power of the creature hum behind her eyes as it held its position, feral gaze gaping back at her. They sized each other up, tasting in the air between them the level of threat each might pose, anticipating how the other might react to a next move.

Fortunately for the creature, Dee's confidence didn't carry over to knowledge of action. Staring back at the form whose edges blended with the foliage around it, Desiree was caught with how human this one looked. She wouldn't have noted this one as anything but human if not for the strange buzzing in her skull. In her head, it felt the same, but its appearance suggested it was something different.

Time stretched as she waited, no idea how to press an offensive. Not forced to react to a rushing assault, Dee had no plan.

"What will you do, strange creature?" The hissing voice was low, a whisper in the trees, each syllable stretched.

Dee gaped, wondering at the mystery of her life that *she* was the *strange creature?*

The thing sensed her hesitancy, the drop in confidence its voice caused.

It sprang.

Even caught unaware, there was enough distance between them for Dee to react. Still, her combatant managed to wrack destruction across her shirt and skin with inhuman claws Dee hadn't noticed while studying its face.

Dee grit her teeth, more against the annoyance of her ineptitude than the pain that was kept at bay by chemicals flooding her system. Her eyes managed to stay on the creature as it rolled away, coming to its feet in one fluid motion, un-phased by her clumsy movements.

-You still have full function of your limbs. Point to you.-

The creature, eyes still focused on her with a furious intensity, spoke again. "You are untrained, even if you are strong. I was sent to test you, but I think instead, I will end you."

Barely contemplating its words, Dee backpedaled from another attack. She flung herself to the side, just out of reach of claws threatening to cause more damage.

This wasn't at all what she'd expected when anticipating another fight. This was more than the snarling, reactionary beasts she'd been able to defend herself into defeating. This was a cognitive fighter, and Dee was in over her head.

-I think this time you really might die.-

Her panic crested beyond her body's capacity to understand.

Then, the fear fell away, overtaken by a numbing calm. The absolute truth that she was facing her death transformed a terrified state into a euphoric experience that brought clarity. This previously unknown lucidity wrapped a stillness around her that allowed her to *see*, a seeing that granted her knowledge to a purposeful path of action.

She was in motion, agile muscles bringing her body up and around, so she was taking the advancing creature by the arm, tugging and swinging, so the body followed, spinning over itself to slam into the earth with a grunt of expelled air.

-Nicely done. See what focus will get you.-

It was a move Dee had learned years ago during a self-defense class. She'd barely been able to make it work then, even with a motionless partner helping her through the movements. They'd laughed at the idea of ever using it in a real-world application, especially for self-defense, but the move had lain in her memory where her focus latched onto it.

The Revenant's underestimation of her was the only reason it worked, and Dee knew it, even as she allowed satisfaction to pass over her.

-How under-appreciated luck is. I wonder when yours will run out?-

The underhanded comment of her inner-cynic broke the spell. Time resumed its breakneck speed. Dee released a breath she felt she'd been holding since first locking eyes with her attacker. The Revenant, as stunned by its meeting with the ground as it was by Dee's ability to survive, stared upwards, eyes widening in a brief register of shock before transforming into spitting rage.

Dee stepped away, bracing for another attack, allowing the Revenant to flip from its back to hands and knees in an accomplishment that emphasized its inhuman agility. The pair stared each other down, Dee waiting for what would come, the other contemplating the odds of a successful attack.

Deciding against it, the attacker took off into the trees. Dee gave chase, thoughts of another night when she'd found herself unconscious in a cemetery outweighed by an instinct that insisted she follow the thing that could kill her.

-Maybe this time will go better?-

She reminded herself that she'd survived that night.

Right on its heels, Dee was taken off guard when it abruptly pivoted. It kicked a leg against the thick trunk of a tree as leverage to spin around to reverse its defensive position to offense.

With just enough time to sidestep, Dee ducked behind a tree. In another surprise move, rather than attack, it continued running in a straight line, back the way they'd just come.

A piece of Dee's mind was grateful for the change in direction. Their heading would have quickly put them out on the main road in town, opening the possibility of witnesses. Another piece of her mind wondered what in the hell the thing was doing.

-Not that it's likely you'll survive this night to have to worry about explaining yourself.-

She didn't argue, but if she let the creature go, she was sure it would be back another night. Heaven forbid it figured out where she lived. *Don't put off 'till tomorrow what you can do today*, her father's voice rang in her head.

The crazed gait of the creature laid a path of broken branches and trampled ferns, so Dee was forced to dodge and jump or risk turning an ankle. When a branch fell in time to hit her in the head, scraping against her face, she instinctively caught it against herself, ready to throw it in a fit of annoyance.She changed her mind when it occurred to her she had no weapon to help kill the thing she chased.

-Hadn't thought that far ahead, huh?-

She hadn't thought ahead at all. There hadn't been a whole lot of thinking going on as far as this entire crazy situation was concerned, but she was too stubborn to give up the chase now.

Gripping the branch as thick as her wrist and as long as her arm, she felt stupid for not having brought a weapon. The one she'd killed in the cemetery hadn't needed its head blown apart, but it had required a tool. She wasn't sure she was up to punching her fist through the things chest or ripping its head off with her bare hands. She wasn't even sure she could do either of those things. She hoped the branch was enough.

She cursed Hamal, part of her glad he hadn't shown up so she could pretend he wasn't some creep with an unknown agenda. His absence allowed her the delusion that his arrival had nothing to do with these things that were after her. The timing of their shared arrival to town was pure coincidence.

-Pretty slim argument.-

Hand clenched around her new weapon, she picked up a burst of speed, pouncing on the thing running full out in front of her.

Hamal came through the trees, scanning the darkness for some visual that would bring him closer to his mark. The sounds he'd followed had gone quiet, so his mind went to the idea that he was too late to save Dee from whatever had found her.

Forcing this from his mind, he stumbled through a thick patch of bramble, stopping fast before tripping over a pair of legs stretched prone in the dark.

Concern that he'd just stumbled over Dee's dead body turned to relief when her voice brought his attention from the forest floor. "Seems to be more of these things around than you let on."

The strain in her voice emphasized the effort she was exerting to ensure the creature never got back up. Hamal looked back to the legs across his path, realizing they belonged to a Revenant that wasn't moving.

Hamal couldn't deny a small part of him was disappointed that he hadn't played the savior once again, while another felt an odd sense of pride that she hadn't needed his help.

He frowned, pushed the thoughts away, and stepped forward so he could see Dee's face.

The scene came into focus. Hamal suppressed a grin. The girl was battling a Revenant already turning to husk. It would not be getting up, though Dee wasn't convinced. Her arms shook with the effort she was applying to the thick branch she'd managed to stick through the creature's chest, so much so, Hamal was sure she'd impaled it to the ground.

He scanned her form, noting the scratches she'd gained from

this new encounter, while also noting there was too much blood to have come from her target alone. How many wounds had she already healed?

Who was this girl?

Struggling to believe Zi and Porrima didn't know about her was secondary to the fact that Hamal's meager human skills were all that stood between this anomaly of a girl and the things coming after her. Hamal could accept the idea that the information hadn't been available at the start of this mission, but the continued silence was feeding his apprehension.

So many thoughts had him miss the opportunity to throw a sarcastic comment about her continued struggle with a corpse.

"This one was *way* smarter than the others. It had a full-on conversation with me. Then, right as I thought I had it, it turned on me. It friggin' tricked me."

Dee's statement pulled another layer of worry over him. A talking Revenant wasn't a Revenant at all, but something else. His mask of mischievous contempt slipped as he processed what this could mean, glad his goggles concealed his face from her questioning eyes.

Was whoever sending these things increasing the aptitude of the hunter? Should he expect an even more skilled assassin to show up next? Or was there more than one player after Dee?

Hamal's hands itched to pick up his phone. He'd never been cut off from a source to gather information, and he realized just how much he counted on the backup. He was good, but against increasingly powerful foes, he'd need to tag out. He wasn't arrogant enough to deny that.

Still, his decision to contact Dee was enough of a breach that he didn't want to complicate his position further by breaking this order of no communication.

Staring at the wilting corpse, he allowed himself the wasted second to wish he'd gotten there just a little earlier so he could have heard the words the creature spoke. If it could talk, it could answer questions.

He remembered hearing of a thing like Dee's words suggested. Those that maintained their conscious minds, despite not being fully transitioned into the Soldiers the process was meant to create. Hamal wasn't privy to the transition rate, but he imagined it couldn't be great. The question of his transition had come up once, Zi's answer that he wouldn't risk such a highly prized asset to such a risky bet.

In his time with Zi, Hamal had gleaned, through conversations he was never supposed to have heard, that only three of the Masters could create Soldiers from humans, Zi one of them. The process was risky, Revenants being one of a handful of possible outcomes if the transition went badly. Advanced Revenants, like what Dee was currently pressing into the earth (if they were called something else, he'd never heard it), were even more rare, with death being the most common overall outcome.

It wasn't often Hamal was at a loss. To say he was frustrated stated it mildly.

"This one isn't getting up again, is it?" Dee's question forced Hamal back to the moment.

With a smooth motion that belied the frustrated energy humming through him, Hamal drew his shotgun, pointing it at the creature's head, the weapon's passing movement ruffling Dee's hair, who threw herself away. "Whoa, whoa, whoa! Can I please get out of this without brains splattered all over me?"

Hamal smiled, a malicious glint of teeth that barely masked his desire to expel some pent-up energy. He paused, giving the dirt-and-blood smeared girl the extra second to move away before firing the weapon into the creature's face. It wouldn't have gotten up, but shooting its face off made him feel better.

Satisfied, he turned his attention to the girl who was brushing at her tight workout pants, unsuccessfully attempting to dislodge the dirt and grime she'd picked up from her fight. Leaves stuck to her like Velcro, pointing out of her hair like some poorly designed crown of thorns.

He chuckled, the sound bringing her gaze sharply to him,

head angled down, so her eyes peered up from beneath lashes shadowing her face. Even with the bright vision his night-vision-goggles allowed, her eyes were pools of black. Another might have felt the hand of terror slide down their spine, but he'd seen too many scarier things. "C'mon. I'll give you a ride home."

When she frowned in response, he stepped forward, dropping the offered hand. "I know you have questions. So do I."

His smile didn't warm her to him. A glint in her eye shone with some unvoiced threat.

He cocked an eyebrow to match the half-grin spread on his lips. "I bet I can even show you a few moves, so you won't get your ass kicked next time one of these things shows up."

The set of her shoulders squared.

Adrenaline surged through him. Would she attack him?

He loosened his knees, readying himself.

When her shoulders sagged, it was obvious whatever fight she'd thought about putting up had fled, as had the opportunity for him to push his way into her world. This former point was probably a good thing. Purposefully ignoring his directive not to make contact, he'd saved her life, a fact he was convinced would excuse indiscretion. But, as much as he'd crossed the line, there was a limit to how badly he could screw this up. She'd just saved him from that.

She searched his face. Maybe for an answer to some internal question? Whatever it was, she didn't find it.

When she walked off into the woods, he didn't try to stop her.

8

Killing him probably was the best option. He'd been watching her, and not in that sexy, flattering kind of way. He'd been on her property, lurking in the shadows when Mike had dropped her off the other night. Adding in his repeated *coincidental* appearances, she was beginning to think it'd been him in the cemetery whose touch had brought her from unconsciousness.

-The first time he failed to facilitate your death.-

She closed her eyes against this rationale she refused to believe. There was no reason for her to accept any of the things Hamal said, but she didn't think he was there as an agent against her.

She chuckled to herself, quieting the voice in her head for the first time in hours as she allowed her panicked anxiety to turn to ironic astonishment. Had it only been five days since the attack that had ended in the graveyard? Six? Her mind had trouble settling on this. It seemed like weeks had passed that included more conversations with the mysteries stalker than two short repartees.

The SUV she'd run past tonight before heading off into the trees was his. She was sure of it. And hadn't she seen it on other nights? It explained how he'd found her in the woods tonight. Even if he shared her same compulsion to jog late at night, he would have no reason to be hiking through the woods.

-*He's seen too much from you. You need to kill him.*-

Even if he had been watching her this whole time, she wasn't killing him. She wasn't killing anyone. There were enough problems with her psyche. She wasn't sure what killing an actual human being would do to her. And she *was* sure, even if his presence was linked with the things attacking her, that he wasn't working against her.

-*Except he knows all about them. Except he's been watching you.* Spying *on you.*-

Her eyes flashed to the windows. Anyone standing in the front yard, even if buried behind the layers of trees that fenced her property from the road, would easily see what she was doing. Not that there was ever anything of note to watch.

Gazing past her reflection in the glass, she wondered if she was staring right at him.

The idea startled her, so she raced from the room towards the back of the house where the open kitchen ended in another windowed wall she had an easier time looking through, as no lights inside the house reflected at her to impede the view. The exterior darkness was thick. Anything could be out there, waiting, biding its time.

Shivering, she turned away from the windows to make her way to her father's office, a place she rarely entered. It was one of a few rooms in the house without windows.

As Dee crept softly over the threshold, her shoulders heaved relief that any prying eyes wouldn't be able to stare at her in this room. Her eyes swept the space. Everything sat as it had on the day he died. It was kept dust free and polished, but not a thing was put away or removed. In all the time she'd been gone, Mike hadn't disturbed anything, and she'd never been inclined to, either.

Comfortable in the oversized leather chair, eyes closed, Dee embraced the memory of the dead to distract herself from thoughts of the living.

A thermal read of the yard indicated nothing around the house that might have spooked her into retreating. The look on her face just before she'd run from the kitchen suggested she'd been thinking too hard about all the things she didn't know. If only she'd let him in, he could answer so many questions. Just maybe, she could answer a few of his.

He reminded himself that was not part of the mission.

Hamal watched her move quickly to the office he'd never seen her enter, glad he'd decided to put up the camera in a room that had appeared unused when he'd initially scoped out the house. That it was a shrine to her father was obvious.

His working theory was that she had some mild amnesia. It explained why she didn't remember who had Initiated her. It explained why she didn't recognize the creatures who'd attacked her, and it explained how she didn't know how to use her gifts. Sure, there were holes in the theory, but the amnesia could explain most.

If he could just have one uninterrupted conversation with her.

Running over arguments and counter-arguments further built up his excitement. He considered just walking up to her front door to force her to accept his explanation of what he was doing there. Sure, she could probably kick his ass. Sure, he was forbidden to do any such thing by his directive. But he'd already disobeyed, and he was committed to gaining her trust and teaching her to survive the next attacks until someone told him otherwise.

The decision he hadn't realized he'd been wrestling with was made. He was going to teach this girl to survive and damn the consequences.

He reminded himself that he couldn't forget that she was dangerous to him. The thought briefly interrupted his planning. If she considered him a threat, would she consider killing him? Would trusting him be worth the risk? In a role reversal, he'd have already killed her. He relied on her naiveté to protect him from such a decision, but would he be wrong?

———

She'd narrowed the Hamal issue down to three possible scenarios. One: he was in cahoots with the creatures trying to kill her, so he was trying to kill her. Two: he was there to try and save her from being killed by the things attacking her. Three: he was sending these things after her so he could play white knight to get close to her.

Part of her leaned towards theory one, while another part didn't agree. He'd seemed genuinely surprised on this last occasion when she'd explained to him about the thing talking to her. Sure, that wasn't enough to sell to a jury, but she didn't feel he was out to get her.

Theory two seemed the most probable, though why wouldn't he just tell her what was going on? It was insulting to her intelligence to think she'd believe the coincidence of it all.

-*Is it, though?*-

Theory three was the one she lingered on the longest. If not for showing up too late to be of any real help on two of three occasions, she might have been sold on this explanation. If she hadn't been able to handle herself, she'd have been dead. Twice. Pretty lousy planning for someone trying to set up a rescue.

-*Unless they were never really going to kill you. Or, he really expected them to kill you, and we're back to the first theory.*-

She frowned. She should have died that first night. Theory one, then?

-*Maybe he knows who you are. Maybe he knew you couldn't be killed. Maybe you can't die.*-

Her breath caught in her throat at this idea of immortality. She'd never considered it, and rather than deal with the swell of emotion the concept brought from the pit of her chest, she tucked it away with all those other things she wouldn't face. Even her inner dialogue was quiet for once.

She sighed, letting her thoughts return to previous concerns. Even if she were wrong in all her theories, killing him would put her back to zero. She was tired of not knowing. Maybe it was time to stop avoiding the whole thing. Forced to search for answers she'd shunned, she wondered why she hadn't just faced the questions to begin with.

Her nightmares reminded her why. On the other side of those fiery flames were answers she was too afraid to see. If she was directly responsible for the deaths of her friends, she didn't want to see that. Didn't want to know.

9

eriously, you can't stay in for one night?-

S   She'd promised Mike she wouldn't go gallivanting all over town. She wasn't even sure gallivanting was something that could be done in a place this small. Either way, she wasn't confident she could resist the temptation to go out, despite her promise.

Pressing her forehead into the cold glass of the sliding doors that would lead from the kitchen to the backyard, she refocused this strange compulsion into an effort to figure out why she had it.

Before this new hobby hit her, she'd never even worked out, let alone felt the need to pound mile after mile of asphalt in marathon running sessions. The habit had started after she'd returned home, and, before now, she'd never questioned it.

She'd tried to keep her promise, going out during the day, or earlier in the evening. It was never the same. She felt intruded upon by the members of town going about their various tasks. It was as if the consciousness of the world encroached upon her solitude.

It made no logical sense, but it wasn't something she'd been able to stop. Even on those days when she'd run until she thought her legs would collapse beneath her, the compulsion to go back out once the sun had long set and the rest of humanity slept was impossible to ignore.

Sighing, she pressed her hands into the glass, interrogating another hard-to-decipher topic: the question of these creatures who hadn't given up in their obsession of taking her out.

-*Vampires?*-

She cringed at the word as if the term made everything crazier. Whatever they were called, they were real. All of this was *really* happening.

Revenants. That's what Hamal had called them, but her mind continued to think of them as the more fictionalized term.

-*A rose by any other name...*-

That they were after her had to be because of what she'd become. Unfortunately, that wasn't a story she could tell. She just couldn't remember. At first, she'd purposefully kept her thoughts from recalling any of it, but now, after digging through feelings she'd wanted nothing but to forget, the truth of what happened seemed lost.

She shuddered, hands shaking from the stress of knowing someone, or something, was trying to kill her. So focused on the minute-to-minute of what was going on, any larger picture had been beyond her to consider. Would this behind-the-scenes puppet-master expect the answers to these questions? Would the fact that she couldn't remember help her or just facilitate her death?

Struggling to breathe, she used the unyielding surface of the glass as an anchor to ensure her legs maintained their roots on the floor.

Was this a panic attack?

-*You went out to fight them of your own volition last night, but tonight the thought of them is immobilizing you with fits of terror?*-

Last night it hadn't been so prevalent that someone was trying to kill her. Not on such a personal level. Last night there was only the knowledge that these strange things existed. Last night, her only goal was to ensure ignorant passers-by wouldn't get attacked.

This line of thinking calmed her mind. She couldn't succumb to cowardice at the expense of someone else. If there were more of them around, even if they were after her, could she live with herself if someone else was attacked?

-If you were worried about the safety of the town, you'd have started your patrol at a time that wouldn't give Mike a heart attack.-

She frowned at the implication her altruism was self-indulgent.

They're here to kill you. The echoing words were something different than the inner-voice whose sarcasm had become standard commentary. This was something else. This was the edge of clinical madness.

She perched in the nearest chair at the large dining table, sorting through her thoughts. Something similar to having her feelings hurt swelled to the front of her emotional upheaval. Someone wanted to kill her. Kill her. KILL Her. Kill. Her. How was she supposed to feel about that? How could she not take that personally?

Her head hurt. She was emotionally exhausted. So many thoughts had shut her body down. Unfortunately, her body shutting down didn't give her a reprieve from the torrent of questions flooding her mind.

There was still no recollection of any details surrounding the house she'd witnessed in flames. She'd never seen it before it was on fire. She had no memory of the interior or meeting her friends there. Ray's beat-up truck, the only transportation the friends had shared, had been in the driveway. It was the deciding factor in why she thought they'd all been there, though she hadn't stuck around to see what the police, or fire department, or anyone, discovered. Had the house ever been found? Were her friend's families still unsure what had ever happened to them? Were they all still lying as dust under the collapsed remains of the building?

Her breaths were heavy, tears streaming down her face, but still, the thoughts came.

When she'd finally left the smoldering pile, it was to move blindly through trees and fields for days. No sleep. No food. But that had to be impossible. It couldn't have been days. She passed this detail off as a side-effect of shock.

She blinked fast, bringing herself back to the kitchen of her father's house.

With slow steps, she moved to the front of the house, pausing with her hand on the doorknob to consider her decision. After a moment's hesitation, she stepped onto the porch. Her eyes searched the treeline. He was there, she knew it.

There were thirty meters between her and the first row of giant oaks, scattered with the thinner beech and pines that climbed high overhead. She could see well enough, despite the blackness of shadows beneath the trees. Hopping the rail, she moved through the yard, confidence, borne from faith in her decision, wrapped around her.

-Don't be stupid.-

She ignored the voice in her head.

"Hamal? I think it's time we talked." Her voice was conversational, not loud, but she knew he would hear. That he would respond was something she also did not doubt.

He stepped from the trees, smile plastered to his face as he looked her up and down. "Thank god. The mosquitos in this place are ridiculous."

A hand waving in the air around his face emphasized his point.

She ignored his attempt at humor. "You can teach me to fight?"

"I think it was my purpose in life to teach you to fight," he replied, smile gone.

She nodded, looking past him into the darkness beyond. "We can start tomorrow?"

His face was blank. "Tomorrow. Early."

Her eyes met his. "Not too early."

He stepped forward, tone lowered, all trace of joviality gone. "Let's be clear. I will train you, but this will not be some random extracurricular activity. This will be your life. You don't have time to treat this as a hobby. We will start *early*."

The change in his demeanor pushed back Dee's confidence. She forced herself to hold her ground and found she couldn't meet his eyes. Fear asked her to renege on her proposal but she'd been scared before. At least this fear would help guide her through the others.

-Or it will kill you by surprise.-

Ignoring her inner cynic, she asked, "What do you mean, *I don't have time?*"

She blinked fast under his penetrating glare before a smile covered whatever he'd excavated from her expression. In spite of the smile, his eyes bore down on her with an intensity that made her squirm. "You know they'll keep coming. And they'll keep getting stronger."

She dropped her chin in the slightest nod. Hamal matched the gesture, looking past her to the grand house. "You know, if I stay here, I'll be able to keep an eye on things. We'll have more time to train."

Dee was unable to keep the dismay off her face. She'd had the same idea, but hearing it from him made it seem like a spectacularly bad one.

-You think?-

He flashed a winning smile, the scar on his face dancing with the movement. "You think about it. I'll be back in the morning."

Moving to walk away, he stopped short. "You stay in tonight. You stay in every night I'm not with you."

She nodded, wondering at the fluttering of butterflies his words uncaged from her stomach.

When he was no longer in sight, her inner voice chastised, *You let him tell you what to do?*

She frowned. She had, but wasn't that what she'd just signed up for?

When she was back inside, she stared at the walls, wondering what she was supposed to do now that she couldn't run.

10

B ack at her house the next morning, Hamal's spirits
soared. Not even thoughts of what might happen to him
when Zi found out he'd disobeyed a direct order could
take away his excitement at finding out firsthand the capabilities
of this girl.

When no one responded to his insistent knocking, his excitement turned to annoyance. No way was she going to change her
mind and stand him up. No way she was going to give him the slip
and take off in the meager few hours he'd allowed himself to
sleep. Talk about a reputation buster.

Easily bypassing the lock on the door for the second time, he
was through the house and up the stairs, barely looking around on
his way. Extensive surveillance had given him a perfect awareness
of the house's layout, so he knew her bedroom was at the far end
of the hall, taking up almost the entire east wing of the upstairs.

Surprised by the locked door of her bedroom, the deterrent
held for only a second before he slammed through it. Not
expecting someone to be just over the threshold, he found himself
flipped to his back.

Staring at the ceiling, he laughed a genuine, full-throated
sound. It'd been a long time since he was taken so completely by

surprise. Apparently, she'd heard him racing up the stairs. She wasn't just some stupid girl, as he continued to forget.

"Christ, Hamal! I almost killed you."

He rolled his head to look at her. "I doubt it. But nice job taking my feet. I never saw it coming."

An oversized t-shirt was all that covered her. Unable to peel his eyes from so much naked skin, he took in the line of her leg that ran to where the edge of the shirt barely covered what lay—

"Alright! Get out! Let me get dressed!"

He rolled away, tearing his eyes from her. "Be out front in two minutes! I can't believe you made me wake you up."

"You never said how early."

He laughed at the shyness now lacing her words, allowing his eyes to travel back in the room as she moved away towards the closet. He was not ashamed to follow her movements as she pulled panties on, then leggings, stripping the shirt off to reveal flawless skin against a femininely-muscular back.

"Next time, I'll be more specific about what early means."

"Good idea," she mumbled.

When she turned, shirt barely over her head, she gasped, jumping back. "Gah! Hamal! You are trying to give me a heart attack! I thought you were in the hall! You always such a creeper?"

"Creeper, huh?" He was smiling again.

"Yeah. Creeper." She'd stopped walking forward, her face alternating between anger and embarrassment.

He turned. "I won't break into your room if you don't oversleep."

Seeing her like this was not the way to start their working relationship. He did not need to think of her as a piece of ass. Unfortunately, his imagination had too much fuel, and it would take more than a few nights away to forget.

Two hours later, he was reassessing that.

She was doing everything in her power to hide her gifts,

and he was furious. He wasn't here to train some random girl self-defense. He was here to prepare a fantastic anomaly how to survive against things equally extraordinary. There wasn't enough time for them to dance around her secrets.

"You know I've been watching you. Why do you think I don't know you're stronger than me? Faster? Quicker? Stop. Dicking. AROUND!"

His words stopped her short, and there was no difficulty interpreting the look of hatred she gave him. He didn't know what she'd expected and didn't care. She could hate him all she wanted as long as she learned to protect herself from whatever else came after her.

Hamal watched her battle with her rage, watched it boil towards the surface. He smiled his trademark expression that was far from cheerful. "There it is. That's good. That's what I need to see. Be mad! Don't just accept what's being thrown at you."

Not letting her stew in her hate, he rushed in with a flurry of punches she managed to dodge by utilizing dexterity.

"There she is." He stopped his assault to give her an approving nod.

Her eyes narrowed.

"Look, I'm here to help you, and that includes helping you from yourself. I get why you hide what you can do, but that time is over. If you don't practice with all your skills now, you'll be off-balance in a real fight."

She continued to study his face, panting from the quick bout of activity.

He continued. "If I were you, I wouldn't trust me either, but we don't have time for that. I need you to take a leap here."

A startled laugh burst from her mouth.

The corner of his mouth turned up in a smile.

His next words washed any feeling of humor from both of them. "There might be Soldiers after you right now. I can *not* help you against them. They will put me down with a flick of their finger. You, though, we might be able to get trained up to survive them."

Dee's eyebrows rose at this exclamation. "Who are you?"

He cocked his head as if not understanding the question.

"Why would you risk so much for me?"

He shrugged.

She gave an overdramatic sigh.

His next words came slowly, carefully, as he succumbed to her frustration. "I was sent to watch you. I think there's still time to save you."

She stared into his face, clearly waiting for further explanation, but he wouldn't tell her more. Couldn't. He'd already stepped too far beyond orders.

She frowned. "Why were you sent to watch me?"

He matched her expression, knowing he didn't contain the bitterness he felt. "Honestly, I'm not sure, though, after seeing you in action, I have a theory."

Again, she waited for more that never came. She sighed again, her frustration clear, pulling another sardonic smile from her teacher. "Any chance you might share your theory with me?"

Ignoring her question, he moved to a fighting position.

She paused, and he was grateful she let go of the thought to face off with him.

O verall, it had been an excellent first day.
Dee lay in the grass, eyes closed. When he'd finally called an end to their training session, she'd slumped to the ground in exhaustion. Jogging was great exercise, but it was nothing compared to what he'd put her through. She'd definitely sleep well tonight.

The thought pulled his eyes to her, remembering this morning, her form barely covered in a t-shirt—

He shook his head, pulling his eyes away to block the path his thoughts took him. If the Rishi's wanted her, there would be no room for him, and they most definitely *would* want her. There were going to be a few fights over whose House acquired this one. There was too much potential in her for her to be overlooked. She'd be like a shiny new toy. Allowing a personal indulgence here, now, while he had her to himself, would only lead to a mess later.

Besides, she was his job. She was the mission. That was all. Overstepping these lines would only sully a reputation he'd worked his entire life to build amongst a group that would always be stronger, faster, and just plain better than him.

Breaking the calm quiet that had settled over them, her words surprised him. "I'm not sure what I can do."

He met her gaze, waiting for more.

Her eyes moved past him to stare at the clear sky. "I'm fast and strong and quick. I've never learned to fight. I'd never even been in a fight until the other night."

"You killed a couple of those Revenants by yourself," he answered in a matter-of-fact tone.

As soon as the words were out, he knew he'd said too much.

Her face brightened before her eyes narrowed. "You were there in the cemetery."

He shrugged admission.

Her eyes closed again before opening slowly to study his face "You were worried I'd died."

She sat up.

He frowned. "Let's not get all mushy. If I'd lost you, my reputation would be shit."

She dropped her chin in a nod. "Right. Yeah." She cleared her throat. "I did kill a couple. But that had more to do with luck than anything."

He laughed. "Well said, but not everything can be given to luck's meddling hands. There's something in you that refused to be bested. That's what I saw. That's why I'm doing this."

Before she could get to questions he couldn't answer, he stepped towards the house. "Alright, I think it's time to eat."

She jumped to her feet, a burst of energy flowing from her in a manner he couldn't help but find endearing. Something had been released from her while they'd trained. It'd been a unique experience for him to witness her anger turn slowly to joy. This joy she found in their training was something he was almost jealous of. The girl who needed to feign arrogance to pretend confidence hadn't surfaced since that moment. In its place was the mold of a confident warrior he was excited to charge.

Still, it was only the first day. Only time would tell if the mold was stable enough not to break under the pressure of holding its contents. It was good she enjoyed training, but he knew the realities of why they were doing it were separate her mind. That would be the hardest thing to sell, and it was the point he was most afraid he wouldn't have time to explain.

"What's a good place to order in from around here?"

Her face fell. "Just pizza."

Did she think he was going to take her to dinner?

"You want to shower?" Her voice held no trace of the disappointment he'd seen on her face.

He kept his face neutral. "That would be great."

She showed him the large bathroom on the first floor after grabbing some clothes that looked like they would fit him. He grinned at her when she handed the pile to him. "Lots of guys leaving things behind?"

"Don't you wish I'd talk to you about my sex life," she snapped, her face flushed with embarrassment.

His grin turned to laughter. "I know you don't have a sex life."

He laughed when her face turned crimson before she fled.

11

He looked around, taking in the luxury of the room that put many of the hotels he'd stayed in to shame. It was, by far, much more elegant than the seedy motel he'd stay in that was the only lodging in this nowhere town. Glad the girl had finally agreed to have him stay with her was quite the understatement.

After showing him the room and where to find towels and toothbrushes, she'd left him to himself. Since his earlier comment about her sex-life, her self-conscious nature was back in play.

He shook his head, loathing that one.

It was why he'd never had any interest in finding a long-term relationship. Most women were unsure of themselves, looking to fill a hole through the reflection of another. The ones that weren't like that had no patience for long bouts of separation his lifestyle would force, a fact he respected enough to not waste their time. He'd never had trouble finding one-night-stands to satisfy his hunger and was too busy to be lonely.

Still, he couldn't keep his mind from conjuring the image of her standing over him in nothing but a shirt that had barely concealed her.

Dee paced back and forth behind her locked door, an action she knew wouldn't stop Hamal if he wanted to get in. Still, it made her feel a little better.

Now what?

-Now what, indeed.-

She should sleep.

Somehow, over pizza, she'd been convinced to let him stay.

-Death-wish, much?-

She didn't think her life was in danger with him here, but her inner-voice continued to try to convince her she should kill him rather than wait to see what he could teach her.

-If you think you're safe with him in the house, what's with the rut you're carving in the floor?-

She *huffed* at the point. It was the second-guessing that had her pacing. Thinking it was safe to let him stay an hour ago was turning into a mess of *what-ifs* in her head.

He'd said something about *Soldiers* and a *something-else* that might come. Another *something* that would try to kill her?

There'd already been four attempts on her life in—how many days had it been since she'd passed out in the cemetery?

-Does that matter?-

Probably not, but she felt figuring out the particulars might slow the crazed thoughts threatening to bash through the dam she'd erected to keep them from overloading her mind. She squeezed her eyes shut in concentration, counting backward slowly.

Seven days. Today was the seventh day since the cemetery.

She took a breath of relief as if working out this detail was a monumental victory.

One week. A week she'd been hiding from her best friend, hoping he wouldn't notice any changes in her.

Her walk back and forth across the room continued, the path

increasing in frenzy as her mind ran with possibilities for her future.

-Freaking out will not help.-

Her footsteps stopped. Her eyes closed. Her body was still for the first time in long hours.

This stillness did not reflect calm. In it, her ability to concentrate on illusions of how her panic might manifest intensified. In her mind's eye, ranting words screamed through the house so the rafters shook, and outbursts of violence wrecked her bedroom to heaps of shattered furniture. The visualization ended with her jumping through the glass of the window, rolling to her feet on the lawn before sprinting away, never to be heard from again.

She opened her eyes. She would not break down.

Instead, she moved from the room, even as she knew she should be forcing sleep on herself. To think rest would come was a fantasy she knew better than to indulge. Instead, she was taking her advice to meet things head-on.

"**B**ottom line is, I don't know why these things are after you." Frown-lines ran deep across her face. "Why are you here?"

"I told you, I was sent to watch you. Figure out what you were."

"What I was?"

"What you are."

"What I am?"

"That's annoying."

"Annoying?" She let out a breath of laughter, and with it, some of the intensity she hadn't meant to be pushing on Hamal with her questions. Neither had she meant to repeat everything he was saying. "What do you mean, what I am?"

"I think you know what I mean."

She paused, letting the answer pass. "Who sent you?"

"I can't tell you that."

Dee watched his face, startled that he'd straight up tell her he couldn't tell her. She wasn't sure if that was better than him lying.

-*Not* better *than him lying?*-

"Why can't you tell me?"

"Some secrets aren't mine to tell."

She nodded, not liking his refusal to answer, but respecting the reason for it.

-*If the reason is actually true, and not some bull to further trap you.*-

Storming down here with little thought to what she would actually say, she found herself struggling to come up with coherent questions.

Before she could come up with something direct to ask, he said, "Essentially, I'm an assassin."

She held his gaze, waiting for a sign that he was making fun of her. When she decided he wouldn't say more on his own, she broke the silence. "An assassin?"

"An assassin."

"How does one become an assassin exactly."

He chuckled, turning to grab a shirt. The movement brought her attention to what should have been obvious the second he opened the door: his naked torso.

How she hadn't noticed he wasn't wearing a shirt seemed impossible when the fact slammed her in the face. Struggling not to stare when he turned back to her, caught not just by his physique, but by the tribal-ram tattoo that covered his chest, reaching from shoulder to shoulder, down both biceps, and to his navel.

-*Cool.*-

The front door to the house opening distracted both of them. Hamal had a gun out, sweeping Dee behind him before she reacted.

"Dee? Whose car is out front?" Mike's voice drifted up the stairs, footsteps telling he was moving towards the back of the house, which meant he was going for the kitchen. It was the only time Dee'd ever been annoyed by the casual relationship the pair had. Mike knew her well enough to think she would be sleeping at this time of night, as well as understand that a hot drink made every visit better. There was always coffee in the kitchen.

Dee moved from the room before Hamal could tell her to wait, flying down the stairs. She almost ran into her friend, who was making his way back from the kitchen to check why he hadn't heard her call back to him. "Mike! Hi! I thought you were out of town."

"Took a late flight rather than wait for the morning one." He studied her for a moment before lifting his eyes to the stairs she'd just bounded from, then back to her, a smile blossoming across his face. "There's someone here."

Dee tried not to look panicked. "There is."

"Is this someone a *gentlemen caller*?" His voice dropped to a teasing whisper, and he made to step around her. She moved in front of him, eyes wide in horror that he might go up and see Hamal.

"Not like you mean."

He stopped, raising an eyebrow as he looked at her. "Oh? How did I mean?"

His eyes glinted with humor, and she dropped her dismay. She even managed a smile, all while continuing to silently ask that Hamal stay upstairs. "He's in the guest room."

Mike's eyebrows rose, his eyes returning to look up the stairs. "Hmm. I'm not sure if that makes me more comfortable. I think I'd rather you had some sleazy one-night-stand than have some random stranger bunking in your house for the night."

"How do you know it's a random stranger?"

He cocked his head with a look that said he knew she knew why he would know that.

She raised her eyebrows in defiance, forcing him to verbalize his answer.

His face turned serious, voice dropping further to ensure Dee's mysterious tenant couldn't overhear. "I'm excited to see you've spoken to another human being that wasn't a server at a restaurant, but I worry."

Dee smiled, matching his whisper. "I know. And I appreciate it. But you don't need to."

Mike looked over her head, and she knew Hamal had appeared. She spun, throwing Hamal a look that expressed her dislike that he'd shown his face, before turning back to Mike to introduce the two, fake smile plastered over her features.

Hamal, managing not to come off with his usual intimidating arrogance, moved forward to shake Mike's hand with a smile that expressed real warmth at meeting Dee's only friend. "Mike, great to meet you. It's real great that Dee's letting me stay here for a couple nights."

-Real great?-

Dee listened carefully to the change in timbre and cadence of Hamal's voice, wondering if this weren't telling of his roots, or just another scary detail about the supposed assassin; that he would change his face as the moment needed. How had he been manipulating her with the masks he chose to wear?

She watched the encounter between the men with attentive eyes.

-I told you to kill him.-

Mike pumped Hamal's hand. "Nice to meet you as well. What brings you to our little slice of nowhere?"

Hamal's smile remained. "Just some relaxing travel. This town is definitely relaxing."

Mike laughed at this, turning away to move back into the kitchen. Hamal trailed after him with Dee staring daggers into the back of his head.

The smell of grounds making their way into the press drew both Dee and Hamal farther into the kitchen, despite the fact it'd been bedtime a few moments before.

Mike continued the conversation as he made coffee. "Relaxing, it is. Sleepy, even. How'd you run into Desiree?"

Dee threw Hamal a look of pleading, relaxing as he answered. "Apparently, we share a love of late-night exercise."

Dee took a seat closest to the sliding doors so she could stare into the darkness. She felt Mike's heavy gaze at the mention of late-night jogs. The very jogs she'd promised to discontinue.

She pretended not to notice, forcing herself not to flinch from his next words. "I see. Strange habit."

Hamal shrugged.

She was surprised when Hamal continued explaining. "Yeah, but it tended to be the only time I could consistently find to fit it in. Now, it's just a habit I haven't bothered to drop."

Mike grunted in pseudo-understanding, pouring the freshly made coffee into three mugs, one which he brought to Dee. Another he set in front of himself while the third remained on the counter. Mike gestured with a head nod. "Milk in the fridge. Sugar just above the coffee, if you need it."

Hamal rescued his mug from the counter and took a seat at the far end of the large wooden table opposite Dee and Mike.

Looking out the window, Dee didn't catch whatever look Hamal must have made that had Mike explaining the large table. "Dee's father owned a large construction and real estate firm. There were always groups of people over for dinner, often staying in the house for a few nights while working on various jobs."

Hamal nodded, surprising Dee again when he continued engaging Mike. "You grew up here, too?"

Mike shook his head. "I didn't grow up here, but I've spent most of the last ten years here. Dee's like a sister to me."

Dee, still staring out the window, felt Hamal's eyes on her. She'd taken her steaming coffee from the table and was blowing on the hot liquid as she avoided the conversation.

-Why is this a good idea? Letting these two talk? Mike doesn't know what Hamal knows, and Hamal doesn't know what Mike knows. Keeping it that way seems like a great idea. Though if you just kill Hamal, there'd be no worrying about it.-

Dee continued to blow on the coffee held close to her face.

-You could at least tell Mike to get out of here. You're going to start saying too much if you get any more tired. Filter shuts off, remember?-

She sipped her coffee. Still too hot.

-Kill Hamal, then take a vacation. Somewhere like the Amazon.-

It wasn't how she'd wanted any of this to go down. Not that she'd had much time to think about it, but she knew that if she had, having Mike meet Hamal wouldn't have come up. That it was happening propelled Dee into a position where she felt more like an observer of her life rather than a participant.

Part of her, most of her, was okay with this, as it allowed her to sit back and watch in a detached manner. A small part of her, the part that was eager to find out what Hamal could tell her, was stymied by Mike's presence. So, as a passively waiting being, she stared out the window, sifting through the words spoken, and unspoken, in the kitchen behind her.

She sipped her coffee again.

"Dee, you'll be alright? I can stay..."

Mike's words brought her attention back to the kitchen. Holding in a sigh, she swiveled around to face the man talking to her. "I'll be fine." Her eyes shifted quickly to Hamal, then back to Mike before dropping to her coffee, taking another sip to give her something to focus on besides the two pairs of eyes asking more than she was willing to provide.

Mike nodded, pausing for a moment before getting up to rinse his mug then put it in the dishwasher. "I'll call you later. Be good, 'Case."

Dee nodded, meeting his eyes and forcing a smile to reach hers. "Sleep tight."

Mike grinned before shooting Hamal a warning look as he left the kitchen.

Dee waited until she could no longer hear Mike's car, a much longer time than Hamal, who was content to wait her out. When Mike's presence had cleared her senses, she turned her attention to the stranger she'd allowed in her house. Part of her wanted to be mad that he'd come downstairs to intrude on her life, but she had invited him here. Also was the matter of how long he would stay if she questioned everything he did.

-Don't do that. Don't give him power over you.-

She understood the truth of this but was too curious to finally find some answers that she ignored the advice. Instead, she bit back her comments of how he'd handled Mike's entrance, concentrating instead on their conversation that had been interrupted.

She took a deep breath to settle her nerves. "You were telling me how one becomes an assassin."

A smile pierced Hamal's neutral mask. "No, you were asking. I hadn't been telling you anything."

Dee's annoyance at this answer flooded her face before she could catch it. With another breath, she forced her face to neutral. "I suppose that's fair."

"Is it?"

He was goading her, and she knew it, but she wasn't sure how far to push.

-He came to you, remember?-

That was true.

"You told me you were an assassin. I didn't ask that."

"You don't believe me?"

Her mouth twitched towards a smile. "Not really. Why would an assassin be sent to gather information?"

Hamal matched her grin. "I wondered the exact same thing. I don't think my being an assassin has anything to do with why I got this job."

Dee raised her eyebrows in question, but Hamal didn't elaborate.

She was bone tired, the energy she had earlier to force this conversation now evaporated. Looking at another full day tomorrow, today rather, brought a new wave of exhaustion over her. "Alright, how about sleep now. We can play twenty questions later."

Hamal shrugged, sipping his coffee like he was there at her sufferance.

-Killing him is still an option.-

Her mind was calm as she wondered just what she had gotten herself into.

"You sleep. I've got some things to take care of, but I'll see you again in the morning." Hamal's words surprised her.

She didn't try to keep the look of distrust off her face. "'Some things to take care of'?"

"You're repeating."

"I'm not repeating. I'm questioning."

"Questioning?"

She glared across the table, head balanced on hands propped up with elbows on the table.

He laughed, standing to put his mug in the sink. "Don't make me wake you again."

12

He was sure she was still hiding things from him. That she'd told him she wasn't sure what her limits were kept him from accusing her of it to her face. Still, he'd changed his strategy.

It wasn't that she was strong. Or fast. Or agile. Or that her reaction times were almost prescient. Those things he was used to seeing in the Soldiers who surrounded his daily living. It was that her muscle memory was so good she merely had to mimic a move a few times to master it. Thus a day of training had been the equivalent of months.

"Alright, so we're going to spend the first part of the day doing some slow-motion training."

"Slow motion training."

"Yes, and you are forbidden ever to repeat what I say."

"Got it, no repeating what you say."

He sent a glare in her direction, letting his annoyance slip when he saw the smile in her eyes.

"Strength is important, but not always more so than leverage."

H amal showed Dee exactly how important this matter of leverage was over the next couple of hours. Her strength was greater than his, but she still found herself flipped, tumbled, and arm locked to immobility. By the end of the day, she wholly agreed that leverage was far superior to strength.

"Had enough?"

She studied his face to see if he was mocking her. "Have *I* had enough?"

"Yeah, have you had enough, or can we go a little longer?"

Her eyes trailed to the house, disappointed the shower calling her name would have to wait. Unwilling to tell Hamal she wanted a break, she brought her eyes back to him. "What did you have in mind?"

"The sun's almost down, not that it needs to be for Revenants to be out and about, but it does make it easier to hide truths from the sheep."

"Truths from the sheep?"

He shot her a glare.

She laughed. Apparently, it was a habit she hadn't realized she had, but it did help her assimilate information. Hamal must have realized this, too, as he hadn't pushed the issue. Much.

"Yeah, truth. Sheep. Let's go find us a hand-to-hand fight."

D ee learned something that night she wouldn't have discovered in a controlled environment like her backyard: Panic moderation.

At the start of the excursion, she was able to focus on the idea that she was looking for a Revenant. Concentrating on the tingling in her head, she was able to open something in her brain that was more reliable than a vague sense of discomfort.

If Hamal picked up on the fact that she was knowingly following one, he didn't let on. Her dictating their path was part of the exercise, so it wasn't a difficult thing to hide. That his shotgun was out, ready for the first sign of attack, had her wondering if he knew something she didn't.

Whether or not he was nervous, she definitely was. The farther away she strode from her yard, the more butterflies opened their wings in her stomach. Concentrating on breathing to keep herself calm was distracting her from tracking, but when she stopped focusing on her breathes, she tended to stop breathing.

He must have noticed her struggles from his position following her. "Relax. You've already survived these things, and you're much better equipped to handle them now. Don't freak yourself out."

She'd stopped moving at the sound of his words. Taking a deep breath in an attempt to follow his advice, she continued forward only to halt after a few steps. The Revenant she was tracking had changed course to move towards them. The thing they hunted was now hunting them.

"You see something?"

"Hear." It was a lie, but the closest thing to the truth she could think to say.

"If it's coming at us, be ready for a flying attack."

She nodded, memory shifting to the tackles she'd endured in the past.

This one didn't come flying through the trees. Instead, it waited, assessing the pair who stared back at it through the darkness.

Hamal had offered a pair of night-vision-goggles to Dee. After trying them out for a few steps, she'd returned them, explaining her vision was more easily navigable without them. He couldn't help wonder how well she really could see that she would turn down the tech he couldn't function without.

His gear was no longer on his mind when the eyes of the creature staring daggers at Dee stopped them fast. She'd told him about the one who'd spoken to her. It'd been hard for him to believe, but watching this one, seeing its face, he was curious about what other things he didn't know. He'd never seen one of these before, surprised it was willing to be used like this if it maintained the amount of intelligence he saw glimmering in its eyes. What lives they must live to be willing slaves to masters ready to send them to their deaths.

Repressing the urge to be mad at Zi for not arming him with better information, Hamal focused on the task at hand. He stifled a flicker of nerves that threatened to undermine the exercise, spawned by the idea that he might not know what they were up against.

N ot sure what to do, Dee stared into the eyes of the thing sent to kill her. Part of her wanted to talk to it. To ask it who had dispatched it, and why.

-*Someone wants to kill you. That's why.*-

The thought had become a daily mantra. Its appearance in her thoughts would send her into a not-quite-out-of-body experience that spun her sideways so she watched herself from a third-person perspective. The concept of someone wanting her dead was still so foreign to her she wasn't sure it was something she truly believed, despite having protected her life from a few of these very creatures that had turned her life into a bad movie.

She started towards it but Hamal's whisper stopped her. "Patience."

Whether because of the hesitation or in time with it, the creature pounced. Dee tensed, every muscle in her body going rigid, everything Hamal had trained her out the window as fear coated her synapses.

Some sense came back to her when the creature hit her, a detached sort of observation and she wondered whether they would barrel into Hamal.

Somehow, she managed to twist her hips, stepping back to

guide the thing around and to the ground. Maintaining the motion, she sliced the long blade Hamal had given her straight through the creature's chest. That she'd managed to pull it, then use it to pin the beast to the ground, was a monumental victory.

Stepping back, eyes wide, breath gasping, she stared down at the quick kill she'd managed. Hamal was clamping her on the back in congratulations, but she couldn't hear him, deaf to the world from the blood rushing through her ears.

Don't throw up. Don't throw up. Don't throw up.

Blinking fast, she looked up, eyes unfocused. Hamal had stepped in front of her, his hands bringing her face close to his in an attempt to force her attention from its daze. "Dee! Dee, you alright? Look at me."

His voice registered as far away. Ironically, when he lowered the pitch of his voice, it broke through her haze. "' Case? You did good."

She met his stare, staring through his goggles to the eyes beneath, using the connection as her tether to reality.

Hamal kept his voice calm. "You're alright, Dee. Relax. You killed the thing. Cake! I told you I was a good teacher."

-I don't recall him ever saying any such thing.-

She brought her hands up to cover his own still pressed around her face, gently guiding them away. Wide eyes continued to stare into the sockets of his goggles, incapable of speech.

His voice filled with concern. "Dee? Don't lose it on me now."

She smiled, eyes glazed. "You don't get to call me 'Case."

He continued to peer into her face, smile not erasing the concern in his eyes. "Who's going to stop me?"

She didn't answer.

Her stare dropped to the body at their feet, and Hamal stepped away.

He handed over a zippo with an expression of pure mischief. "The honor is yours."

Still not out of her daze, Dee took the lighter, crouching to the corpse, letting the flame lick the skin of its hand. The flame caught quickly, surprising her, so she fell back. Landing hard, the majesty of the fire caught her eye and drew her into a past of vague imagery and broken feelings

---

S he'd performed fantastically. Except for the post-kill anxiety he wasn't sure what to make of, there was nothing he could tell her that would have made the fight better.

Now, watching her stare, stunned, at the burning corpse, he huffed. He probably could have warned her about how flammable they were. He knelt to her. "Dee? Time to go."

She rose without pause, her eyes still glassy as they strolled back through the woods towards her backyard. He hoped she wasn't going into shock.

"Hamal?"

He looked at her, startled by the quiet tone of her voice.

"Why are they trying to kill me?"

He'd told her so much already, why not this? "I don't really think they are."

"So, this has all been a test?" Her voice remained breathy but gained some force at hearing he didn't think they were trying to kill her.

"I think so. If one of them really wanted you dead, they'd have sent something better after the first Revenant failed."

She frowned. "You're here because someone knew someone else was checking me out and wanted to know what the deal was?"

He grimaced that she'd deduced his part in this. "Basically."

"But you can't tell me who sent you, or who you think was checking me out?"

His silence was answer enough.

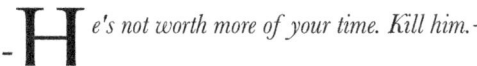 H *e's not worth more of your time. Kill him.-*

Dee almost laughed out loud. What would the point be now?

-The point would be to get the hell away from where they know you are.-

If she thought it would matter, she might consider killing Hamal, then skipping town. But if they'd found her after the fire when she was hiding, then found her again here, she wasn't sure any amount of running would help.

-I hear they're manning a mission to Mars. Maybe get on that?-

This time she did laugh.

Hamal's eyebrows rose.

"Sorry, I was just thinking how maybe if I got in on that Mars colonization plan, I might be able to hide from these guys."

"I don't think that would even do it."

His comment brought total stillness to her. If that were true, it meant she was in more trouble than she thought.

"Are they aliens?"

It was his turn to laugh. "No, but they've been around for a looong time. Money, even in the amounts that planning, creating, and manning a search to Mars would take, is nothing to them. I'm pretty sure they have access to technology that's not even developed yet."

"How is that possible?"

"With money, you can fund R&D. With life spans as long as I think they have, they have memories of tech long forgotten by the rest of us."

Long forgotten tech?

"R & D?"

"Research and Development."

Her heart jumped into her throat. "So, I'm screwed."

"It depends what they want. Right now, you're simply a curiosity. Maybe they'll get over you, and you can go back to your life."

"How likely is that to happen?"

He didn't meet her eyes, pointedly looking straight ahead. "I can't say."

Dee closed her eyes. "So, we just sit around and wait for whoever to decide what they want to do with me to do it?"

"Basically."

"Basically?"

"Basically."

"I'm not sure I like that."

Hamal shrugged, too nonchalant for Dee.

She slowed her steps, watching him walk farther away from her, before catching up again. "Well, can I go meet any of these—"

"Rishis."

"Rishis?"

"Not until they ask."

"I have to wait to be invited? Sending—things—to kill me isn't invitation enough?"

"They're not really meant to be an invitation, no. And, like I said, I don't think they're here to kill you."

"Are you making fun of me?" Her voice pitched towards hysteria.

He stopped walking. After a couple of steps, she stopped too. Taking his goggles off, he met her eye. "I promise I'm not making fun of you."

"How can you be so—calm?!"

"Should I be yelling too?!" He stretched his arms to the sky, leaning in, so his words shouted into her face. His suddenly loud voice startled her, throwing her heart to racing, his encroaching posture setting her a step back. After a second of being surprised, she laughed, stress tears flowing down her face in opposition to her laughter.

Hamal started walking again, moving more slowly without his goggles to light the path. "Tomorrow, we'll train, and the next day, and again, until we get more information."

Dee nodded, following him. "Train and train and train."

13

Hamal pushed her hard. With so many training hours and his vigilant oversight, he gave Dee no time for anything else. Other than a few calls to Mike, her life was wake, train, eat, train, sleep. Over and over for a month, Dee struggled to remember what life had been like before this tyrannical mentor had moved into her house.

Hamal had no trouble finding time for extracurriculars. Most nights saw him slipping out after they'd gone to bed. Dee knew well enough what he was up to by the smell of the women wafting off him when he returned. An odd sense to have heightened, and an awkward way to realize it, the recognition of what he was doing with his time left her bitter that he could go out but she was forbidden to leave.

-Right, 'cause you're in no way jealous.-

Just like he never explained to her where he'd been, she didn't tell him she knew. It was the perfect reminder for her to keep her eye on the ball. When her thoughts slipped to the idea that she was never going to meet someone else who had a handle on a supernatural world that wasn't supposed to exist, whenever she felt herself slipping to the idea that he might be the ideal partner for her, she remembered his nightly adventures.

-He probably thinks you're a freak. You're just his pet project.-

Standing in the kitchen, coffee in her hands steaming her face, she stared absently at a point in the room. She'd gotten up early to train, but Hamal wasn't even there.

-You should have killed him.-

He'd spent another night away, making it the third night this week. The second week after he'd moved in, he'd gone out once. The next week, twice. These last two weeks had seen him gone more than he was there.

Face set in stoic nonchalance, she moved to the front of the house, curling herself onto the porch swing to wait for his arrival.

-Right, this is you not *caring.-*

It was illogical and dangerous for her to be jealous. She knew it. Her brain knew it, but other parts of her had been lonely—

She pulled out the long knife Hamal had gifted her, turning it in her hands, watching how the sun glinted off the blade, wondering why a knife, and not a gun, would be the thing he gave to her.

He'd called it Damascus steel, explaining the eight-inch blade's dark and light patterns were formed in the process of melting the different metals together. She thought the designs were reminiscent of flowing water, the ivory handle elegant in its simplicity. Her fingers traced the patterns lightly.

There were no serrated edges as she imagined a long hunting knife should have, the curved edge of the blade sharp enough that she didn't touch it. Not again. The straight side of the knife beveled towards the sharp edge, and it was here her fingers caressed.

Hamal's SUV rolling up the driveway pulled her attention. She had little trouble masking her face with the same contemptuous humor he was so good at, her body language relaxed, almost catlike in its curled position on the bench seat.

Until now, she'd needed Hamal to stay. She hadn't asked too many questions. Hadn't done anything that might scare him. In short, she'd been on pins and needles, not rocking the boat that was him training her to not die.

This morning, all that had vanished, buried beneath her annoyance.

His eyes didn't rise to meet hers until he was climbing the porch steps. That he was brandishing gourmet coffee and bagels meant he'd traveled over an hour to procure breakfast. If there'd been any question about where he'd been, this fact answered it.

Dee smiled, a look she hoped portrayed contempt for where he'd been as well as a confident aloofness that it didn't matter. Maybe a little bit, she hoped to scare him.

"I brought treats." He kept his voice friendly, a mask to guard against what he saw reflected in her eye. The attitude she was throwing him hit him with a sharp pain he didn't understand. He refused to believe he felt regretful.

She flowed off the bench, movements more feline than human. He'd only seen her move like that this in their training sessions, those moments when she forgot to hide a part of herself. This was something more.

A twang of fear rolled over his shoulders.

Who was this girl? Even after the weeks he'd been there, that thing he sensed hiding beneath the surface remained elusive. Was the girl standing in front of him now a glimmer of what that thing was?

As she moved closer, his breath held. She seemed taller, larger. Something more powerful than any Soldier. Maybe training her hadn't been the best idea.

"I like treats."

Her voice shook him from the paralysis that had come over him. The mocking arrogance she'd shown only a second before vanished under the smile she now wore.

She took the tray of coffees and bag of bagels from him into the house.

His eyes lingered, caught on the mug she'd left on the floorboards of the deck, but his concentration was on where she'd brushed him as she'd passed. Electrified by the passing contact, he was afraid to move after her just yet.

Was there a subtle threat in her posturing? Had it turned to flirting?

Since the first morning he'd returned from the arms of his conquest of the week, Dee'd never let slip that he was anything more than a teacher to her. It was another part of what forced him away. That thing about wanting what you can't have? It was real. More and more often, he had to give himself the pep talk about why she was off-limits. Why any involvement the two might succumb to could only end badly. More likely for him than her.

Badly was a word he kept himself away from when dealing with Rishi business.

The threat he'd seen in her was worse than this hypothetical *bad*. He knew he couldn't take her if she made up her mind to get rid of him. The thought had crossed his mind that she might decide he was too dangerous to live. That was before he'd moved in. Now, he'd just be more careful.

He followed her path to the kitchen. She'd settled with a cup of his procured coffee, still warm despite the long drive from where he'd picked it up. He stared at the remaining cup in its holder, set on the table next to the bagels she'd placed near a tray of butter. Had he really brought her breakfast, like they were a couple or something?

He shook his head, eyes flickering to her to see if she'd caught his reaction before moving to the coffee. She wasn't paying him any attention, her gaze out the window consistent with her usual mien. There was no trace of whatever had overcome her outside.

Sipping coffee, he walled himself from the excitement the girl who'd met him on the porch sparked. That hint of something wild, untempered, underneath the veneer of an unlearned damsel was the girl who would be fit to survive the Rishis' games. A girl much more than a girl who he was not allowed to have.

Energized by this sense of Dee's future, Hamal left his coffee untouched to make his way upstairs to a shower where he washed off the remnants of last nights foray. Letting the water pelt over his face, squeezing his eyes against what was forbidden, he struggled to find his center.

It was only when he allowed anger to overwhelm him that he broke from the forbidden. Anger that he couldn't control his feelings. Anger that they'd put him in this situation. Anger that he wasn't strong enough to do what might be necessary to keep Dee safe.

Anger that he couldn't take what he wanted.

Finally, he turned off the shower, stepping out with thoughts focused on what needed to be done. Today would be another hard day. It was what was demanded.

He'd finally heard from home-base. Porrima, a Rishi who'd given up control of her own House a millennia ago to assist Zibanitu in maintaining order, had contacted him. Her dislike for Hamal was no secret. Even as a boy he'd known to avoid her.

It had been her who'd approached him about this mission. The last person he'd ever expected to see at his door, she'd wielded an open laptop without saying a word. Zibanitu's face waiting patiently on the screen was the only reason he'd let her in. To have her perched rigidly on his sofa, face a mask of discontent for all Zi was telling him, had made it difficult to concentrate.

Short and chubby with mousy brown hair, her pinched face forever told how superior she was over everyone. If not for Zi's personally asking him to take this job, Hamal would have been elated to tell her to shove it.

Her self-important tone on the phone this morning couldn't ruin his cheer about receiving details about this simple task that had grown complicated. But when he heard what she had to say, everything was worse.

There would be Revenants in the area, most likely sent to test if Dee was something more than she seemed.

Hamal had laughed, unable to speak, stomach and face hurting from the outburst. Giving in to the humor of it had stayed his rage. Laughter might be forgiven. His temper wouldn't have been.

Porrima had been angry enough with his laughter that she'd hung up on him. He could handle that. When she called back, most likely at the insistence of Zi, she allowed Hamal to explain the reason for his response.

She was less happy when she learned how old their intel was, then threatened his life when she found out he'd made contact with the girl. Silence settled over the line when he explained how he'd been training her to protect herself for weeks.

As dangerous a game as he was playing, Hamal couldn't help but grin that he'd rendered the Rishi speechless.

When she found her voice, Porrima explained how she would use this opportunity as leverage to see him extradited from the House.

He hadn't been worried.

Not *that* worried.

The third call surprised him. This time she explained, in a voice tight with displeasure, that Zi approved of Hamal's decision to get involved with the girl. Of course, she didn't expect continued competent choices, especially considering his reputation with human women.

He'd laughed at her again. She'd hung up on him again. That was more than fine with him. He'd already forgotten her threats. What he hadn't forgotten was how old their intel was that left him with a sense of foreboding. If Hamal was on his own, they were screwed.

He moved down the stairs, thoughts shuffling through the little he'd learned since taking this mission, forced to continue to speculate on what was going on. He'd been running this mission on conjecture from the beginning, always with the idea that eventually he'd have answers.

Whoever had been sending tests at Dee had to be deciding their next move. He didn't believe she was in the clear, regardless of these quiet weeks that suggested just that. Still, he saw the prudence in laying low. Any movement, whether bringing Dee to Zibanitu or sending Soldiers here to protect her, might draw attention. This attention could force someone's hand that might otherwise remain still.

Given the Rishis vast network of spies and information gathering, few secrets stayed so for long. It was why Hamal continued to be grateful that a swarm hadn't descended. Once that happened, Zi would have to decide whether to bring her in or take her out.

It was another thought that sent a curious sensation through him. His feet paused as he hit the first floor. He was far from capable as her only protector if Soldiers started showing up. He was Zibanitu's pet human, allowed here because his presence couldn't cause a diplomatic riot.

Zibanitu's pet human. The words rang through Hamal's head in Porrima's annoying, matter-of-fact tone. The phrase no longer annoyed him as it had in his youth. Zibanitu was the reason he knew all he did, was capable of all he was, and allowed the life he never regretted. Even if this mission ended as his last, there was nothing he'd choose differently.

When he entered the kitchen, his head was settled.

Dee was bouncing on her toes, staring out the wall of windows into the backyard. She turned to him as he grabbed the coffee he'd left on the counter.

Her eyes widened in surprise. "You're going to make me wait longer? Let's go. Let's go."

Her words were light, but the energy leaking off of her told of her need to get moving.

So far, she'd obeyed his decree to stay inside, despite him not following his own orders. He was surprised she'd followed his rule.

He'd spent most nights away staring at the hidden camera feeds in her house ensuring she obeyed.

"It's not that late. I figured you'd still be in bed."

She raised her eyebrow at his deflection. "Well, I'm not still in bed."

She looked into the backyard. "How about I get out there and loosen up while you let the rest of whatever stink that is fade off you."

His posture went rigid, but she was out the back door, tumbling nimbly through the grass before he could mouth off a comeback.

Pressing his lips together, it occurred to him that sending an attack while he was gone all night was the perfect opportunity for whatever might come next. His selfish need had superseded the question about whether or not she'd be safe to protect herself.

That his first reaction was embarrassment-turned-guilt pissed him off, so the anger he thought he'd mastered left him seething.

Who he was mad at, he wouldn't admit to anyone.

14

——————

Dee's muscles were plenty warm by the time Hamal made his way outside. She stood as close to the treeline as she could without actually being in the trees. The slow movements of the kata Hamal had shown her had progressed to the quicker, tightened motions that made the exercise strenuous enough that she had a sheen of sweat coating her body.

She felt his eyes on her as he walked across the yard.

As usual, she deciphered nothing of what he might be thinking from his body language. His face, always impossible to read behind a mask of arrogant mocking, did nothing to help her either. Did he know she knew he was studying her? Not that he wasn't doing it every moment they were training, but there was something different about this.

-He was sent here to watch you. He admitted this to you, but you're wondering why he's studying you?-

That he'd never explained all his motives for helping her wasn't a point she'd forgotten. Sometimes it slipped her mind, snapping back when she found herself doing, or saying, something to him only friends might do.

They weren't friends. She repeated to herself, every morning and again every night. At some point, whatever game he was playing would came to light, and she knew she'd be glad she drew this line.

Still, it was hard keeping him at a distance. His relaxed manner, quick wit, and enveloping confidence enfolded her to him, even as he taught her to protect herself against creatures she still struggled to wrap her mind around. Maybe it was harder because of that.

She pulled her attention back to the trees in front of her, letting their comforting wall give her a sense of protectiveness.

-In your own backyard, you need protection, yet in the darkest hours of the night, you're okay jogging around town?-

She admitted to herself there wasn't much logic in the nuances of her paranoia. No one could see her in the backyard of the house set far from the road, circled by woods but her subconscious didn't care, which was why she always moved closer to the tree line when she could. If Hamal had come outside first, they'd be in the center of the large clearing that was her backyard.

As his approach neared, she stopped her warm-up to turn her full attention to him. Meeting his eye made her self-conscious, so she turned away before the blush could consume her face. To hide the movement, she swung her arms back and forth across her body to stretch and keep her muscles loose.

Taking a long, cylindrical bag from its position draped across his back, Hamal pulled two long, curved swords. Dee wanted to call them katanas but didn't know enough about bladed weapons to say so out loud. Whatever they were, their presence sparked new excitement that she'd be learning something different today.

The weapons glinted in the sun. "The only way to be sure they're really dead is for them to lose their heads. Super sharp, bladed weapons is the only way to guarantee that."

"We haven't decapitated anything so far."

"The things you've seen will seem like toddlers to what might be coming."

Keeping the terrified scream sounding in her brain at Hamal's words quarantined, Dee took the blade Hamal handed her, noting its blunt edges. "I thought you weren't supposed to bring a knife to a gunfight."

"Who said anything about a gunfight?"

She shrugged, concentration focused on the way the grip felt in her hand, pulled by the weight of the metal as it trailed away from her. "You've mentioned *Soldiers*. You said you wouldn't be able to protect me from them. I guess I just assumed they used guns."

"They do, actually."

Dee sighed, dropping her attention from her new toy. "So, I ask again, why bring a knife to a gunfight?"

Hamal laughed. "Well, this is a sword, not a knife, and, you should bring as many weapons as you can to every fight. At least, that's what I say. I also say, don't get in a fight with things that can kill you with a bullet but won't die the same way. Your chances of getting close enough to use the beheading trick are usually not good." He shrugged. "Sometimes, you have no choice."

Thinking of another point, Dee frowned. "I've been learning hand-to-hand defense to protect myself from things that don't fight hand-to-hand?"

"None of the Revenants had weapons. That's who you were learning to defend against."

"But now I might need to fight these Soldiers?"

"Possibly."

"Jesus."

"No."

Dee blinked fast. "Was that a joke?"

His face was unreadable. "Was it funny?"

She ignored him, thinking about how close she'd come to death when facing the B-team. Learning these other guys, these Soldiers, whose only purpose was to fight other supernatural supers would be coming after her did not stimulate confidence.

-*We could still kill him and make a run for it.*-

Her eyes darted around the yard, heart rate spiking. They

might be in the trees, watching right now. Surely, it wasn't safe to stay there.

"Don't get soft on me, Dee. We've made a lot of progress. This is nothing to worry about."

Her eyebrows rose in disbelief, the comment breaking her from her spiral down fear's path. "Nothing to worry about, huh?"

Hamal expressed a vague non-answer, moving away so he could begin his warm-up.

Dee continued her questions, matching his pace as he jogged around the perimeter of the yard. "They can only kill each other with blades, but they all carry guns?"

"Yeah, they're usually decked out in all the newest, coolest toys."

"But, they can't kill each other with bullets?" She re-asked the question to focus her thoughts from panic.

"The bullets *might* kill them, but have you ever been shot? Not pleasant. They feel pain. Injuries still debilitate. They just, *probably*, won't die from them."

Dee envisioned spray from an automatic weapon keeping some super-soldier wielding a sword at bay. Hamal's words seeped further, and she shot her eyes to his face. "Probably?"

He shrugged. "Sometimes a freak thing happens. It's rare, but it happens a Soldier dies from bullet wounds. Not all Soldiers come out—the same."

"Come out?"

He shrugged again, and she wasn't sure if he didn't have more of an answer because he didn't know or if he wasn't willing to tell.

She closed her eyes, trusting her body to follow Hamal's rhythm around the yard without tripping while she settled her thoughts. Her eyes popped open. "The Revenants can't use guns, can they?"

She wasn't looking forward to the possibility of being shot at. Her healing abilities were outstanding but she didn't want to find out if a bullet would kill her.

"Well—" Hamal hesitated, forcing Dee's attention to observe

his face. Here was a rare instance when she was sure he was weighing what he was willing to tell her. After a moment's pause, he decided to answer. The shock of it almost had her miss what he said.

"There are a few, let's call them *levels*, of Revenants. The one you got in the cemetery was a Level One. These talking ones— well, honestly, I'm not sure what they are. The talking ones don't typically show signs of heightened strength, not without other problems..." he trailed off, eyes going distant before he pulled himself back. "Just trust me. There are a few that would be able to carry a gun and use it adequately, but I can't believe they'd be sent here."

"Use it *adequately*?"

"Able to shoot you. Adequately. Shoot you. To death."

Dee found it in herself to chuckle. "I feel like it's a terrifying thing that these things are running around capable of handling weapons *adequately*. No police force or government agency has figured out these things are out there?"

If her comment had been enough to give away her disbelief in his story, her tone more than made up for it.

It was Hamal's turn to chuckle, a glint in his eyes that sucked the breath from her. "Who says they haven't?"

The comment stopped Dee's push for information, hearing the possibility in his words of secret agencies tasked to deal with the hidden problem of monsters. Her attention turned from his face to stare at the trees beyond.

He'd been hiding information from her, she'd known that, but this spin opened a line of possibilities she'd never considered. It was information that validated his secrets.

-Is that what you're getting out of this? His right *not to tell you things?-*

Her attention returned to his face. "Are you working with an agency like that?"

"No." There was nothing to read in the answer. Nothing registered on his face or in his voice that might suggest he was lying or had more to offer that he refused to give.

She huffed. "Whatever. You were going to show me how to cut people's heads off or something."

Dee's learning curve with the weapon excited them both. Once he explained that the movements were the same from the hand-to-hand forms, there was no stopping her.

He'd learned weapons first, hand-to-hand last. The point was to kill things, and these tools enhanced that. Forced to fight without a weapon meant you were having an especially bad day. He hadn't started Dee with a sword because as much as he acknowledged he was disobeying his orders, he hadn't wanted to put himself in a position where he might have armed the very thing that might need killing. Now that he'd gotten permission, it was time to level the playing field.

Backpedaling faster than his legs could keep up, Hamal fell. Lashing out with his weapon, hoping to catch her with an unexpected attack as a last resort even in the moment of his failure, she managed, with a speed he'd not yet seen, to deflect the attack. Her eyes, too intent on her prey to let up, showed how far she'd drifted into the zone of the fight. A ripple of fear slid over him. Not for what might happen here, but for what she would be if he continued to push her. What she could be if they continued to force her towards the thing she would need to be to survive them. Or, if any of the others got her, what she might be when they molded her to their desires.

Landing on his back, breath bursting from his body.

Dee followed, falling on top of him, and wiping all thought from his head.

A part of her brain registered that she'd gained the upper hand, pushing Hamal back as he fought to maintain his defense. When he tripped, a sound that might have been glee sounded in her brain but wasn't enough to bring her from the flow. Hamal had mentioned this place where one's body moved perfectly of its own volition without the mind getting in the way. It was terrific. Her body chased the feeling, unwilling to let it go.

He struck out at her, a move that should have taken her by surprise, but her flow would not be redirected. Parrying the move, she found herself falling with Hamal, barely catching herself before the front of her head smashed into his face.

-*Flow, huh?*-

Breathless, Dee smiled in pride that she'd taken Hamal down, searching his expression for recognition of her achievement. What she saw in his face hit her like a slap.

It wasn't pride in the skills he'd taught her. It wasn't even annoyance that she'd won in so clumsy a manner.

What beamed back at her was pure lust.

———

This was the very thing Hamal had been avoiding. Thoughts he was able to distract himself from were thrown in his face in a heap he couldn't just flip off. Her body pressing against him reminded him of the glimpse he'd gotten of her naked form under an oversized t-shirt on the morning he'd arrived. Not to mention the camera's he'd hidden all over this house that showed she rarely wore clothes while moving about her dreary existence.

They were sights that haunted his nights. They were sights that made it tricky for him to remain in this role of aloof tutor. Her eyes, blue spheres that drew him in, pierced his own, so the only thing he could manage was complete stillness while he waited for her to remove herself from him.

Only she wasn't moving. She was going to kiss him. The idea threw a smattering of emotions through him that moved quickly from panic to indifference. He deserved to take what he wanted, even if it would only be for a few moments.

Mind blank, he lifted his head to find her lips with his. She never hesitated, their first touch sparking the desire they'd both repressed to a blazing need. Taking her head in his hands, his kisses turned forceful, taking as much from his indulgence as he could. Her weight pushed further into him when she moved her hands from holding herself off of him to press over his own framing her face.

In a sudden move, he flipped them, so he was pressing into her, their mouths never disconnecting, bodies moving together as they reacted to their hosts' desires.

Then, he was standing, breathless. He stared down at her for a brief second before turning to stride purposefully into the house.

Dee listened to him rush away, following his path in her mind. She heard him move through the house, then out the front door.

She continued to lay in the grass, eyes never straying from their stare into the pale blue sky, even after his SUV, screaming down the road, was no longer heard.

-That was stupid.-

That was stupid.

-So much for your——-

Shut it.

She rolled slowly to her feet, relishing the endorphins even as she waited for them to subside. She hoped the memory wouldn't betray her the next time such a situation arose.

-Don't let there be a next time.-

Sage advice.

She had been avoiding it, but here it had happened anyway.

15

"**P**laytime's over! Get your shit together. Go again!"

-Well, at least things didn't get weird.-

This was more than weirdness. She wasn't sure what it was, exactly, but it wasn't that.

Something had happened in the few hours he was gone. When she'd asked, he'd just gone on and on about how if she wanted to survive, there needed to be less talking, less worrying about everyone's feelings, and more sweat dripping.

Yes, dripping sweat was essential to the cause of her not dying.

-Definitely seems like weirdness.-

She ignored the voice in her head. It wasn't that. At least, it wasn't only that. Hamal was worried. No, he was scared.

The thought terrified her.

They'd been training relentlessly for over an hour. She was surprised his voice hadn't gone hoarse with so much battering of her ego. If her confidence hadn't hit an all-time high with the introduction of the sword, she might be fighting off tears. Still, despite his exceptionally harsh treatment, he was teaching her to survive.

"Why are you stopping!"

Dee's answer was quiet, eyes staring towards the front of the house. "Mike's pulling up the driveway."

Hamal threw up his hands. "Of course, he is."

A frustrated snap of his wrist sent his sword piercing the ground and his steps *stomped* towards the house like a three-year old's tantrum. The glass door vibrated in its frame when it slammed shut behind him. Dee flinched but didn't follow.

Leaving worry over Hamal's reaction for another time, Dee walked around the house to meet Mike. She refused to let him see her stress, forcing cheerfulness into her voice. "Hey, Stranger. Early day?"

His gaze took in her sweaty, grass-stained clothes, but he kept his questions to himself. "Something like that. I'm actually on my way out of town. Have lunch with me before I go?"

Dee stole a glance at the house, seeing if she could catch Hamal's watchful eye on her. "I'm sure that can be arranged. Have time for me to shower?"

He looked her up and down. "I will make time."

She laughed, slapping his arm playfully as she turned to the house. Mike followed, his gaze lingering on Hamal's SUV still parked in her driveway. "Roommate working out?"

"He's teaching me some things."

She'd avoided talking about Hamal the few times Mike asked. She knew he was dying to know what the deal was, but she wasn't a good enough lier to alleviate his questions. So, she didn't talk about it.

"Gardening?" He motioned to the dirt and grass stains covering her clothes.

She laughed. "No, some self-defense stuff."

He went rigid.

-*The next time someones asks if you're gardening, you. Say. Yes!*-

Mike's voice was quiet. "You're being safe? Not running around in the middle of the night?"

"No, Hamal keeps me in at night." Her face turned crimson. She whirled around. "Not like that. We're not—"

Mike was laughing. "Relax, 'Case! I'm not your dad. I'd be ecstatic if you were having sex."

Her face blazed. "Wow! Awkward much?"

He laughed again. "We're friends. I can say that."

She laughed too. "Yeah, I guess you can."

Mike made a beeline for the kitchen as Dee went upstairs to start a shower, surprised Hamal wasn't waiting for them as they came in. He wasn't in his room, either.

With only a slight pause and a shake of her head, she continued to her room and the momentary bliss of a shower.

I mpulsivity he'd had as a child had been tempered by the implicitly understood fact that he would always be outmanned. Add that to the fact that few bothered to look at him as much more than a pet, Hamal had quickly learned to hold his opinions to himself. That he hadn't stifled his reaction earlier with the girl was a bad thing. It was an impulse he'd expressly forbidden himself.

This case was messing with him. Out of the loop, out of sight of his betters, and out of contact with those who persisted in guiding him, he'd made his own decisions. Many, based on emotion. He could admit that. Impulsive, emotional decisions. Still, they were choices he didn't necessarily regret even when set against the fact that they would probably cause him a lot of grief.

Who was he kidding? They were already causing him grief.

He walked faster, pushing through the woods, intent on finding something. Anything to progress from this unending *waiting*.

From the newest intel he'd received, he figured they had another day before Han's Soldier showed up. Or, someone was already here, checking on them; spying on them.

The thought sent a nervous chill up his spine. His phone call with Porrima had given him the heads up. It's what had him acting crazy. It's what had him afraid.

The snide bitch had relayed the information as if telling him what she had for lunch. Zibanitu's hard line of neutrality wouldn't allow him to interfere directly with the girl they still didn't know enough about to warrant the risk.

Hamal kicked at the bramble as he walked. That Sabik Han had resurfaced seemed reason enough to get involved? Han's House had been silent for centuries. Hamal only knew of him from stories whispered in secret, the name not even allowed in Porrima's presence.

He was scary. Capital *S-C-A-R-Y*.

Zibanitu worked hard to maintain peace between the Houses, whose millennia-old feuds could easily destroy pockets of the human world that had risen around the ashes of their culture's demise. Hamal appreciated the effort. As a member of the human race, he didn't want to see it destroyed because of ancient disagreements never lost to time.

Not that he'd spent much time with his kin, but there was enough of a connection that he didn't want humanity swept up in the dangerous underground world he'd grown up in.

The peace Zi had shouldered through thousands of lifetimes was priority enough that even Hamal's death, the pet-human, wouldn't shake the Rishi from his decision. Hamal's end would mean nothing when weighed against this bigger picture. Dee's would mean nothing.

Even after discovering the fantastic anomaly that she was, Zi wouldn't sway from breaking his own arbitrary rules. Hamal was sure there was nothing that ever would. It was probably the reason *the* Rishi among Rishis had been able to hold on as long as he had. Few others else could boast similar perseverance.

Hanging tightly to anger kept his fear at bay. Hamal was no match for the Soldiers, their heightened strength and speed combined with unmatched training would put even Dee to shame. There was no way Hamal could keep Dee safe if one of them were on their way. That it was one of Sabik Han's only meant the likelihood of survival was significantly less.

Even so, he never once thought he should leave. It hadn't been suggested that he do so, nor had Porrima offered any helpful advice. That they were *working on it* didn't instill confidence. They'd been working on it since before he'd arrived.

This was the first time he'd ever considered the fact that they weren't omnipotent.

He scowled, thinking of Dee off with Mike. Didn't she understand the danger?

He stopped, the quiet of the forest pressing around him.

Of course, she didn't understand. Sure, she was scared. There were even moments when that fear threatened to turn into all-consuming terror, but she didn't realize what was going on. How could she? He'd been so worried about not overwhelming her, added to the gag order he had on most topics, he hadn't relayed the danger the Rishis, and their armies, posed. He assumed she'd understand when she finally saw it all herself. Unfortunately, it looked like the only time she'd be able to see it would be the same time it was killing her.

Fishing his phone from his pocket, he made a call, hoping he wasn't sealing his death warrant.

16

She gave herself a moment to tilt her head back, to breathe in the humid air of late summer, to watch the stars twinkle from so far away before she looked towards the trees. A lifetime ago, her existence had consisted of lounging around the house, waiting for the sun to go down so she could lose herself in the running. A lifetime ago, her life hadn't been in constant danger.

-A lifetime ago you were bored to tears.-

There was something peculiar about tonight's exercise, something that settled a somber calm over her. Maybe it was from the way Hamal explained she would lead. Or the manner in which he'd introduced so many new gadgets for a seemingly simple exercise. Maybe it was just because he'd been acting strange all day.

Whatever it was, this wasn't like the last time. That had been a learning exercise. This was something else and Dee wasn't sure what to make of it.

-You can still just kill him.-

Dee ignored the voice's distrust. It was an irrelevant position at this point. She'd decided to put her faith in Hamal and was too far down that path to back out now. It didn't make sense that he would go through all this trouble if he did have some nefarious plan.

-Because you don't see it doesn't mean it's not there.-

She met Hamal's eyes briefly before moving towards the trees, putting her hands to the straps of her new backpack, as he'd done to his own. Both had triple-checked the draw speed of their weapons, feeling in their core that there would be need of them. There was something in the air that told Dee this night would be unlike any other.

-Maybe it's telling you to stay inside.-

She moved away from town, directing their path towards the thick woods that ran South and a little West for miles without break. She kept her mind open, listening for any hint of an impression that something was out there.

She imagined she felt Hamal's anxiety, the questions of something he hadn't told her burning to be asked. But something held her tongue, kept her pushing forward towards more unknowns.

"What is it?" He'd noticed her slow their pace.

Her head panned back and forth as she peered into the shadows, posture hunched, knees ready to spring. Something wasn't right.

"Something's not right."

Dee's sweat pooled between her shoulder blades where her pack pressed against her. She wanted nothing more than to strip out of the immobilizing load.

The air pressed around her.

-Don't tell him. He already knows too much about what you can do.-

Dee sighed, a release of frustration at the need to keep secrets.

There was a major difference in the one she sensed. Something *more* from the other Revenants she'd tracked. If she hadn't known better, she would have said the thing she felt wasn't a Revenant at all.

-Great. A whole new kind of creepy-scary?-

"Hamal, what else could be out here?"

He moved up next to her. "What do you mean?"

"I mean, what else could be out here. You said there were different levels of Revenants. Could they be out here?"

He opened his mouth to answer but closed it without saying what he was thinking. His goggled face turned to stare into hers. "You know when they're around? You can—*feel*—them or something."

The look on her face was answer enough.

His next words surprised her. "I think pulling your weapons might be a good idea."

She did as she was told. As he slid his shotgun to his back, replacing it with the rifle he carried, Dee pulled the long knife he'd gifted her in her left hand, the 9mm H&K she favored in her right. Despite him insisting she needed a smaller weapon to aim more accurately if she planned on using a one-handed grip, it was the one she'd decided on. The smaller Walther was snug at her back, all recent gifts from Hamal.

He took a breath. "Alright, where to?"

-You really suck at keeping secrets.-

There was nothing to be done about it now.

That he was nervous made her almost pass out from fright. It took a few seconds and a lot of inner-coaching for her to convince her feet to move forward. Once they did, she fell into a zone that took over her senses as she allowed herself to be pulled along by instincts, quietly leading the way through the trees as if she'd been doing it her whole life.

Hamal's slower pace had him quickly falling behind. If she heard his whispers for her to slow down, she ignored them. Torn between his fear of not being there to help her and the worry that he'd give away their position by being too loud, he hurried after her.

Moving silently through the woods was an exercise in futility. Everywhere he placed his feet, noise followed, so he was forced to move painfully slowly. He was a city boy; his targets typically taken out in much more urban landscapes.

When Dee came back into view, she was crouched behind a tree, as still as a cat about to pounce on its prey. His nerves frayed, he took a breath to ensure his words wouldn't come out in a yelling blitz as he moved next to her. "The point of the exercise is to have the teacher near-by so he can *teach*."

She nodded, but he sensed she wasn't paying attention. He took another breath to berate her attitude, cut off when she motioned ahead with her chin. "It's almost to us."

Hamal peered through the white-phosphorous world, waiting to see what it was they'd been tracking. He had the distinct feeling it was hunting them.

As if in answer to his thoughts, Dee spoke again. "It knows we're here, but I don't think it can see as well as I can."

Hamal glanced at Dee, this time worried for an entirely different reason. It was like she'd shed some mask of the girl he'd been training and revealed the warrior underneath, cold, calculating, and unwaveringly focused. He shivered at the confident energy radiating off of her, at the matter-of-fact tone to her voice.

In a burst of speed too fast for him to keep her in place, she was attacking. She was half-way to her target before he saw who it was.

He shouted a warning that fell on deaf ears.

The finely crafted golden snake symbol of the Ophiuchus' House hung around the perpetrator's neck to his waist. The few similar items Hamal had glimpsed, only in pictures, hadn't been this grand. Whoever this was, was at the top of the food chain.

Standing fast, Hamal anchored his shoulder to the tree while training his weapon forward. Real fear for Desiree washed his senses in a dampening fog. Not even Zibanitu's men would face off against one of Han's men without ensuring they had favorable numbers. Dee had no chance of winning and Hamal had no chance of successfully helping.

But he wouldn't just stand by and do nothing.

He slid through the trees, taking Dee out of his line of fire.

D ee's focus was sure, her plan clear. There was no place in her mind where doubt distracted her from felling this foe, though later, she would marvel at the fact.

When none of her shots landed, the face of her prey smiled in delight, his laughter ringing around her. Still, she moved forward.

Dropping her pistol after the last bullet failed to land the evasive target, she noticed the long blade hidden against his leg. Shifting her knife to her strong-hand, she left her sword sheathed in the possibility she might surprise him with it later.

She launched herself into the air, aiming to pass over him, twirling, so her eyes never left her opponent. She sliced out with her knife, felt the blade grab cloth, then skin, before his movement took him away from the blade's bite.

She landed with bent knees, transitioning directly into a lunging second attack.

But he was ready. He easily parried. The wound from where her knife had found his shoulder not slowing him in the least. His expression told her that he'd allowed her to finish her acrobatics rather than end her as he could have.

But Dee wasn't ready to concede defeat. She launched herself to the side, rolling behind the trees for cover.

From her left, she heard the *tap-tap-tap* of Hamal's rifle fire.

The newcomer spun away from her with a growl. "Hamal! I'll get to you!" His voice dropped, so he seemed to be talking to himself. "Stupid human has no reason to be here. Smart of Zibanitu to send you, though. No one plays politics better than Zi. Too bad The Ophiuchus cares nothing for his rules."

Only a part of Dee's attention was on this little speech as she stalked towards him. Deciding on offense, Dee came at him with sword drawn.

At the last second, he whirled, his blade easily defending.

Then, he ran.

Dee followed, adrenaline pounding through her.

The Ophiuchus' man turned abruptly, but Dee was ready. He missed a step, forced to backpedal against Dee's flurry of strikes.

Despite his failed attack, a smile crept across his concentrated features. Clearly enjoying himself his non-lethal attitude pushed aside much of Dee's attitude of violence.

A rustle charged through the trees distracting them both

They broke apart to look at what was coming, both ready to face some new foe.

The newest threat closer, Dee's opponent abandoned his mission.

Dee wasn't ready to let him go, but at Hamal's command she let the stranger disappear into the trees to turn and face the newest threat.

17

Hamal was explaining the evening's events to the bronze-skinned newcomer, while Dee pretended not to freak out. That this stranger was here on Hamal's request had her seething. Hamal's quick explanation, centered around the idea that he'd wanted to show Dee the reality of what she was up against in a controlled environment, hadn't pacified her.

-Controlled, my ass... what was with that other guy?-

That other guy was Barnard. Sent by The Ophiuchus, an enemy to all the Houses. No one was sure how he'd gotten word of Desiree's existence. This was all according to the stranger standing in her kitchen was Atkins, a Soldier from another House. Not one of Zi's. Not one of the Ophi guy.

-Fortuitous they arrived on the same night.-

Atkins studied Dee for a moment before returning his attention to Hamal. "I don't think a secret has ever been so well kept. If you hadn't called, we still wouldn't have any idea this drama was unfolding."

Dee kept quiet, afraid her anger would erupt in a violent outburst if she allowed herself to speak. That and the press of power radiating from Atkins was unlike anything she'd ever felt. It scared her in a way not even Barnard's presence had. There'd been no question in her mind she could take that one, as misleading as it might have been. With Atkins, her only impulse was to run.

Atkins continued to speak to Hamal. "Amalthea's first questions dug up the hint that Zosma's been looking into some girl who might possess skills akin to our Soldiers. This is probably what tipped The Ophiuchus off. Whatever other answers that may have been uncovered came after I left to come here."

Hamal nodded at Atkins' while glancing at Dee. She hoped her casual posture, eyes staring into the coming dawn as if she wasn't paying attention to the conversation, was enough to hide the fact that she wanted nothing more than to kick them out of the house. She wondered if they would leave if she asked, even as she contemplated if that was the best idea. Things had escalated from bad to nasty. She'd need backup if more Barnard's came for her.

Hamal's next words peaked her attention. "It was Zosma who knew enough to test her? Sending the Revenants? The Ophiuchus wouldn't waste the time. He'd have just come and taken her." He paused. "How did he find out when no one else had caught on?"

"Zibanitu caught on," Atkins replied.

When no one filled the gap in conversation, Dee turned, repressed energy expelling her voice too loudly. "So, this Zosma, why would he want to test me?"

Hamal and Atkins shared a look that Dee couldn't decipher.

Her eyes narrowed. "Will there ever be a time when I can know what's going on?"

Hamal choked on a laugh, managing chagrin when Dee threw him a venomous look. "Sorry. It's not funny, but you still don't understand who these things are or what their attention might mean for you."

Atkins raised an eyebrow.

"Sorry, Atkins, but you know what I'm saying."

Dee looked at Atkins, wondering what Hamal had apologized for, unless—Atkins was one of the *things* Hamal was referring to.

She froze, awed curiosity mixed with fear rendering her inert. Until now, the things sent after her had remained separate from whoever, or whatever was dispatching them. Now, finding herself next to one of the things that might be controlling from behind the curtain, she wasn't sure what to do.

The two continued to talk, Atkins' calm grating Dee's nerves. It held her attention, forced her to acknowledge the itchy feeling at the base of her skill was from him.

"...no one will want her in his hands. They'll come together to protect her from him. Assuming they don't consider her a threat."

"I'm right here," she barked.

Atkins looked at her with his weighted stare, that spoke of carefully contained violence. She squirmed under his focus, pulling her eyes to Hamal under the pressure.

Her breath held, only letting go when his eyes moved off her.

"I'm sure my Mistress will take her, but we'll need backup to transport her. Barnard won't simply tuck tail and run."

Hamal's voice was distracted. "I didn't think he was a Soldier."

Atkins turned to peer out the windows, staring into the brightening sky that painted the trees from black to green. "He's not."

Dee's stomach dropped. Atkins wasn't a Master? Barnard wasn't a Soldier? She wasn't sure how to prepare herself to meet a Rishi.

Refusing the pull of despair, she focused on Atkins feature by feature, using the exercise to still her mind.

Auburn hair fell past well-muscled shoulders. He was taller than Hamal's six-foot by at least four inches, towering like some ancient statue given life. His upper body was covered only by a leather vest that reminded her of some primitive tribal clothing. Cris-crossing his chest under this outer layer were straps that held bladed weapons of all sizes.

Trailing her eyes back to his face, she realized he'd been watching her study him.

Panicked, she rushed from the room. "I'm going to pack some things."

-Yeah? Were going with them?-
As if she could say no.

H amal was astonished when she didn't put up a fight, though after her run-in with Barnard, maybe she'd figured there was no other option. He stared at her retreating form, forcing himself not to follow. After this evenings fight, he wasn't keen on letting her out of his sight.

He listened as her steps faded up the stairs, trying hard to keep tabs on her this way.

"She's not what I thought she'd be." Atkins' quiet voice brought Hamal back to the kitchen.

"I'm surprised you gave it any thought at all."

A trace of a smile showed itself, equivalent to a hearty laugh for the ancient Soldier. "If she is what is rumored, it has been millennia in coming. Long have my people tried to do this very thing. How she managed to go so long under everyone's radar is a story I'm very curious to hear."

"What do you think she is?"

Atkins' contemplative stare was Hamal's only answer.

Hamal had to admit it didn't seem such a bad thing, whatever had happened to her. He would have sacrificed much to gain what she'd received. But, if she'd been created differently, if she were something other, things would get messy fast. A mess that might be enough to break the truce Zibanitu had maintained for so many centuries.

The suddenness of sprinting steps from upstairs turned their attention.

Dee's blurred shape was down the stairs and out the door before Hamal could react. Atkins, super-abilities on par with Dee, right behind her.

Hamal called out, but neither paid him any attention.

T hough he could have stopped her, Atkins was curious to see what had incited such a reaction. He stayed behind, not distracting her forward attention, watching her pull a pistol in her left hand and a beautiful eight-inch knife in the other. Whatever had called to her, it was not something she found friendly.

After following her through the trees, across the road, and through more trees, he understood what was going on. She'd caught one of their scents, remembering that Hamal had mentioned this was a trick of hers.

Unfortunately, the scent she'd caught was not of an enemy.

Atkins opened his mouth to explain, but it was too late. Dee had fired the 9mm rounds while picking up a burst of speed.

Daniel and Dimitri, Soldiers sent from Zibanitu's House, jumped and dodged the attack, their voices, first Dimitri's then Daniel's, rising over the burst of gunfire in the night air.

"Damn. Wait! Stop! We're—"

Her last shot landed, spinning Daniel around, though he managed to keep his feet.

He roared to the sky, "Ahhhh! That hurts, you crazy bitch! We're here—"

He turned back just in time to meet Dee's downward sword arc with his wrists.

Atkins breathed relief that the Soldier had bothered to wear his gear. The vambraces were standard issue, as the sword was the scariest weapon to face for a creature who might evade death by any other means.

Dimitri, hesitating, stood motionless through the engagement. Casting a glance at Atkins, he looked relieved that the elder Soldier reached the fight just in time to interfere with Dee's follow-up blow.

Atkins pulled her sword from her in a move that defied physics before he stepped between Dee and the newcomers. His free hand pushed into Daniel's chest, so he stumbled backward, still cursing his injury to the night.

———————

"**R**elax, everyone, please." Atkins' voice was level, lacking the volume the stress of the situation might have invoked from another. Still, his words were obeyed without hesitation.

Dee, breathing hard, stepped back a few paces. Standing in the middle of the woods with a trio of supernatural creatures, she wondered if running out like a crazy person had been the best idea.

-We need to work on your impulse control.-

"Daniel. Dimitri. We haven't had time to brief her." Atkins' calm voice further settled the group's nerves.

-Brief? They've been brief, *alright. Vague even.-*

The Soldiers nodded. Dimitri glanced around Atkins to throw Dee a sheepish look. "Sorry. We would have waited until you were in the loop, but we were told there's a severe time crunch."

-That's why the walk through the woods and not a car ride up the driveway?-

Daniel, his hand prodding his shoulder where her bullet had hit him, was less forgiving. He hissed, turning annoyed eyes to Dee's face. "How'd you even know we were here?"

Dee didn't answer. Her eyes drifted back the way they'd come. Hamal was still minutes from reaching them, and she wondered if she should go help him along. The sun had risen, but not much light breached the trees.

The Soldiers stood patiently, awaiting orders, already settled from the surprise engagement.

Atkins seemed confident Dee wouldn't continue to try to kill the newcomers. "Dee, my apologies for the manner this has been sprung on you. I imagine everything will be fully explained, in its time. Right now, we need to get you out of here before the Ophiuchus' people come in force."

Dee, who'd only been half-listening as she tracked Hamal's progress towards them, snapped her head around. "There might be *more* on the way?"

Atkins answered plainly. "Barnard will have called in reinforcements. They won't be afraid to fight for you, especially now that we're closing their window of opportunity."

"How does Sabik Han even know she's here?"

Dimitri's words were mumbled, but Atkins answered as if the question weren't rhetorical. "I imagine the same way your Master knows."

Dee looked between the three Soldiers. "I thought the Ophie guy sent Barnard."

Daniel let out a sound that might have been a choked laugh. Dee's eyes flickered to him, then back to Atkins, nerves too far gone to care if they were laughing at her.

Atkins answered, ignoring Daniel. "Sabik Han is The Ophiuchus, a title given him when he unmade the world."

-Unmade the world?-

"Who're these guys?" She stared at the pair of new arrivals, one light-haired where the other was dark, both over six feet tall and covered in tactical gear. She eyed the coverings on their arms that had allowed Daniel to block her sword, wondering where she might get a pair of her own.

"Dimitri and Daniel are the forward guards." Light then dark.

-Two guys?-

"Two guys."

Atkins nodded, ignoring the implied question. He set off at a walk that translated to a jog for Dee's shorter stride, back towards the house.

When they came to Hamal, he said nothing, only paused to meet Atkins' eye, then run his gaze over Dee injuries, before matching his pace with the group.

Daniel smiled upon seeing Hamal. "Well, well. No wonder this was kept quiet for so long."

Hamal *humphed*.

Dimitri's face revealed nothing.

-Nice to know they're all on the same page.-

Dee hated agreeing with her naggy inner sidekick. It was like no one knew what was going on, everyone stepping on everyone else's toes.

Thinking how else they might get to her, she turned to Hamal, expression fearful. "They won't involve Mike, will they?"

Hamal kept his gaze ahead, deliberately not meeting her look. "They shouldn't."

"Shouldn't? Like, shouldn't: they won't, or shouldn't: I can't tell you he's in danger because you'll freak out?"

Daniel answered, "They'll only involve him if it's absolutely necessary. He's safe today."

She whirled on the newcomer, forcing the others to crowd her. They wouldn't put their hands on her if they didn't have to, knowing it might encourage her anger, but neither did they want her to attack the newest member of their group for a second time.

"What do you even know about it?! I would hand myself over without a thought if they threatened to do anything to Mike."

Daniel glanced past her and Hamal to Atkins. "She's sparky." His eyes met hers. "I like her."

Her eyes narrowed, and she took a step forward, stopping when she pushed against Hamal. As fun as it might be to fight them all, the headache pounding behind her eyes told her now was not the time.

"Careful, Daniel."

Daniel's eyebrows rose, eyes turning to meet Hamal's with a look of both surprise and respect. He chuckled. "Well, well. Curiouser and curiouser." He returned his gaze to Dee, but it was Dimitri who spoke to her, head gesturing towards Hamal. "Don't settle for this one. You haven't even begun to see what's out there. Zibanitu's charity case could never keep up with you. You're one of us."

Daniel opened his mouth to say more, but Dimitri's hand on his shoulder stopped him. Daniel held Dee's eye for a moment, before stepping through the group to stride confidently towards the house.

Dee turned to watch the pair walk away, unsure what she'd seen in Daniel's gaze. Something like humor, but also anger, and —lust? The same she'd deciphered in Hamal's voice.

She shook her head to fling it all away.

PART 2

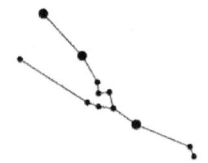

18

Dee was in the backseat, sandwiched between Dimitri and Daniel. Slamming the door against his objection to the seating arrangements, Daniel had stared Hamal down through the window as if daring him to object.

Hamal hadn't risen to the bait. Taking the passenger seat with Atkins as driver, he should have been ecstatic. His mission was about to end. Once they dropped Dee off at Amalthea's, he would never have to worry about her again. He'd never have to think of her. He should be relieved, but instead, he felt—pensive?

It had started an hour ago when Dimitri convinced Dee to arm wrestle. It was an absurd request that she'd refused. When the Soldier hadn't let it go, egged on by Daniel, she'd finally agreed just to shut them up. Even Hamal hadn't believed she could win. These guys could, literally, dodge bullets. Daniel had healed the wound to his shoulder so quickly it was like it'd never happened. Arm wrestling seemed irrelevant after that.

But she'd won.

She beat both Dimitri and Daniel.

They hadn't let her out of their sight since. Their purpose there was to ensure her safety, but after her display of strength, there was something more in the way they watched her.

Hamal wasn't sure why this bothered him so much.

Atkins had expressed the futility of the wasted time but hadn't pressed the issue. Neither had he acknowledged the way the pair latched on to their charge. To keep from making a fool of himself, Hamal had stayed in the corner, keeping himself aloof as the Soldiers acclimated to their assignment.

Buckled in the front seat, Hamal's eyes narrowed out the windshield, remembering the moment when Daniel had jumped up, excited rather than indignant that he'd lost the Neanderthal battle. He'd hugged a bewildered Dee, spinning her around until she couldn't help but laugh. What did he care if Daniel liked her? Or Dimitri? The Soldiers wouldn't be around long, either. They'd be joining Hamal back with Zibanitu.

Except, that might not be true.

Amalthea had allowed Atkins to come when Hamal had broken the rules and called the Soldier. She then agreed to open her doors to them, where Zi couldn't. As the self-proclaimed head of all the Houses, Zibanitu would be forced to explain Dee's existence and strange attributes. Keeping her from his House would allow him to feign ignorance. That Hamal was human, so not technically one of them, was a loophole that had allowed him to be here without worry. Zi would never have to answer questions about the human's whereabouts.

Amalthea, in turn, was allowed to call on Zibanitu for help. That help came in the form of Soldiers, since she was unable to create any of her own. A couple of Soldiers given on loan wasn't something Zi would be compelled to explain. That he'd only sent two of his youngest highlighted how cautiously he was treating this situation. Theoretically, two Soldiers could be on loan for an indefinite period without turning heads.

Both Dimitri and Daniel, born human, had survived the stressful change to superhuman. Zibanitu had never allowed the conversation that Hamal attempt this transition. Until today, Hamal had never thought to push it. Hamal had always considered himself lucky in this regard, enjoying the freedom his aloofness gave him. Now, sensing the pulse of the three behind him, noting how much like them Dee was and how quickly she'd fit into the world he only fringed, he wondered if his time had come.

Four dark SUVs, identical to the one they were in, were pulled over at the entrance to the upcoming rest stop. Dee leaned forward between the front seats. "Who are they?"

Hamal turned his head to answer, surprised to find her so close. His hand clenched the door to battle the feelings that swarmed.

Before he could answer, Dimitri sandwiched his head between theirs. "It's the cavalry!"

The Soldier's eyes shone with good humor, and Dee smiled with him. She sat back as Atkins slowed their vehicle to let two of the caravan pull ahead of them, the other two following. Without stopping, they all merged back onto the highway as if they'd been traveling together all along.

Dee asked, "Are they all Soldiers?"

Daniel answered, "Probably. There might be a medic or two, but I'm not sure if they'd care about anything but firepower—"

"Daniel." The one word from Atkins stopped Daniel's speech.

Dimitri made a sound that was followed by a chuckle from Dee.

Dimitri faked a whining tone. "You guys are always so serious."

"Only about serious things." Atkins' eyes never left the road.

Thinking back, she couldn't be sure if it was the sound of impacting cars, or the jostle of her body as it was thrown from the vehicle, that woke her. When her crazed motion came to a sudden halt, she struggled to remember how to even open her eyes.

The *tap-tap-tap* of suppressed semi-automatic fire pulled her from the brink of unconsciousness, though her eyes remained closed. Through the pandemonium of sound, she heard her name shouted, focusing on it as a tether to pull her fully awake.

Eyes snapping open, cheek pressed to the asphalt, her first clear vision was of the caved-in roof of one of the SUVs close to her face. She tentatively pulled her arms from her sides to press palms into the ground.

"Dee! Wait! Stay down!"

She complied, not sure whose voice she obeyed, not even sure she could have found the strength to push herself up. A hand on her back told her someone had come up beside her. "You alright?"

She managed a groan, which elicited a laugh from whoever was near. The sound told her it was Dimitri. She was surprised how deep her relief was that he was okay, her thoughts quickly turning to the others. If she was in this bad of shape, how would Hamal be?

"Good. I'm—" A burst of weapons fire cut him off, the thundering noise of his return assault deafening. In the sudden wash of silence, he spoke in a rush. "Okay, I'm going to keep shooting at the bad guys. You run into the trees there. I think Hamal made it. I saw Metis with him." He glanced down to make sure Dee was listening. "I know, I can't believe she let him out of her sight either."

Not having a clue who, or what, he was talking about, Dee managed to sit herself up, strength coming back in exponential returns. She felt her body knitting itself together, prompting another groan. This process was not exactly painful, but painful was the only word she had for it.

The Soldier recognized her confused expression. "You don't know what I'm talking about. Why would you?" He laughed, a strange sound juxtaposed against the raging of battle around her. He was crouched, firing over the overturned SUV that had been too close to Dee's face.

Dee ducked her head against the loud *popping* exploding through her eardrums, the echoes of the reports making it impossible to figure out where they were coming from. Estimating how many were out here was also impossible.

A part of her brain recognized that she should be dead. The damage to the truck suggested it, and her body lying on the pavement reinforced the idea. A second flipped vehicle was near enough that she wondered if it had rolled over her.

-Yup, you should definitely not be alive.-

Sensory overload was pushing her to panic, so she continued to analyze these data points in a detached way to maintain the eerie calm she was experiencing. If she was forced to engage with her surroundings, she just might lose it.

"Ready?" Daniel slid in beside them, the scraping sound of his clothes against the asphalt pulling Dee's attention.

She rose to a crouch, balancing on the balls of her feet, adrenaline pulling her further from her daze as her super-charged blood finished repairing her injuries.

Trying to block out the loudness of wild bursts of gunfire followed by indecipherable yells from Soldiers, she focused on Daniel, nodding that she was ready. What she was ready for, she wasn't entirely sure.

Through the shattered windows of the totaled truck, she mapped the place Dimitri had pointed for her to go. She didn't see anyone there, but having no better plan, she trusted he knew what he was talking about.

-There's that trust *word again.-*

"Didn't I say you were one of us?" Daniel laughed, firing a burst behind her as Dimitri fired to the side. He let the clip fall to be replaced by a fresh one while yelling, "Go go go!"

The first *GO* already had her on her way, stumbling the first two steps before her body remembered its dexterity. In two breaths, she was in the brush.

A malthea watched the chaos on multiple screens spread across the long wall.

While the Rishi prided herself on an estate full of bright, airy rooms filled with plants and flowers, this room she'd had purposefully built beneath the others in sterile grays and whites. Only through secondary sources could information of the exterior world be beamed onto one of a plethora of monitors around the room. The wall she now stared at, twenty feet of 3D capable viewing, was linked to the Soldiers she'd sent after the girl.

Each Soldier's visual display showed the fight from their point-of-view, along with the skewed feeds from the dash-mounted cameras inside the vehicles, most tilted at ninety or one-hundred eighty degrees, as well as a satellite feed Phecda had managed to commandeer.

Processing all the information wasn't enough to calm her. Watching had never been her thing.

She spoke into her headset, a direct link to Ainn, who'd she'd put in charge of the retrieval. "Twenty minutes until pick-up."

"Roger."

There were eighteen of the Rishi's people on-site, plus Hamal and Desiree, at the time of the ambush. Amalthea hadn't seen the hit, but the aftermath marked the events she'd missed. Her people were in trouble, and all she could do was pace back and forth in front of the screens, listening to the chaos.

In twenty minutes, there might not be anyone left to assist.

———

"You really are tougher than you look." Hamal's voice came from farther in the brush.

Dee turned to find him supported by the most unnaturally attractive man she had ever seen. She tried to focus on her mentor, glad he wasn't dead, though not unscathed, but her eyes continued to return to the other man's face.

"What happened?" The calmness of her voice surprised her.

The beautiful man answered, supporting Hamal's weight with no sign of difficulty. "The Ophiuchus sent his troops. We knew he would. We'd hoped to make it back to the estate before he caught up to us."

His demeanor was different than the other Soldiers she'd met; his energy something else, as Atkins' had first seemed. Whatever this new variation might be, he felt powerful enough to be just as scary.

Remembering Dimitri mentioned Metis had pulled Hamal from the wreckage, Dee assumed that's who she was looking at.

She studied Metis' face, his skin the same bronzed tone as Atkins, hoping to find something there that might explain the difference she felt in him. His beauty lay in the flawless skin that almost glowed, as well as eyes that shone with an inner light she'd never imagined was more than hyperbole. Maybe he was one the infamous Rishis. No, he felt too much like Barnard and they'd said he was no master.

A shout pierced the din of chaos behind her, bringing her attention back to the direness of their situation.

She turned, using a tree as cover as she peered out towards the fighting. "Are we winning?"

Hamal answered, his voice breathy and forced. "Hard to tell, but with Atkins and Vali out there, I wouldn't bet against us."

"Vali?"

Her question was interrupted when a spray of bullets flew through their cover, peppering bits of bark and leaves around them.

Metis deposited Hamal on the ground. Hamal grimaced, now propped against a thick tree, eyes closed, breaths ragged. Metis moved next to Dee, pausing to study the battlefield. She looked out as well, unsure what she was looking for.

A rasping cough from Hamal had Dee move to him. She stooped next to him, wincing at the struggles his lungs were having. She didn't have to know much about his injuries to assess they needed to get him out of there. His leg was broken, and by the shortness of his breaths, she guessed a few ribs, too. Hopefully, the raspiness she heard wasn't a punctured lung.

She patted his arm awkwardly, not sure what else to do. His eyes remained closed, face pinched.

Feeling useless, Dee looked back at Metis who pulled a pair of short swords from his waist before jumping into the fray. Dee imagined she could hear his weapons cut the air as he slashed and stabbed their attackers.

Returning her attention to Hamal, she found he'd fallen to unconsciousness. Knowing there was nothing she could do to help him, she stood. A motion to pull her weapons reminded her that they'd been taken and put in the trunk of Hamal's SUV.

Frustrated, she clenched her fists, contemplating adding her fists to the fight. But, she'd just be in the way. They could handle themselves.

-But it would be so much fun if we did.-

Not consciously listening to the voice, her feet brought her closer to the road. It was just so she could better see the conflict on the street.

Three of the five trucks in their caravan had flipped, blocking both lanes of traffic. A pair of mammoth trucks explained how the caravan was accosted. Flipped, crushed, she wondered how they'd managed to be so thoroughly ambushed. On the far side of the road, she saw where these vehicles must have lain in wait. A construction site cleared of trees was big enough to have hidden them.

A lull in gunfire exploded in a new assault. She ducked reflexively, echoes ricocheting through the trees, so she had no idea which direction might mean safety. Remembering what Hamal had explained about why they used guns and that the weapons probably wouldn't kill any of them, gave her a modicum of comfort. The real fighting wouldn't begin until the gunfire stopped.

Fidgeting from foot to foot, trying to repress the urge to join the fight, she looked out over the carnage of vehicles. Tracking the best route to it, analyzing her chance of success, weighing whether Hamal's tutelage would make her a helper or only hinder her side.

When someone leaped across her view, turning to fire at whoever was giving chase, she realized she'd never be able to distinguish between those on her side and those trying to take her. Except for Daniel, Dimitri, Atkins, and Metis, she didn't know the faces of who fought for her. Apparently, tactical gear didn't come in *good guy* and *bad guy* colors.

From the satellite feed, Amalthea saw the girl responsible for this storm peek her head from the tree cover.

She whispered to the girl on the screen, "Stay put. We're here to keep you safe. Don't make our job harder."

Dee wasn't convincing herself it was worth the risk to make a move for her weapons, body crouched out of sight, when a voice called out to her. Dee's eyes panned the chaos for who it was.

His dark clothing blended with the shadows of twilight pressing on them, and no longer did he wear the golden torque that painted him as one of Sabik Han's. Still, she'd never forget that grinning face from the trees near her house.

Barnard.

From twenty meters down the road, his back pressed against a vehicle that managed to stay upright, he met her eyes. Something in his gaze held Dee's. Something in his presence called her forward.

She hadn't noticed his beard when they'd battled in the woods. It seemed an obvious thing not to see. She could understand why his striking cheekbones wouldn't have registered, or that his piercing eyes were an almost unnatural shade of amber, both characteristics that should have labeled him handsome but somehow didn't.

Barnard extended a hand as if she could just take it as a child to be led away. It was a gesture of welcome, of safety. It seemed absurd not to go with him.

-Don't be nuts.-

But how would it be more nuts than what she was doing? Maybe going with Barnard would stop the fighting. Maybe Barnard was the good guy. If he'd gotten to Dee before Hamal, would this situation be reversed?

B arnard. It wasn't a surprise to see him there. He was the one Han had sent to meet Dee near her house.

Still, Amalthea was astonished to see Han's right-hand so near danger. Barnard was never one to throw himself into battle. He served an advisory role to the Ophiuchus, who was not known to take much counsel. She wondered, not for the first time, about the nature of their arrangement that kept the servant relevant.

Used to not getting answers to the hard questions, she watched the Messenger's hand come out in a gesture that spoke his desire for the girl to go with him. If Desiree decided to go along, there was no one near to stop her.

In quick staccato, Amalthea prompted the computer, "DOR-THY, ping the nearest operative to Desiree."

Immediately, the electronic voice replied, "I have pinged Operative Ellie."

Barely a second passed. "Ellie here, Rishi."

"Ellie, Barnard is on-site and currently engaging the contact. He's—"

"I see them."

Startled at being cut off, she settled her feelings as she watched the female Soldier's camera move stealthily through the engagement to intercept her target.

A barrage of bullets turned Dee's attention. Dimitri sprinted towards her, his super-speed blurring his steps until he was crouched next to her.

"Deja vu?" His voice was conversational, but his glance asked what the hell she was doing.

"I thought I might be able to help."

Daniel was suddenly on her other side, studying her as if seeing her for the first time. "Since it's you they're after, I think laying low is the best idea. Wouldn't want them to sneak up on you and steal you away while we were trying not to die."

He was right. They were both right. She'd known it, but she'd wanted to get away from the sound of Hamal's injuries. She'd needed to feel something other than useless. That , and a pair oof her was excited at the idea of being in the fight.

Daniel sent a barrage of gunfire towards the center of chaos.

Dimitri spoke between bursts of fire. "We've got reinforcements on the way to pick you up. Atkins and Vali are doing just fine taking Han's forces out while the rest of us keep them inside the funhouse of wrecked cars. Everything will be fine."

Amalthea sighed in relief when Dimitri and Daniel distracted the private interaction between Desiree and their enemy. From Ellie's camera, Amalthea watched Barnard come into view, the visual lost when the camera swung around to meet an engagement from a trio of Han's men. Ellie fired a couple of quick bursts, diving behind cover and low crawling to a new position.

Amalthea searched the other feeds, looking for Desiree from

another's point-of-view. It was good news that she didn't find the girl quickly. It meant she was far enough away from the battle to be out of sight of those engaged. Still, she couldn't help a twinge of nerves that it also meant the girl could be taken right from under their noses.

Ellie's feed showed that she'd finally flanked Han's trio. Atkins and Vali, whirling beings of violence, helped the Soldier take them out.

Amalthea breathed relief before returning her attention to the satellite images that were the only source for Desiree's location.

The girl now stood flanked by Zibanitu's Soldiers.

Barnard had vanished.

D ee looked to where Barnard had stood. He was gone, along with his offer to take her out of there. Returning her attention to her direct surroundings, noting how carefully Dimitri and Daniel protected her, she wondered how exactly she had planned on helping them.

-I think your plan stopped at retrieving your weapons from the back of the SUV.-

Her gaze returned to the truck lying on its hood, its crunched body making her wonder if she'd even be able to open the back if she made it there. "My weapons are in the back of that car."

"Okay?" Daniel was searching the wreckage through the scope of his rifle.

Sliding from the cover of the trees, Dee stayed crouched, preparing to beeline for the spot in the center of the wreckage. Daniel's arm on hers spun her back to cover. "Whoa there. Your weapons can be replaced. I'm not letting you go out there."

Dee huffed, eyes moving behind Daniel to rest on Hamal hunched against the tree. She focused, desperate to see some movement that told her he was still alive, but there was too much background sound for her to get a good read.

The noise was getting to her, grinding on her nerves so much she wished she'd stayed unconscious. Its intensity forced a sense of vertigo through her, and she stumbled forward. Her hand flung out to catch herself, landing on Daniel's shoulder.

"Is she hit?" Dimitri's voice behind her was panicked while Daniel's hands frantically groped her to deduce if she was hurt.

When he relaxed his hold on her to reassure his partner she was okay, she pulled away, sprinting towards the crashed SUV and her weapons.

-Yes! Let's get down and dirty!-

Both Dimitri and Daniel lost a critical second as they stared uncomprehendingly after her before following, guns blazing a path of cover for the girl who seemed to have lost her mind.

Slamming into the crushed vehicle jolted some of her sense to the forefront of her brain, but it was too late to take back her decision. Daniel slammed into the truck next to her while Dimitri crouched away from the vehicle to cover their back. Daniel's fire over their cover barraged her brain, so she squeezed her eyes closed.

Breathing deep to help mute the sounds, she searched for just a nanosecond of calm.

A nanosecond was all she got.

Amalthea's eyes remained on Dee. She couldn't tear her eyes from Zibanitu's pair keeping close watch over her, even as the others kept enemies away.

Unfortunately the trio coming from the girl's home hadn't been equipped with surveillance and communications gear. Dimitri and Daniel had never had the opportunity, and Atkins had left too quickly for them to think this far ahead. If they'd been able to comm-up, the Rishi could have warned them they were hunted.

She rushed to ping Ainn, knowing there wouldn't be time.

Daniel soared backward from a kick to the chest. Dee turned to help, but a second assaulter rounded their cover, weapon peppering him. Behind her, more gunfire told her the same had happened to Dimitri.

She may have screamed.

Jumping the one assaulting Daniel, Dee spear-tackled him at the waist. She used the momentum to swing around and throw Daniel's assailant to the ground, burying her elbow in his face. His arms came up to stop her, bringing the tactical knife strapped to his forearm to her hand.

She broke it free from the snap that held it to bury it in his neck, wrenching it across in an attempt to sever his head from his body, actions born from pure adrenalized instinct.

The knife wasn't long enough for a clean-cut, nor was she in the right position to cleave through both muscle and bone. Still, he was sufficiently incapacitated that she could turn to the others.

Leaping to her feet, facing where Daniel had fallen, knife in hand, she ducked instinctively when another burst of weapon fire went off, nearer then before. She kicked with all her might into the ribs of a second attacker now straddling Daniel, long blade poised to strike a killing blow. The Soldier flew, spinning down the road to bounce roughly against one of the overturned SUV's.

She turned to those engaging Dimitri. She managed to disarm and disable one but was too late to stop the lethality of the other assault on her bodyguard.

Amalthea stared at the screen, mouth open in astonishment. These were The Ophiuchus's soldiers. Even against her best, they were nothing to be trifled with, and this girl had just taken out three of them.

147

"Rishi?" Ainn had been waiting for orders, confused when her open comm remained silent.

"Get to the girl. She's in the center of the wreckage. Dimitri and Daniel are down. She's a sitting duck."

"Understood."

———

Bullet holes peppered their torsos. Daniel's neck looked like the guy Dee had ripped her knife through. The bullet wounds looked remarkably similar to the bladed wound. How munition weapons might kill the hard-to-kill was now clear.

But they weren't dead.

-*Yet.*-

Dimitri was unconscious, but Daniel's panicked eyes flashed to her as she dropped to his side. She took his hand, an instinctive reaction to bring him comfort even as she was loath to touch him and cause him more pain.

"Daniel?" She whispered. It carried all the questions she'd never asked, all the sympathy she'd ever felt, and all the hope that they'd all be alright.

He closed his eyes, face slack. Dee was afraid she'd witnessed his last breath. Tears welled in her eyes as a fierce rage swelled within her.

Looking around for someone who could help, she watched the enemy Soldier she'd kicked get up, glaring at her as he held his ribs. She knew she'd broken them, but his healing factor would be knitting them back together. That was unacceptable.

Daniel's sword lay in its sheath half underneath him. Dee retrieved it, moving towards the enemy Soldier, the naked blade resting loosely in her hand, fear washed from her mind.

"We're here to take you with us," the Soldier explained, but Dee was beyond hearing. Barely registering his words, their sounds muted by the rush of blood through her system, she stalked closer. The murderer's eyes went wide, seeing his death in her face.

He pushed his hands in front of him. "Wait! I won't hurt you. We were told to bring you unharmed. You no longer have to be deceived by the others."

His words came in a rushed babble, but Dee did not hear. She leaped at the Soldier who didn't defend himself. Whether out of strict obedience to orders or because he didn't believe she would kill him, she didn't pause to consider.

A quick twirl gave enough force to cleanly cut through the pleading Soldier's neck. His head dropped from his body, eyes staring in surprise as it was tossed through the air. Barely giving him a second look, she turned back to the Soldier whose head she'd mostly cut off with his own knife.

There was nothing to worry about from him. A statuesque Soldier who hadn't been there a moment ago, a Soldier Dee assumed was on her side, stood over his torso, finishing the job Dee had started.

Dee paused, intimidated by the newcomer, but Daniel's throaty cough washed it beneath worry and guilt. The newcomer stepped to Daniel's side to maintain a watchful eye on their surroundings as Dee fell to her knees next to her injured guard.

She barely looked up when another soldier knelt opposite Daniel's body. This one was petite as the other was giant. Long auburn hair spilled down her back when she ripped off her combat helmet.

"**D**ORTHY, how are we with local law enforcement?"

The computerized voice responded after barely a second's pause, "We've intercepted all calls to emergency services. The road continues to stay closed to potential witnesses."

Amalthea's voice was sharp. "Who called it in then?"

"Noise of a firefight like this will travel. This isn't as remote a location as the surroundings may suggest." It wasn't the computer who answered.

Amalthea turned to greet the woman entering the room, welcoming her presence with a smile. "Phecda. I thought you'd left."

The taller woman stepped next to Amalthea, eyes scanning the monitors behind neat glasses designed for aesthetic, rather than practical, use. None of the Rishis had ever suffered trivialities of mortality such as fading eyesight.

The rest of the Rishi's appearance matched this clean look. Expensive business suit tailored perfectly to her trim form, hair carefully managed in a sensible ponytail, tasteful make-up highlighting her features perfectly but not overtly. Phecda was ever practical. Ever aware of effectiveness and efficiency.

"I couldn't miss the excitement of what my intel spawned."

Amalthea's smile deepened. Though it was often buried, she knew Phecda had a heart concealed beneath her cold outer layer. "Find anything else?"

Phecda's lips turned up.

Amalthea chuckled. She'd never been good at playing Phecda's game. *The* game. Amalthea communicated too directly to effectively play at subtlety. Phecda dealt in information, and it wasn't good business to give away her commodity for free, even to a friend.

What she'd done for Amalthea would cost, but Amalthea was sure it would be worth it.

"Atkins and Zi's guys went in without gear?" Phecda's smile vanished, eyes ingesting the information on the wall in front of her.

Amalthea nodded. "We hadn't thought to send gear. Things happened too fast."

Phecda frowned. "Still, the other cars would have been stocked with backups they could've used." Her frown deepened. "Vali has tactical command?"

"Vali's too interested in his personal body-count to ever have tactical command."

Phecda nodded. Amalthea wasn't known for military strategy. There'd been few times in the whole of their history that Amalthea'd been directly involved in any fighting. Zero where her House had been in a point position. It was why Phecda was here. The curiosity of watching Amalthea direct a tactical mission was an opportunity that may never arise again.

"Ainn has command."

Phecda scanned the screens, noting stress levels from the biometric feeds, combat styles of individual Soldiers, anything that might prove useful later. She said nothing more. It was her habit to gather information.

The female Soldier was pouring powder into the holes littering Daniel's body while he squeezed his eyes shut, struggling to breathe. Dee watched helplessly as guilt ate at her. If not for her, none of them would be getting shot at, and Dimitri and Daniel wouldn't be dying on some backroad in the middle of gods-knew-where.

Dee squeezed his hand.

His neck wounds were closing on their own, the introduction of the powder speeding the process. Dee wondered what it was but wouldn't interrupt the medic's tasks. She watched as it soaked and clotted the blood, quickly turning his bleeding wounds to pinkish marks across his body.

The woman handed a thick wad of gauze to Dee. "Here. Hold this in his neck. Press hard."

"*In* the wound?" Dee looked down, stifling her urge to throw up. The girl nodded, continuing her triage. Another had been working on Dimitri, and Dee's gaze went to him, wondering how he was hanging on.

She put the gauze to Daniel's neck, gasping when his eyes flew open in pain.

"It hurts, but it's better than him dying," the medic said without looking up from her work.

Dee pressed on the neck wound, closing her eyes so she wouldn't have to see Daniel's expression of agony.

———

"**D**id we get everyone out?"

Ainn's voice paused. "We lost Tau. Injuries were sustained all around."

Each Soldier was monitored closely when they were in the field, but there was always the possibility of equipment failure. Ainn's confirmation only validated what was displayed in front of them.

Amalthea's voice was sad. "You all fought well. We were strong. Against the best, we succeeded in our mission."

"Thank you, Rishi." Ainn's comm channel closed.

Phecda watched Amalthea's face, judged the truth of the feeling saturating her response. What she saw there convinced her of its validity. Affection had always been a part of Amalthea's personality, but after so long, Phecda was surprised to see it still held a place so close to the surface. Too many of them had forgotten who they were and hid behind masks they'd perfected over so much time. She wondered if any remembered their roots. She even wondered it of herself.

The Keeper of Secrets made a mental note not to stay away so long. Personal visits could be useful for other kinds of intel.

"How many of Han's are down?" Phecda stepped back to Amalthea's side after checking over the equipment she'd loaned to get the satellite surveillance up and running.

Amalthea repeated the question, so the VI would respond, "DORTHY? How many enemy units are down?"

"My estimation is eight, Rishi," the computerized voice was loud in the quiet aftermath of the chaos.

"It seemed we were able to get Dee out too easily." Amalthea's voice was quiet, contemplative.

The computer continued its assessment. "The enemy seemed unwilling to risk harm to the target. They only engaged at a distance, enabling your units to keep them away. The reinforcing caravan was able to pick up the first team with little difficulty."

Phecda nodded. "They didn't push their perimeter. They weren't expecting such a defensive force."

"A mistake I'm sure Han won't make again."

"Han," Phecda whispered the name as if speaking it for the first time. It'd been so long since the name attached to The Ophiuchus' title had been uttered so brazenly.

"That is his name." Amalthea's voice was laced with annoyance.

Phecda nodded, tilting her head as she filed this information away. Was the human platitude *time heals all* relevant even for them?

Looking back at the monitors showed vehicles leaving the battle zone with the asset secured. Phecda contemplated what other things this new revelation might breed among the Houses, and how she might anticipate them so her market would be full when the time came.

19

"Hamal did an outstanding job prepping her. You weren't there. She was downright scary."

"I don't know what girl you saw, but that one up there is as frightened and clueless as any I've ever come across."

Amalthea listened to the conversation, never pausing her pruning of the rose bushes that ran the length of the low wall surrounding her garden patio. They needed their time to sort things out before she would come in with the final word. And, she wasn't embarrassed to admit, she was interested in hearing about the strange girl from those who had seen her in action.

Zibanitu's unwillingness to commit himself to direct involvement had offered Amalthea this chance. That, and the fact that Phecda had been close at hand when she'd received information that The Ophiuchus had planned a military strike.

Even with that information, they'd been unaware of Barnard's visit to Dee. Atkins' call alerted them, already too late to be of use. It was fortuitous that Hamal had broken orders by calling on Atkins. It was the only thing that had saved the human's life, and maybe even the girl's. Assuming Hamal survived his injuries, Zibanitu might forgive the transgression his pet had made when he'd called on another House for aid. Simply to thwart a plan of The Ophiuchus, even Zibanitu would over-look his pet's misdeed.

Sending her own people had been a risk the likes of which she hadn't taken in recent memory. Amalthea had no way to replace her numbers if they fell. Only through favors and goodwill had she managed to amass the small army that made up her House. Tau's fall would be felt for decades. Maybe longer.

Daniel, though still alive, didn't seem to be healing. Although stable, he was in bad shape and mystifying her medical staff. There were questions about whether The Ophiuchus (Han, she scolded herself) had found some poison that somehow slowed the healing process. That Daniel had survived his wounds at all suggested not, but Amalthea was already battling the rumors. Thankfully, none sitting here had brought it up. Her temper would have ignited like Vesuvius if they had.

Time had taught her, rather ungracefully, the benefit of prudence, so she stilled her turmoil. The next forty-eight hours were crucial, both in what they did about the girl and how they reacted to Sabik Han's strike. The likelihood that Han would attack her estate was low, but this probability depended on how badly he wanted the strange girl. The girl who, until yesterday, far fewer had known existed.

Hoping the others didn't catch wind of what was going on, Zi agreed with Amalthea that they lay low. The more who got involved, the messier things would be for everyone. Zibanitu's compound was more secure than her estate, but that wouldn't matter if they couldn't get her there safely. They'd already seen what could happen, and the distance to get her to Zi's was much more significant.

It also afforded Zibanitu more time to decide how he would formally address the issue. Having the girl stay here meant he had no one to answer to. Han's attack might have forced his hand, so he was glad not to have to take responsibility just yet.

Amalthea's thoughts drifted back a few hours to when the caravan, full of amped-up Soldiers, had arrived, along with one of her own dead, and three of Zi's severely injured. A team had met the incoming group, opening doors even before the trucks had come to a full stop to bring the wounded to the on-site hospital. Those uninjured had stood guard, every cell on high alert in case another assault pressed them on their home turf.

Dee had sat on the far side of the Humvee she'd shared with Atkins and a driver, facing away from the thickest of the commotion, seeming oblivious to the frenzied movement around her. Any attempt to remove her from the vehicle was met with no response. Not wanting to risk frightening her even more, they'd let her be.

Amalthea had come to greet her. The Rishi had watched quietly as the remaining medic looked up in frustration that she couldn't get the girl to respond, let alone leave the truck. Amalthea met the medic's gaze and shook her head, allowing the medic to back off to attend other duties.

The sudden silence hadn't brought the girl from her trance either.

Amalthea had remained on the opposite side of the girl, able to see directly through the truck to where she sat in the back seat. All the doors were open, the driver impatiently waiting until he could pull the SUV out of sight.

It was Amalthea's turn to try to convince the girl to come with her. Voice pitched to motherly kindness she coaxed, "It'd be best if we could get you inside."

She remembered the girl's fighting prowess from the video feeds, so was loath to push too hard and risk inciting defensive wrath. But, if the girl were in shock, they'd need to get her inside right away.

"Desiree? Is it okay if I sit with you?" Amalthea took the nonresponse as a yes. Climbing into the back seat, she sat with her shoulders squared to the front, even as she kept Dee in her periphery.

She hadn't bothered to really look at the girl when the fighting was taking place, so Amalthea used this time to examine her guest, who continued to stare unseeing into the surroundings. If she hadn't seen her with her own eyes, Amalthea's skepticism would have been high, along with her anger that she'd risked so many to save this one.

She replayed the scene in her head: Dee moving quickly, too fast for any pure-blooded human, to meet the threat that had taken out Dimitri and Daniel.

Was she a rogue Soldier? It wasn't common, but there were stories...

And if she were a Soldier, her skills were already catching up to those few who'd been alive since the beginning. It meant a strength of blood long lost.

Hamal's mentorship was evident in her movements, the slight variations of the style of Zibanitu's House tailored for his less physical skill. Hamal had learned much in his years among them but could never match the enhancements of the Initiated. Yet, in this case, he'd been the only one who could have started this adventure with this strange girl.

She smiled despite herself, wondering how much foresight Zibanitu conjured, or if his over-preparedness only suggested prescience. Had he known all along who this girl was? Had he held the information close to his chest for the rest of them to flesh out on their own? Had he only interceded when another's move forced his hand?

Silent minutes passed.

Amalthea extended her hand. "It's time to go inside."

Dee didn't move, and Amalthea was afraid they'd have to force her out of the truck, a move that would do nothing good for building trust. Just as that seemed to be the last option, Dee asked, "Who are you?"

The girl's quiet voice held a trace of that strength Amalthea had witnessed from the field. The Rishi smiled, glad the girl would be walking from the truck of her own volition. "I'm Amalthea. I am the Rishi of this House."

Dee's head turned towards her, face tilted slightly, eyes focused far away. "Rishi?"

Amalthea gave a faint nod. As the words were processed, Dee went rigid, breath catching in her throat.

Maybe she wouldn't be leaving the truck.

That the girl understood the title meant Hamal had taken more than one liberty with his mission. Amalthea held her anger in check for a more appropriate time.

Atkins moved towards them, stopping in front of the SUV so he could meet his Master's eyes through the windshield, ensuring he wasn't stepping on her toes before he moved around to Dee's side of the vehicle. Amalthea wasn't sure what he thought he could do but allowed him his experiment. She was loath to have to resort to violent means to extradite the girl from the vehicle.

Coming around to Dee's door, he knelt so his head was level with her thighs. Dee's eyes followed him, head now dropped to look at the Soldier.

"We're safe here." His voice was a whisper. The rigidity that Amalthea had incited faded until slowly Dee allowed Atkins to help her from the truck.

Atkins escorted her through the large estate, leading her over the acres of front yard before entering the towering house that sprawled in a half-circle away from them. Their arms remained entwined like he was escorting her to a school dance, pulling her gently to the rooms Amalthea had prepared for her.

Desiree had been upstairs, in a suite on the other side of the house, ever since.

The Rishi's thoughts snapped back to the present. She returned her shears to their place before taking her seat with the others. Metis made to rise, but a gesture from her assured him she needed nothing.

She held his eye for a moment, exceedingly grateful he hadn't been harmed. There were only a few times in their long history that he'd defied her, and going with the team to rescue this girl was one of them. The decision had shocked her, but it said much about the curiosity this girl brought to them all.

The others quieted as she sat, her attention on the thin file that had been Hamal's in front of her. Her eyes scanned the meager contents before closing it. Desiree Galen. How had anyone caught on to the idea that she should be watched? Not even Phecda had a theory.

Amalthea smiled kindly, meeting each of their eyes before speaking. "What have we done about the possibility of him attacking us here?"

"Our perimeter monitoring system is being extended as we speak. Phecda has promised eyes on any known locations where he might send troops from. Everyone is up, securing the estate, but—"

Amalthea nodded. "But, we are too few."

The speaker nodded gravely, sitting back as their Master's attention turned to Metis. "Nothing still from the prisoners?"

"When the threat of death is all we have, and they know we won't kill them, interrogation has no power."

It was as she'd expected. Only the young soldiers were susceptible to interrogation. When your memories stretch back over centuries, time holds an entirely different significance. Lengthy torture sessions became more harmful to the interrogator than the prisoner, so it was impossible to get data from those who weren't already of a mind to give it.

It was just as well. She'd rather her people stay away from the horrible things that happened in the throes of attempting to break one's will.

"I have a meeting scheduled with the Air God. We'll see if he can help us fortify."

"Will he be angry we lost Dimitri?"

Amalthea took a breath, holding it for a moment before releasing it slowly. Dimitri hadn't survived. Daniel was critical. These were points she wasn't looking forward to relaying, especially as she'd only lost one of her own. Still, it couldn't be avoided.

Hamal was still in surgery. She wondered if he would care more about that.

"He won't be mad enough to risk the safety of the girl."

20

Dee didn't sleep long. Nightmares of gunfire kept her sleep light and unrestful. Jolted from slumber for the last time by a dream filled with explosions and decapitation, she stopped trying. Instead, she stared into the darkness, blinking away the fading images of horror that clung like cobwebs. The more she batted at them in a silent war to erase them from her mind, the tighter they wove into a tangled mess until there was nowhere she could look she didn't see some horror.

But what if the nightmare had been the last couple of months? Maybe, she'd finally woken. Maybe this darkness was the spawn of a new life where the pain of vague memories could no longer hurt her.

The room was silent. Still enough, she latched onto this thought, allowed it to spin, to grow to belief. The chaos and panic her nightmares left replaced by a sense of peace she hadn't known in years. Snuggling further into bed, she closed her eyes, her brain quiet, relishing the serenity.

But her body wouldn't let her stay in bed forever. No longer able to ignore the call to the bathroom, Dee begrudgingly brought her feet to the floor. Her toes curled against the unfamiliar feeling of the smooth surface, her steps unsure as she moved towards a white door cracked open ahead of her. Eyes adjusting to the shadows, tuned in that she was in a strange place, knocked any allowance her brain had given her that she was no longer in danger. Her momentary delusion that all was well faded under an alarm that rose from the depths of her psyche to push the tranquil calm under a tide of fear.

Her inner-voice was uncharacteristically quiet, though its contempt at her attempt to forget the last twenty-four hours, the entire previous year, screamed loud in its silence.

Reaching past the door, arm extended to its max, she found the light switch to this other room and flicked it on. Hanging onto the doorframe, she blinked blurry sight around the bathroom that was as large as the bedroom behind her. A sunk-in-tub she could swim laps in was at the far end, polished porcelain shining brightly against the darker tile of the surrounding walls. Hanging plants flowed from the ceiling above it, a few fronds close to the floor. The left wall was taken up by a glass box that was the most immense shower she'd ever seen. Potted trees rimmed the glass, and she imagined that bathing inside the cage would feel like showering under a waterfall of the Amazon Jungle.

With a smile, she stepped into the room.

She turned to the mirrored wall on her right, and her smile fell. Her reflected image hovered over a double sink nestled into a floating counter and showed a face patchy with bruises. Cheeks, jaws, and eyes, even her nose was rubbed raw. All were painted in the yellow-green palette of healing. Scabs along the left side showed where the road had claimed her hide almost to the bone. She couldn't imagine how awful she'd looked a few hours ago.

-*You look awful now.*-

With a gasped breath, she fell forward into the counter, catching herself on straight arms, head falling against her chest, eyes closed as the entirety of the last twenty-four hours overcame her.

Dimitri and Daniel showing up in the woods near the house.

Her attacking them.

The ambush on the road.

Dimitri.

Daniel.

…Hamal.

Where they alive?

Rishi.

The word shot through her, shattering all other thought, snapping her eyes open. This strange word was the title for whoever was after her. For the one who'd sent Hamal to watch her. For the Master of this place where she now stood.

She took slow breaths.

-We should have killed Hamal.-

She couldn't help a bark of laughter. The event that had started everything could be argued as that moment when he'd walked into her world, though, really, he'd only been a symptom of the more significant problem. A problem still not clearly defined.

-Sure, but killing him would have alleviated the need for a gun battle on some back road. How do they cover that up, anyway?-

The question only supported the idea that these Masters, these Rishis, were powerful on a level she'd never considered, able to act outside of a system Dee had thought controlled everything. She'd never considered there were multiple systems. There should only be *one* system.

Avoiding looking at herself in the mirror, she turned, leaning back against the counter, eyes panning the room, this time for something she could arm herself with.

Finding nothing, she returned to the dark bedroom.

The curtains pulled against the picture window allowed no light to pass, attaching a sense of timelessness to the room, so she wasn't sure if the day had given to night, or back to day, or if she was in a place where the sun never shone.

Her brain asked her to move across the room to check, but her legs refused.

What was she doing? What was happening?

-You think Hamal was teaching you how to fight these things for fun?-

She hadn't thought about it, to be honest. Even as she'd known Hamal was training her for this very scenario, her brain ignored the fact that bigger things were going on. Here, these bigger things were no longer too obscure to ignore, and she hadn't been prepared to handle it.

She was in the house of a Rishi.

A shiver came over her, then another as she remembered sinking a blade into the Soldiers who'd attacked Dimitri and Daniel, the feel of the blade catching on bone, the sticky warmth of so much blood.

Dimitri. Daniel. Hamal. She still didn't know if they had made it.

-You have *been mostly unconscious.-*

She shuffled to a second door, one she hoped would let her escape this room. Just as she turned the doorknob, a young girl, no more than twelve years old, pushed into the room. Startled, she stared up at Dee with wide eyes.

The girl recovered first. She bowed her head, soft voice explaining that the mistress had asked her not to leave the suite.

"So, I'm a prisoner?"

Startled, the girl stammered, "I don't think so, just, they weren't sure you were feeling well."

Dee's voice was stern. "I'm feeling great. I want to check on Hamal and Daniel and Dimitri."

The girl's shoulders relaxed. "Hamal will be fine. He isn't quite ready to move yet." Her tone softened. "Daniel... they're still not sure what will happen with him."

Dee's shoulders fell. Unsure why she felt such protection over the Soldier she barely knew, she peered at the girl staring at the floor as if reading her face might procure more information.

-Guilt. That's all it is. Misplaced emotions. You don't care about any of them.-

She ignored the voice, whose callous words tore through her heart.

-If you kill this one, you can leave.-

Dee pressed her eyes closed against the voice, speaking quickly to drown it out.

"What about Dimitri?"

The girl's silence was answer enough.

Dee's steps took her falling back to the bed. Sobs found their way from her throat. She covered her mouth with her hands as if she could stop the torrent of grief. She'd barely known him. He'd hardly known her, but still, he'd fought to protect her. He'd died doing that very thing.

Eyes pressed together, she fought against the swell of emotion; fought against the hard reality of what she was involved in; fought against a despair that threatened to render her mind unable to deal with it all.

The need to move, to get out, pushed her to her feet, so she was making for the door so fast the girl could voice no objection. Dee threw herself into the next room, moving into a large living area, barely noting the lavish space as she continued on to the next door.

She was at the exit in a flash, the double mahogany doors more robust than those separating her from the bedroom. Expecting the doors to be locked, she was excited when they opened, a breath of tension releasing that she wasn't a prisoner.

Flinging both doors inward, so they rapped loudly against the wall, she stepped into a vast hall. With a passing glance, she noted plants decorating every spare inch of space. Across from the doors was a chaise lounge Atkins stood from.

His calm gaze took in her mood. "We thought you might not take an order to relax without questions."

Dee stared at the warrior, remembering it had been he who'd escorted her here when they'd arrived. She hadn't been afraid of him then like she was now.

She took a breath, hoping her voice wouldn't waver. "Dimitri didn't make it."

The warrior had the courtesy to look mournful. "He did not. He fought bravely."

"And Daniel? Hamal?" Her anger grew and the only outlet for it was the Soldier in the hall.

"Hamal is in fine condition. Daniel," his voice dropped, and he seemed reluctant to add anything. "We don't know what will happen with Daniel."

Her hands balled into fists as she realized the futility of engaging the being in front of her, who was easily twice her size and exponentially more skilled.

-Or maybe you're just a coward.-

She scowled, turning her attention from Atkins to look up and down the hall. "I was told I'm not a prisoner."

"That's true."

"Can I walk around?"

"Yes, but not yet."

She frowned, her eyes locking on his, before snapping away from the intimidating weight of his stare.

"Hamal? Can I see him?"

"I'm sure this will be the first place he visits when he's allowed to get out of bed." Atkins took a step towards her. She got the impression she was being herded back to the room. She took a breath, holding it as a wall against the pressure of his stature.

His tone dropped, soothing, "There is nothing to fear here, but we are concerned for your safety. It is why we ask you to stay in your rooms. It is easier for us to secure you this way."

"Secure me?"

Atkins nodded, taking another step towards her.

Dee looked up and down the hall again, knowing there was no way to defy the Soldier but stalling all the same as if some idea would come to her that would allow her to change his mind. Atkins' eyes never strayed from her. She was sure he would stand there, unmoving, until the end of time, if she remained there as well.

Resigned to this, she sighed, accepting her fate. "So, I just hang out here then?"

He made no move or gesture, nor did any expression brush his face, but Dee knew his answer was affirmative.

Defeated, she turned back to step into the room that was her prison, regardless of what they called it.

-At least no one's tackled you yet.-

It was true, she seemed safe, but at what cost? Being sequestered wasn't the same as being safe, was it?

-Is it time for philosophy then; freedom versus safety?-

Ignoring the voice, she wondered just how *secure* she was. Was she not being housed by the very thing she should be running from?

-A little late for that.-

Doors still open behind her, she turned, questions about her security and who they were securing her from dying on her lips. Atkins remained standing in the center of the hall. He was one of them. How could she trust anything any of them told her? Maybe she should have gone with Barnard.

-Point-of-fact: Barnard is also one of them.-

Atkins spoke quietly. "Why should you trust us? That is not something I can answer. It is not something anyone can ever answer. Had you gone with Barnard, he would not have been able to answer it any better, nor his Master. You are in the unique position of being at the mercy of those you can't know if you should trust or not. You have only the guidance of Hamal to reflect on, another who you may have trusted unwisely. Only time will show if you made any correct decision. But remember, if you find your position here a mark for gratification, it was Hamal who made it so."

Dee stared at her feet, caught by his calm wisdom, wondering if he'd read her mind. She wanted to like him. To trust him. Hamal trusted him enough to betray his orders and ask for Atkins' help. .

-We. Don't. Trust. Hamal.-

Was that true?

Her inner voice's declaration forced a sense of isolated self-preservation. She stood straighter under the knowledge that she might be on her own, needing to rely on all she'd been taught to get her out of there.

Whatever Atkins saw in her at that moment brought him to alertness, but Dee knew it was not the time to fight.

Dee turned, shutting herself in the suite. Leaning her head back against the thick wood of the door, she closed her eyes. Leaving this place wouldn't solve anything. She'd be running forever if she started now, or until they were bored of her.

-Or kill you.-

They wouldn't get bored without extensive analyses, which running would only prolong. When she thought of it like that, the overzealous protection seemed entirely benign.

-At least you're not a lab rat in some dank dungeon... yet.-

Ultimately, she was at their whim. Facing Atkins in the hall was one thing. She might stand a chance against one warrior unwilling to kill her, but she wasn't strong enough to take them all on.

-Sounds a lot like being imprisoned.-

She didn't disagree, but it was irrelevant.

She opened her eyes to the room, finding the girl watching her.

Taking a step from the door, Dee spoke to her. "So, what is there to do around here?"

"Maybe you're hungry?"

Dee smiled at the quick speech pattern of the child. "What do I call you?"

The girl blushed, eyes dropping to her feet. "I'm called Paige."

"Paige. Nice to meet you." Dee's eyes traveled around the room, this time to take it all in.

Plants covered the room, lining the floor, hanging from the ceiling, draping over the wall of windows opposite the door. Others, dispersed throughout the elegant seating and waiting areas, clustered together on the white-marble floor that reflected the green of the plants back to the room, so it glowed with a refreshing light.

"Wow. This place is really something."

Paige smiled.

Dee moved to the windows that showed a sweeping expanse of manicured lawns, decorated with flower gardens and mazes of greenery that stretched to a forest at the horizon. Dee couldn't begin to guess at the amount of acreage she was overlooking, never doubting that all she saw was the Rishi's jurisdiction.

"Where are we?" she asked.

"This is Amaltheum."

"Amaltheum?" Dee said the word slowly, recalling the Rishi she'd met at her arrival. "Amalthea lives in Amaltheum?"

Her inner-voice chuckled for them both, but the girl was unaware of Dee's mocking.

"Where is Amaltheum? Are we still on the East Coast?"

When the girl didn't answer, Dee turned to find her confused.

"You don't understand what I'm asking?" Dee's voice was gentle, even as shock laced her words.

The girl shook her head, wringing her hands.

Dee shrugged, smiling to show the girl there was nothing to worry about, filing away the odd information. "I think I will eat. Would you join me?"

Paige looked horrified and insisted it wasn't appropriate. Finally, Dee let the matter drop, but only because the girl seemed so uncomfortable.

Paige smiled, relieved, and moved towards the bedroom door. "I'll draw a bath. There are clothes for you as well. Food will be ready when you're finished."

Laughing to herself that asking for food had been interpreted as bath-time, Dee followed Paige, afraid to start another conversation that might fluster the girl.

21

Hamal was grateful for the highest-tech medical care in the world, but his injuries were still taking too long to heal. Not only that, Amalthea refused to allow him to get out of bed, though he was more than fine enough to walk, even if he needed crutches to do so.

He was worried about Dee.

He was concerned about his worry about Dee.

He knew this worry was the only reason the forced bed rest had him agitated, but the knowledge didn't alleviate it.

Coming across Barnard in the woods had brought a fear to his veins he'd never felt before: fear for another's well-being.

Hamal closed his eyes against the memory of that night, thinking instead of his upcoming trip home that would allow him to leave this mess for the Rishis to figure out. His involvement had long outplayed itself. His part had ended as soon as Dimitri and Daniel had walked on the scene.

He filled his lungs, ignoring the sharp pain, holding it for a couple of seconds before releasing it, calming himself as he'd been taught to do. Days. Days and he would be back at Zi's, his life able to resume normalcy.

She'd asked about him. They made sure he was aware of this

fact, and he was curious why they would make such a point to tell him. They'd have placated her by saying she would be able to see him when he was well enough. He wondered if he would be well enough before he shipped out.

Amalthea strolled into the room, trailed by Metis, Atkins, and Ainn, each nodding a greeting that he returned. He searched for signs of how dire matters were in the world beyond this room. Not surprising, there was nothing to read from their expressions.

The Rishi moved to his side, grasping his shoulder in a motherly gesture only she could get away with. He smiled to mask the annoyance he felt. Here was the interrogation he'd been waiting for, what they would call a *debrief.*

"Hamal, they tell me you're recovering wonderfully. How do you feel?"

"Wonderful."

Ignoring his dry humor, or maybe missing it altogether, Amalthea left his side to claim one of the chairs that had been brought in behind the interrogators. Atkins shot Hamal a look of warning.

Rather than wait for the questioning to begin, Hamal took the initiative, speaking directly to Amalthea. "I should thank you for giving me time to rest before bringing in the Inquisition."

Ainn smiled, turning her face to Atkins to hide it from Amalthea and Metis, who were less than pleased by Hamal's attitude. Atkins wasn't amused either, though his reaction held a note of concern. Hamal was allowed much leeway in his own House, but here, with all that was going on, the leash would be much tighter.

"The Inquisition? I'm sure you wouldn't compare us to that farce if you'd been there." Amalthea kept her voice pleasantly conversational, though the flash in her eyes couldn't be mistaken. "And I'm absolutely sure you don't want to give us any ideas about how to handle your lack of respect."

Hamal's eyes swept the four seated in a semi-circle near his bedside. "Maybe not, but I still can't help thinking I'm about to have all sorts of information extricated from my head."

"A bit dramatic, no?" Hamal was surprised to hear Metis speak. Ever at Amalthea's side, his reputation was only as a silent observer, as if his supernatural good looks were all the threat necessary. If he'd ever been anything but a pretty face, Hamal had never heard the story.

Hamal shrugged. "We shall see, yes?"

Metis' eyes tightened but otherwise resumed his silence.

Amalthea's voice remained patient. "We'd like you to tell us about your time with Dee."

Hamal closed his eyes, setting his head back on his pillow. After a moment, he turned his head to look at Amalthea. "You know I can't say anything until it's cleared by Zibanitu."

The answer was expected; none flustered in the least that he did not readily give them information.

The Rishi spoke again. "Tell us what happened after you were ambushed on the road three days ago."

Had it been three days?

"What happened after two huge fucking trucks hit us? I can tell you that. My right side was crushed, then we were all flipping. Dee got ejected somehow. I'm still trying to figure out how that happened. At the time, I was sure she was dead." His voice broke so he paused, taking a few breathes before continuing. "I was sure the truck was going to roll right over her. I still think it did. Atkins wasn't in the car anymore either, but I figured he'd just climbed out while the car was flipping." Hamal's eyes met Atkins'. "You're like a superhero, man."

Atkins gave the barest of nods. The others did not appreciate Hamal's deviation from the facts, so he continued, knowing not to press his luck.

"Gunfire started from the treeline. I assume from the direction the trucks came from, but I couldn't see, and the damn echo made it impossible to pinpoint where. The screeching of trucks crunching across the asphalt was a little distracting. As were my lungs being punctured. Then, I was being carried through the brush by Metis."

He gave Metis a nod, thanks he hadn't been able to provide until now.

"Did you see any of the fighting?" Amalthea's question turned his attention.

Hamal shook his head. "I heard the gunfire. Dee made it to me, but after Metis left us, she took off back towards the fighting."

The Rishi leaned forward, genuinely curious about how the human might answer. "Why would she do that?"

He blinked, surprised by the question.

"I taught her to fight. She must have thought she could help."

"You heard about the ones she took out on her own?"

He hadn't, and he knew Amalthea knew that. Any information that would have made it to him in this isolated room would only do so because she willed it. She'd asked the question to judge his reaction.

Used to dealing with this kind of subtle underhandedness from Porrima, and having mastered the art of controlling what his face portrayed because of it, he betrayed nothing. Dee had learned quickly, but her after-the-fact reactions to the stress of combat had continued to worry him. It was much of the reason he wanted to see her as soon as possible. She was probably sitting alone in some room, freaking herself out.

He ignored Amalthea's studious gaze.

Ainn explained. "Dimitri and Daniel were guarding her. Four of the Ophiuchus' Soldiers attacked. Dimitri and Daniel were both down. Dee retaliated. Protected them. She's the only reason they weren't KIA."

Hamal allowed surprise to show. "They were both hurt?"

Ainn nodded. "Daniel's just regained consciousness. He'll be alright. Dimitri didn't make it."

Hamal's head fell back to his pillow, his chest constricting under the realization of how close Dee had come to her last day.

He picked his head back up. "Dee took out the ones that took out Dimitri and Daniel? Alone? She's alright, though?"

The words were out before he caught his error. They'd interpret too much of his feelings through his questions.

Taking another breath, he lay his head back on the pillow, closing his eyes to give himself a moment of feigned weakness to collect himself. His injuries were severe enough that it would be expected. Silently, he chastised himself for caring.

"Dee's fine. She received no wounds from battle." Atkins' blunt response brought Hamal's eyes to him. Though the closest thing the Soldier had to a friend, Hamal was no such thing in this situation. Atkins was a commander of Amalthea's forces, here to play his role in debriefing the outsider.

As grateful as Hamal was for the information, it did little to relieve his anxiety. What did Atkins mean, *no wounds from battle*? Had something else happened, or was he merely answering the question as it was asked?

Hamal forced himself to express only benign calm. He wasn't sure why Amalthea's people would care what he felt about Dee. Except, he was never sure what mattered to the Rishis, never sure what information was stored away for later use as ammunition in manipulating others.

He focused on the facts of Dee taking out the Ophiuchus' Soldiers. Of all the units to meet in combat, The Ophiuchus' were the most feared. Or so he'd heard.

Pride that it had been his training that had kept her alive came over him and he did nothing to hide the reflection of it from his expression. Kudos to her teacher."

His self-congratulatory smile went ignored, but he continued to grin.

"Had she had any training before yours?" Finn inquired.

"None. That's what she told me, anyway."

"You don't believe that to be true?"

"I believe her. She's not a good liar."

"How long did you train her?"

Hamal met Ainn's eye, then Amalthea's. "No disrespect, Rishi, but I'll need Zibanitu's approval before I can talk to you. I'm sure I've already said more than he'd appreciate."

Amalthea looked at him for a moment, visibly judging how far she might push him and what ramifications the pushing might have on her. Dimitri was already dead, having died under her roof. Until very recently, Daniel's state of health was unsure. Badgering his pet human might not be the smartest thing at this point, at least not until the human had had a chance to be debriefed by his own Master.

She stood, and the others followed. "Thank you, Hamal. We'll let you see Dee as soon as you can be out of bed."

"You won't let her here to see me?" The words fell from his mouth before he could stop them.

Ignored, he was left alone in his prison.

22

F or four days, Dee stayed in her rooms, sleeping, eating, resting, before sleeping some more, stewing in all the unknowns. Her mind raced to put together the limited information she had. Staring out the window was her main hobby, but even the beatific view didn't help her pull what she didn't know from thin air.

Hamal still wasn't out of bed.

Daniel was doing much better, but she wasn't allowed to see him either.

Finally, on the morning of the fifth day, while Dee stood in the center of the large room, repeating the katas Hamal had showed her, body sick of the lack of activity, Amalthea sent word: Dee would continue her training here. Dee was grateful, if for no other reason than to be allowed outside.

She thought Hamal had been a harsh master, but she wasn't prepared for the pair Amalthea set on her.

On a quiet, secluded patch of yard on Amalthea's immense estate, Ellie and Ainn worked her mercilessly. Their speed and power easily surpassed her own, so she was in a position she'd never faced before. With Hamal, she'd continuously pulled her punches and slowed her movements, but with these two, those habits were only getting her into trouble.

"Get up! Let's go again."

Dee pushed herself upright, eating dirt before she'd even found her feet, the petite redhead pacing around her.

"Again!"

Ainn was tough, bringing tears to Dee's eyes more than once. She pushed through, more frustrated than hurt, unused to this level of severity. She might have complained if there was anyone to complain to.

-Complain they're teaching you how to stay alive?-

Dee blocked the swift attack, then another, and another, before seeing an opening to push an offensive.

Then, she was face down on the ground.

"I can't believe you're this slow."

"You had everyone fooled."

Dee glared at her trainers as she pushed up from the ground. Ainn threw a laugh, at her expense, towards Ellie.

Without thinking, Dee threw herself forward, forcing Ainn to defend against a flurry of attacks. Coming together in a cross-block, Ainn smiled. "I knew you were holding out."

They stepped back from each other, breathless, Dee stunned at what she'd done when she'd stopped thinking so hard.

"Think you can do that again?" Ellie stepped in behind Dee.

Dee turned to the taller, fairer of the pair. "Let's see."

The Soldiers put Dee through the paces, working with her the better part of the afternoon before they released her.

"You really were holding out on me." Hamal's voice called to her from his perch on the low wall that wove its way through Amalthea's land.

Dee smiled until she thought her lips might split.

He hobbled from his perch and she wrapped her arms around him in a bear hug.

They broke apart, Dee smiling apologetically. "Sorry. It's just really good to see a face I recognize." She looked him up and down, assessing his recovery. "I wasn't sure when they'd let you out. They said you were hurt pretty bad. Surgery?"

He nodded. "I couldn't stay cooped up any longer. Besides, I needed to make sure they were taking care of you."

An awkward moment hit them, something in his words bringing Dee's memory to the kiss they'd shared, while her inner-voice grumbled she should have killed him.

He smiled his cocky grin. "I think there's much we have to tell each other."

Her eyebrows rose in disbelief. "Can that happen now?"

He shrugged ambiguously while his laughing eyes declared affirmation.

Dee's spirits soared as they made their way towards the house.

Coming in through the French doors, the pair was stopped by Amalthea, who sat in the corner of the large receiving room, camouflaged by the plants that were ever abundant. The Rishi stood, forcing the pair to greet her. Hamal surprised Dee when he bowed respectfully.

Amalthea smiled graciously in response. "It's nice to see you up and about, Hamal. I hope your visit with your previous charge won't hinder anyone's plans."

Dee noticed Hamal stiffen, her attention turning to his face to see what she might read there, but his face was a blank slate. She looked from her mentor to her hostess, and back again, waiting for their eye contact to break. Whatever was said in their silent subtext, Dee wasn't privy to.

Another moment passed before Amalthea turned to Dee, satisfied by what she'd read in Hamal's face. The Rishi took Dee's hands. "I hear your training is coming along wonderfully. Already a breakthrough." She smiled, warm and bright, bringing the same expression from Dee despite her uneasiness about what had transpired with Hamal. "I've sent word to Paige that you're bringing a friend for supper. Enjoy yourselves."

The pair watched the Rishi disappear through the adjoining rooms.

-That was weird.-

"That was weird, right?" She cast a glance at Hamal's stiff posture. They crossed multiple rooms and were up the stairs before Dee broke the silence again. "You alright?"

Hamal's attention was distant.

She sighed. "You can't talk to me, can you?"

Hamal looked at her, surprised.

"It's the only thing she could have been talking about. Reminding you of your duty. And the silent stare down? Why else would she need to interfere? Am I wrong?"

Hamal's eyes were locked straight ahead, not looking at her. "You're not wrong."

Dee sighed again. "Any way anyone will ever tell me what's going on?"

Hamal chuckled. "I wish I could answer that. Even I don't know most of what's going on."

"Can you tell me who attacked us on the road?"

Hamal was shocked. "Amalthea hasn't spoken to you?"

"Not really. She's explained to me that I'm safe, that I won't be here very long, though she didn't give me any context about what very long might mean. All my questions have been pushed off for another time."

Hamal shrugged as if this information was perfectly reasonable. "She's technically a neutral party and bound by the same rules as I am."

What no one seemed to remember was that Dee hadn't spent her life inside the circle of whatever world this was. Her frustration rang clearly in her tone. "So? What does that *mean*?"

Hamal looked Dee over as they reached the closed doors to her rooms, her sweat-stained shirt clinging to a body that'd only grown more toned since that first day he'd begun following her. Her gaze no longer held that tint of insecurity he'd hated.

Even stuck in a place she didn't know, surrounded by beings that probably scared the hell out of her, hadn't broken her. He was proud of her.

The thought pushed a strange feeling through him. He pulled his eyes away.

"It means she doesn't know enough to tell you. Amalthea won't answer your questions because her own questions haven't been answered. None of the Rishis have answers."

He was glad Dee turned to push the door open so she wouldn't read the mix of emotions battling within.

The room was bright with the lingering sunlight of the fading day. Hamal swept the room with a cursory glance, taking in the hanging plants, the ivory furniture tossed playfully with colored pillows that matched the blooming flowers scattered throughout. Compared to his room, which contained only a bed and night-stand, this was a palace.

Off to their left a small, round table was set for two. A girl stood near, smiling shyly.

Dee's eyes lingered on the table of food. "Hamal, this is Paige. She basically watches my every move and feeds me."

Hamal nodded, startled by the child's presence.

"Do I have time to shower?"

Hamal wondered who Dee was asking, but Paige's answer, in a quiet voice, almost made him laugh. "Of course. Supper is ready whenever you want it."

Dee shared a look with Hamal that said, *see what I have to deal with.*

This time, Hamal did laugh. "Oh, you've got it rough."

Dee rolled her eyes and walked into the adjoining room.

Gone, Hamal slumped, struggling. He had gone against his better judgment and allowed himself to engage with Desiree. He should have just watched from the shadows, ensuring she was safe but not letting her see him. Now, he couldn't find it in himself to leave, even as his brain listed all the reasons it was a better idea.

He couldn't leave the estate. It had been deemed too big of a security risk for anyone to come or go until they had more information on what forces were massing nearby. His injuries kept him from the training field and left him no outlet for his mounting frustrated energy. That was why he struggled with his base desires. Desires he'd always freely indulged.

He stood nose to the window, staring out over the green land that spread across his view. He barely saw what was in front of him; instead following Dee's movements in the shower with his mind's eye.

He'd never had a problem keeping a benign eye on what belonged to the Rishis. Dee clearly fit in this category, yet he was finding it more and more challenging to remember it. She'd stopped being his mission the day Daniel and Dimitri showed up. There was no reason for him to worry about her. The reins had been passed to superior protectors. He shouldn't even be here, and as annoyed with Amalthea as he was for her interference downstairs just now, her visit was justified. In fact, he should thank her. She already knew what he was still arguing with himself.

Why had he even come here? He'd told himself it was just to make sure she was alright. But of course, she was. No one had ever been as well cared for as she would be here. He didn't need to see her to know that. Amalthea wouldn't do anything to harm the precious cargo she'd managed to secure. And, even if she had, or orders had come down the line that Hamal didn't like, he was in no position to say, or do, anything about it.

D ee came out of the bedroom smiling. "Compared to the guest bedrooms at my house, this place is—"

She looked around, catching Paige's eye, who was resetting the table for one.

Hurt, Dee knew it was for the best. After Amalthea's silent gag order, she wasn't sure they had anything to talk about.

Even so, Hamal's absence caused a wrenching ache to form.

Her breath caught, and she found herself sobbing, still standing on the threshold of the rooms.

She was alone here. She was alone in a life that had become a stranger's, and there was no way for her to figure out what was going on except to sit back and wait for information to fall in her lap.

-*Absorb what you can for now. A time will come.*-

She wasn't sure she had the fortitude for that approach.

-*As if you have a choice.*-

She wanted to call Mike, except that was forbidden as well. There were too many security risks with contacting him, though she had been allowed to leave him a message as they'd left town with a lame explanation of why she'd left in such a hurry.

So much for her promise to be the best best friend. .

Her tears fell harder.

23

"I don't understand. You got involved, but Zibanitu can't get involved? Didn't he send Hamal, then Dimitri and Daniel?"

Dee's head hurt. She was finally having an actual conversation about what was going on, yet she wasn't sure any of the answers were helping her make sense of any of it. It seemed to her the Rishis were a bunch of rich busy-bodies so concerned with what the others were doing, they couldn't enjoy their own lives. Or let her enjoy hers.

"Hamal's part is easily overlooked. He is not one of us, so can not technically be viewed as an asset of a House. Dimitri and Daniel were sent to assist me, which is allowed, and a pair of young Soldiers sent to assist a House without its own army isn't likely to be noticed."

Dee leaned over, elbows on knees, hands covering her face. "Okay. So, the Ophi—Han?—"

"The Ophiuchus. Sabik Han."

"Sure. That guy. He's the one who came after me on the way here?"

Amalthea nodded, ever patient. "He sent Barnard to you. And the ambush, yes."

"But Zosma was sending those Revenants after me?"

"That is still the question to be answered."

"It was definitely not The Off—Han."

Amalthea smiled. "Oh-fee-YOU-kus. Ophiuchus."

Dee nodded, knowing she still wouldn't be able to remember the pronunciation. The word didn't flow right off her tongue. Leaning back in the chair, laid out in the oversized seat, she sighed. "Basically, I'm not going home anytime soon."

Amalthea shook her head, face set in an expression of compassion that Dee wouldn't like her answer. "Even I wouldn't agree to let you return home at this time."

"*Even* you?"

Amalthea's motherly expression made Dee suspicious despite never receiving anything from the Rishi other than kindness. "I am curious about you, yes. As will the others be, when they learn of you, but I have no agenda outside of that. I wish you no ill will, regardless of what the answers to your questions might be."

"The others wish me *ill will?*" Dee perked as fear knifed through her.

Amalthea shrugged, a strange gesture from the ancient Master, so it almost took on a different meaning. What that meaning might be, Dee couldn't decipher.

"If one of them wants you, there will be another that wants to take you from them. There are twelve of us, thirteen when you count Han, and with family, there is always at least one that has to rock the boat."

-And you thought you weren't learning anything.-

Dee shuddered. What happened when they all knew about her? As far as she could tell, only four Rishi knew she existed, and her life was already in chaos.

-You'll be running forever.-

"With Han deciding to play, the game may erupt to war. The very thing Zibanitu has been working against since the beginning."

Dee buried her face back in her hands, not sure what she was supposed to do with information that was more stifling than enlightening.

Sure, she was comfortable, for now, but Amalthea was talking about the possibility of *war*. Could she sit around and wait for that to happen because of her? But where could she go? How could she stop it?

-We could always get on this Ophiuchus' side of things.-

She didn't think that would be allowed, even if she did decide that was a good idea.

-You should have killed Hamal.-

If her inner-voice was a tangible being, she'd have slapped it. Why her head always went back to that point made her crazy. There was no way to look at any of this that would make that point valid.

Rubbing her eyes, Dee looked back to the world to find that Ainn and Ellie were waiting for her to recover herself.

"Ready to work?" Ainn's tone brokered no room for a negative response.

———

Her mind whirled with thoughts of what a war between these creatures, with her at the center, would mean. So distracted by it, she didn't notice the group converge on their training spot.

Nervous, Dee spoke towards Ellie in a low tone, "Everyone's training with us today?"

Ellie smiled. "Something like that."

-They're bringing out the big guns to show you just how powerless you are.-

She forced her feet to keep moving, to continue following Ellie, knowing Ainn would just push her from behind if she stopped walking. Drilling with the girls had significantly improved Dee's adeptness in the training ring, but she was still far from consistent enough to be tested. She hoped the others were only there to stare at the freak.

Donning the mantle of arrogance she'd learned from Hamal to feign confidence, she said, "Didn't think I was getting enough of an ass-kicking from you two on the daily, you had to bring in the rest of the troops?" She made sure her voice was loud enough to be overheard by the others.

Ellie chuckled. "Actually, no, but since you don't seem to mind the idea, maybe we'll switch the day's plans."

-Good one. How 'bout we make it a rule not to be sarcastic with the uber-powerful, psycho Soldiers?-

Dee made a mental note to keep her mouth shut.

Her lack of control had been bothering her since she'd arrived. As well as she was being treated, she never forgot the fact that she was a prisoner. She could only do what was asked of her, not knowing enough to contradict anything she was told. Even if she could slip away, there was nowhere she could go they couldn't follow. Sabik Han probably had guys waiting right out the front door for when she did something impulsive like that. Then, she would be his, no harm, no foul.

-Unless you plan to jump the fence right now, you might want to pay attention to everyone standing around waiting for a piece of your noobishness.-

Her eyes moved around the ring of Soldiers, counting bodies as she did. She'd only made it to four when she realized she was staring at Daniel.

Her face broke out into a smile. "Daniel! No one told me you were out and about."

He laughed, pleased by her reaction. "Why would they?"

She hugged him. She hadn't planned to, but with so few familiar faces around, it was just a natural reaction. He embraced her warmly, ignoring the catcalls from the others. "I'm not one of Amalthea's, remember? I'm sure no one thought you'd care."

"You saved me."

"I hear you saved me."

Dee's eyes swept over his neck, remembering the wound she'd thought would kill him. "They said you weren't healing."

"I guess it just took longer than they thought it would."

Dee was too happy to see him to care about the specifics.

Daniel looked over Dee's head. "I'm surprised Hamal isn't with you."

Dee shrugged, thinking of Dimitri, wondering what she could say to express how sorry she was. She was cut off from further speech when Ainn whistled loudly, bringing everyone's attention back to why they were there. "I'm glad the reunion is going so well, but it's time to work!"

Daniel rolled his eyes playfully, stepping back to his place in the circle. "Sure thing, Sarge."

If Ainn was annoyed by his flippancy, she didn't show it. "Alright, Desiree. I know you think we've brought everyone out to get a shot at you, but the real reason is so you can watch other Soldiers fight. We want you to see what you can do. Our theory is that your preconceptions are holding you back."

-They really think you're one of them? Interesting.-

A million questions came to her, but it wasn't the time for talk. Instead, she moved to take a spot in the circle, watching as two Soldiers moved to the center, long staffs held like they were born with them in their hands.

The way they maintained an above-human speed was the first thing that caught her. She knew she could move as fast, but had only managed it in quick bursts. She buzzed with curiosity to see if she could do what she was seeing. She allowed the energy to echo through her legs, bouncing on her toes, watching with wide-eyes the display of athleticism that defied anything she'd ever dreamed possible.

-I'm not sure they're human.-

It was a point she'd shied away from, not understanding, or wanting to understand, what these Ancient Rishis were, and by account, what the Soldiers were. By all appearances, they were human. Dee hadn't seen Amalthea do anything to suggest otherwise, despite the humming in her head that told her there was great power there. She couldn't even define what that power was, so it was just some vague concept that brokered fear.

By the time the third pair stepped to the center of the training ring, Dee was pacing the perimeter of the circle, analyzing everything she was seeing. She encoded to memory the feats of agility she witnessed, recognizing things Hamal had shown her, expanded upon by Ainn and Ellie, and again by those she now watched.

Acrobatics stitched seamlessly into the forms she'd been taught through katas opened her mind to new ways of blending styles. Commentary from those watching gave her insight into what happened in the ring as well.

"Always keep your feet. If you jump, you're much too vulnerable."

"You have to keep your opponent guessing! The leaping and spinning keeps them off balance."

"Too much ground-work. Someone'll come behind you and *tap-tap* the back of your skull."

Dee filed it all away, eyes dissecting the play in the circle.

As the last pair came to the end of their exhibition, Ellie called to Dee, "You ready for a go?"

Dee hesitated, the excitement that had built in the watching erased in the face of performance anxiety. But Ellie didn't give her a chance to say no.

She grabbed the staff Ellie tossed her from the air. The feel of the smooth wood in her hand erased the doubts surfacing. She twirled the bo with a smile, knowing Ainn would yell at her for disrespecting her weapon, but it was time for a little exhibition.

-Careful. Don't get cocky.-

Rather than use a verbal reprimand, Ainn stepped into the circle, her staff buzzing with offensive motion to berate her student physically. Dee brought her weapon up to block, stepping and twisting as she did, forcing muscles to respond more quickly than she'd considered allowing them before. If these Soldiers, whose every waking moment was fixated on honing themselves into the best possible fighters, thought she was more than she'd shown, she was going to trust they knew what they were talking about. Here she was going to see just how capable she was. She was going to show them they couldn't hold her. She was going to show them she didn't need protection. She was going to show them to leave her to the quiet life she never realized how much she enjoyed.

-Right, because you were living quietly, rather than hiding.-

Egged on by the pestering in her head, she continued to up the ante, pushing herself until she no longer needed pushing, following the flow that had set over her when her mind allowed her body to be free.

She wasn't sure how long they sparred, neither getting a hit on the other. Given that Dee was used to lasting only as long as it took her to get to her feet, this was a vast improvement.

Much of her vision, a sense relied on more than any other, was lost in the whirling motion of their accelerated action, yet, there was no disadvantage. As if her muscles had sight, some fore-knowledge of the oncoming blows, there was no need for her eyes to perceive what her body naturally sensed.

The fight's pace quickened. Murmurs flowed around the central pair, but neither of the two engaged took notice.

It was Ellie who called for a halt.

Panting, Dee stood, bo held with one end resting on the ground, ignoring the impressed reactions from those surrounding her as she relished the feeling of her body. Energized, she bounced on her toes, giving Ellie her attention, who beamed. "Dee, never had I imagined our exhibition would bear such fruitful results. Would you like to see more, or continue playing with what you've learned about yourself?"

-Let's play!-

"I'd like to play." She tried to adopt the severe nature of her newest tutors, but her smiling face betrayed her.

The Soldier matched her smile, pleased with Dee's answer. "Alright, then let's continue. Who'd like to join Dee in the circle?"

Daniel ignored the others whose hands rose or voices called out to leap forward, sword drawn. "Had much sword practice?"

"Not much." Dee stared at the weapon in his hand, heart fluttering, thinking of the katana gifted by Hamal, now lost on some backcountry road. The sword stalking towards her was a different style, and she found herself curious how it might feel in her hand.

He looked to Ainn, ensuring he had permission to continue. The trainer had already pulled a pair of practice swords for them, tossing one to Dee, then the other to Daniel as he sheathed his own. Absently, Dee nodded thanks, testing the weight of the new weapon before returning her attention to Daniel. "Promise not to maim me?"

He chuckled. "No promises, but I will try very hard not to scar you for life."

She might have laughed with him, but the gleam in his eye as he began circling her was anything but mirthful. This was a solemn duel.

She spun in a slow, tight circle as Daniel stalked her, his movements smooth and fluid, sword point never wavering from his target.

Her memory flashed to their first meeting. The same night she'd faced Barnard in the woods, and the first time she'd ever wielded a sword with the intent to kill. How much easier would her nights have been if she'd carried one all along? She would have had no problem killing a few Revenants.

-Or you would have accidentally slit your own throat.-

Daniel moved forward using a stuttering step to feint, a move designed to pull her head into the fight. A silent bereavement at her wandering attention.

His feint spiked her adrenaline, as well as a tinge of embarrassment that he'd shaken her. She scrambled to make a move. Coming at him in a blur of speed, her eyes searching for the counter she was sure he'd throw, she wasn't prepared for the simplicity of his action.

As her muscles created movement out of the disordered plan in her mind, he adjusted his position, moving only enough, right at the last moment, to avoid the hit. There was a split second when she thought she would win with a first strike.

Then, she was on her face, reminded of those first days working with Ainn and Ellie.

Leaping back to her feet, she spun to a smiling Daniel. "Not thinking is not the same as not having a plan," he admonished.

Dee stood in a fighting stance, not lowering her guard as she tilted her head at his words. "Oh?"

His sword arm dropped, his stance relaxing from his fighting position. "You reacted emotionally. Not that I can blame you, but in a fight, leave emotion off the table."

Her lips were pressed together in a tight line of annoyance. "I did not react emotionally."

His eyebrows rose. "What did you feel right before you sprinted at me with no plan of attack other than irrational outburst?"

She met his eye, her embarrassment rising. Grasping for any explanation that might make sense, she shrugged, realizing his assessment was correct.

"You were embarrassed. I get it." He pointed his sword straight out, turning to each of those standing around them. "We all get it. We all started as beginners with the worst better than us. Being embarrassed at not knowing should be erased from your mind. How could you know? Why shouldn't you be beaten by all of us who have decades of experience over you? Why shouldn't I show you up? You should simply walk out on the field and already know how to play? You are here to learn. Learn!"

He was speeding towards her before the last word had cleared the air, but she was ready, his words wiping her mind of background distractions. All those eyes on her, and their potential for judgment, were forgotten. Regardless of other motives, at this moment, they were there to teach her. Right here, right now, she could allow them their influence as it would make her stronger, more able to face the chaos beyond this circle.

And so it went, Dee amplifying what she knew as each Soldier met her in the circle. They only stopped when the last of the sun's rays passed from sight.

Bowing to each other before wandering off in groups and pairs, Dee found herself standing in a hushed twilight, staring up at the star-riddled sky, her body aching deliciously from working so hard.

"You were great." Daniel's words implied multiple meanings. She wondered if he flirted with everyone like this.

"I think I have you to thank for that." She turned her head to look at him before returning her gaze to the sky. "Learn!" She shouted it into the night, laughing. "Everyone was inspired. And everyone remembered to give me some slack for being such a noob."

He chuckled. "Noob. That you are." His voice dropped as if talking to himself, "I wonder how many of them would under-stand the term."

She studied his face as his attention moved to the stars. From many of the Soldiers, there was a sense of timelessness, similar to what she felt from Atkins, but Daniel wasn't like that. He appeared no more than thirty, and until this moment, she'd never considered he might be precisely how old he seemed. His jovial nature was in contrast to the others whose stoicism allowed only focused work. Could that be due to his more modern heritage?

"How long have you been one of them?"

Daniel wasn't surprised by her question, but didn't answer, instead smiling at the sky.

The remaining Soldiers continued to shuffle away. When the air surrounding them was filled with only sounds of croaking frogs and chirping cicadas, he answered, "A few decades. I'm a baby. *The* baby, actually." He laughed, turning his attention to her. "I think it was why Dimitri and I were chosen as the first to come to your aid. I'm a little more relatable than these old-timers. Plus, sending your weakest Soldier on a mission this important is counter-intuitive. My showing up is easily deflected as unrelated to the curiosity surrounding *the anomaly*."

His eyes studied her's with an intensity she wasn't sure how to define.

Forcibly, she maintained eye contact with the young Soldier. "So, you're *Baby*, and I'm *Anomaly*."

He laughed, and Dee couldn't help but join him. When their laughter faded, they were both looking at the sky.

"So, were you also sent because your playful attitude might endear you to me?" Dee had been playing his words over in her head.

Daniel chuckled. "Playful attitude, huh?"

She smiled, eyes remaining on the sky.

"I think that's a reason, yes. Zibanitu's been manipulating both humans and—whatever it is we are—for so long, I'm not sure we could measure it. There are always layers to his actions. And non-actions."

Dee nodded, wondering how he was manipulating her. Had he wanted her here with Amalthea for reasons other than to circumvent a diplomatic incident she still didn't understand?

Daniel's words gave her a thought. "So, Zibanitu's waiting for someone to make a mistake. For someone to come forward, at which point they'll be forced to explain what's going on."

Daniel shrugged. "I just work here."

She frowned, knowing he had his theories. Knowing it wasn't his place to say, despite him having offered his cryptic insights up to this point, didn't make his silence any less frustrating.

"When will you be going back?" She wasn't sure what she felt that Hamal would be leaving, and she probably would never see him again.

Daniel shrugged again, looking over at her, his playful demeanor turned on full. "Why? Think you'll miss me?"

Dee chuckled, rolling her eyes. "If you can leave, maybe I can leave."

The playfulness washed from his face as he studied her. It was there, in his expression, in the seriousness of one so genial, that she saw her infinite imprisonment. He might only just work there, but even he knew what her fate would be.

"Why did you," her hands moved in front of her as she searched for verbiage, "become one of them?"

"Zibanitu keeps tight control over how large any House gets. It's rare, well—it's rare *now*—that Soldiers need replacing. There's not enough conflict that kills us off, so there's not much Initiating going on."

Dee frowned. "You say that like you wish that weren't the case."

He shrugged, eyes still on the sky. "I was created to fight. What does one do when their purpose is no longer purposeful?"

Dee had never had purpose. She had no way to relate.

Daniel continued. "They take humans. The better warriors they are, the more they're sought after. Then, it's like they infuse whatever they are into us, and we come out like this." He lifted his arms to the side to gesture to himself, eyes falling to Dee's face, eyes guarded against whatever emotion bubbled underneath.

"What do they do?" Dee's voice was soft, not sure if she had the right to ask.

Daniel's gaze was internal now. "I have no idea. I just know I woke up after a few weeks, and I was this."

"A few weeks?"

He shrugged again, eyes returning to the sky. "There's not a whole lot of explaining that goes on. Soldiers obey. Explaining the whys and why-nots tends to muddy the water. That's how mutinies start, and players switch sides. Not good for business, those things."

Dee's scrutiny moved from his face to the sky. "Don't want your troops knowing the heinous shit they're responsible for?"

He smiled. "Exactly. But, I knew coming in. We're not just

plucked from our lives, prisoners to their will. Only after does our will become theirs."

-Must be nice.-

Her eyes lit with surprise, her attention returning to studying his face. "So, you knew them before you agreed to the change? You knew what they were—are, whatever."

"I still don't know what they *are*. Not really. But yeah, I knew they were something—else. I was allowed a genuine decision, to stay and be more than I could *ever* be without them, or continue with my old life. I saw what these Soldiers could do. Watched their training. Saw where they slept. How they lived. After that, there was nothing the Rishis could have shown me that would have made me say no."

Steps through the grass, coming from the house, turned their attention.

Dee hadn't seen Hamal since he'd left her room a handful of days ago. She struggled to remember exactly how long it had been, each day here seeming a week, the last few weeks a lifetime.

Part of her was elated to see him, but it was buried beneath another part that didn't know what she was supposed to say after he'd abandoned her. They stared at each other, his blank mask covering any clue to what he might be thinking.

She grit her teeth against the disappointment growing inside her.

Daniel was the first to speak, noting Hamal's tense posture, the way his eyes moved over the pair in search of something going on. Daniel hid his smile, realizing the truth of the rumored infatuation Hamal had with the anomaly, knowing it wasn't something to throw in his face unless the Soldier wanted a real fight.

The idea brought a smile to his lips, but Daniel knew better than to test the Rishi's patience with something so juvenile. Besides, what if he hurt the human?

The Soldier peeked a glance at Dee before deciding on a course of action. Was this infatuation reciprocated? Daniel was sure the plan was never for the two to become enamored of each other. But, with Zibanitu, one never knew true motive.

Dee's face was stone. The effort it took to hide what she felt evident, though Daniel couldn't determine which emotions she was hiding. Did she detest the man who'd been forced to lie to her, blaming him for bringing her into all of this? Or was she secretly in love with her mentor?

"Hamal, good to see you up and about." Daniel's tone was friendly, genuine.

Hamal's was less so. "Daniel. Word of your impending death was greatly exaggerated. An interesting story that'll be told for centuries, I'm sure."

"Just what I need, a story of my almost dying proceeding me. Hopefully, I'll fight another day to fix my reputation to something a bit sexier."

Dee chuckled, a sound that brought a frown to Hamal's face.

Tension rose over the group.

After a beat of silence, Hamal asked Dee, "Everyone treating you well?"

She nodded.

Daniel took Dee's hand, watching Hamal's face. "We were on our way to supper. Would you like to join?"

Hamal's eyes went to their clasped hands. Daniel watched the war in the human's eyes as he struggled with how to respond. It told Daniel all he needed to know.

Dee wasn't sure what she felt as Hamal walked away, her hand still clasped in Daniel's, who was working small circles on her wrist with his thumb.

Snatching her hand away, she continued to stare after Hamal. "What the hell was that?"

Daniel chuckled. "Just messing with him. And proving a point to the both of us. You'll both be glad of it, trust me."

She turned to face him. "What point?"

"His feelings for you. They need to be tempered. If you share his interest, you, too, need to forget it."

Dee opened her mouth to speak but found no words. Too many emotions swirled through her. Surprise that Hamal cared for her. Anger that Daniel would interfere, and even greater indignation that he would tell her how she was allowed to feel. Not least of all, longing for the thing she'd already known she couldn't have.

She tapped down her anger, kept her thoughts to herself. She told herself Daniel wasn't interfering. He was explaining how it was. Not liking the reality of it didn't make the truth any different. This latter statement she heard in her father's voice.

"Daniel? Who am I?"

She felt his assessing gaze in the pause before he answered.

"Honestly, I'm not sure anyone can answer that. I didn't know anything about you until I showed up at your house, dodging bullets before I was even sure I'd found the right place."

Dee smiled, remembering well her attack on him.

-And Dimitri.-

And Dimitri. One already dead because of trying to help her. How many more would there be before the end?

"You aren't one of us." Daniel pointed his finger at his chest. "But neither are you one of *them.* I'd place my bets that you are something else."

24

Prepared for her typical quiet, solitary morning eating a quiet, solitary breakfast, Dee stopped fast when she found Amalthea seated in one of the oversized chairs that faced the windows in the living area of her suite. The Rishi sat calmly as if her presence there was a daily occurrence.

"Come, sit with me." Amalthea motioned with a hand that lay lazily on an arm of the chair.

Hesitating long enough to cast a sweep of eyes over the room, Dee did as she was told, falling into a chair and turning her gaze to follow Amalthea's.

They stared out over the lands of the estate. Fall had descended over the landscape to redefine color. How she'd never noticed the uncountable shades of green, that there was yellow in the red and brown in the green. How bright colors were only so because of the contrast from the duller leaves.

Minutes stretched in this silent observance until Amalthea's soft voice eased into the quiet. "It has been my pleasure to have you here. Not only have I ensured myself a place in this story, but I've found you to be a most gracious guest."

Dee smiled.

"Thank you, Rishi."

Amalthea smiled back, and Dee relaxed.

As the Rishi looked her over, Dee wondered what she was seeing, or what she might be looking for. She thought to ask but held her tongue. Speaking with Amalthea was not the same as talking with Daniel or Hamal.

"As I've said, I'm excited to finally be part of one of the grand stories my brothers and sisters play out. Even so, there is no script, and as patient as I can be, I do not like to sit around and wait to see what might happen. I like to touch things, feel them, experience them. Stories are no good if they have no life."

Rising, Amalthea stood tall at the window, her full five foot two frame casting a shadow across her guest. Dee went rigid, fear born from instinct slicing through her. But, the Rishi only stared out of the glass. "It is time to show you what this is. This world we've dragged you into. A world, I believe, you have no knowledge of, regardless of whether others think you're playing a game of ignorance."

Dee opened her mouth to defend herself. This was the first she'd heard that anyone thought she'd been lying.

Amalthea held up a hand, still not looking at her. "There is no need to explain to me. I believe you. Hamal believes you. For now, that is good enough."

She turned from the window to face Dee. "I will show you what I can about the things you've seen. It may give you some insight into our world, though there will be much more to learn."

The Rishi studied Dee for a moment, and Dee got the impression she was debating something to herself. When she spoke, Dee knew that whatever it was, she had decided against it. "Eat. Get dressed. We will be hiking many miles today. I will send an escort when we are ready to go."

-Hiking?-

An hour later, Dee was walking through the very hills she'd been staring across that morning, matching steps with Daniel, her assigned bodyguard. Dee wasn't sure why she needed private security detail when they were safely on Amalthea's land, surrounded by the Rishi's Soldiers, and she didn't ask. Still, her heart hadn't lowered to a regular beat since leaving the shadows of the house.

Hamal hadn't been chosen to come with them. Or had decided not to. Dee pointedly did not ask about him, though she couldn't deny the loss his absence created.

Still, a few hours later, she realized she was enjoying herself. A much more meditative activity than jogging, she wished she'd started hiking years ago. How different her life might have been.

-*Sure, you'd be dead down some gorge after being tackled off a cliff.*-

Her imagination envisioned just that happening so vividly she shuddered, prompting Daniel's question, "Hanging in there?"

"I'm great, actually." She took a deep breath of the clean air to emphasize her point.

They walked side by side, behind Ellie and Vali, who followed another pair Dee recognized, though she didn't know their names. Behind her, Amalthea walked with Metis, and behind them, Atkins and Ainn.

Glancing behind her to judge how quietly she could speak for the pair behind her not to hear, not entirely sure such a thing was possible, she caught Metis watching her. His carefully crafted expression betrayed nothing. Since seeing him at the battle on the road, which the others now referred to as Road-side, she'd caught only glimpses of Amalthea's beautiful right hand.

She wasn't sure what it meant that he was the Rishi's *right hand*. What things did Amalthea's House deal with that the Rishi would need someone to act in this manner, and how powerful was he that he could fill that role?

There were still so many questions. She was excited that this trip might fill in some gaps.

-Careful. So far, every time you've learned anything, it's only created more questions.-

This was true, but there had to be a point when answers would start yielding information rather than further muddy what she thought she knew.

Daniel bumped her casually. "You're fidgeting."

"Sorry, I'm not sure I can talk without everyone hearing me."

"Would it matter?"

She thought about it. "I guess not."

She shot another glance over her shoulder to find the Rishi, and Metis engaged in hushed conversation. Could she eavesdrop on them if she focused?

Another bump from Daniel refocused her thoughts on her own conversation. "Where are we going?"

"That one's easy. I thought Amalthea told you."

"She told me she was going to show me *about the world I've been dragged into.*" Dee air-quoted.

He chuckled. "Typical. We're hiking through the hills to a secure location. We're still on her property, but removed from the rest of the estate."

"Secure location? I thought the house was secure."

Daniel swept out a hand to encompass their surroundings. "Sure, but this is secure from anyone knowing about it."

"Except us."

He smiled. "Except us."

"I'm surprised she'd let you know the location of this secret location."

He shrugged. "I just work here, remember." He paused before continuing. "I'm sure there was a conversation with Zibanitu. Hamal wouldn't come, so it had to be me."

Dee's heart dropped, and she chastised herself for it. *Wouldn't* come?

-Who cares. You should have killed him.-

If Daniel noticed her deflation, he let it pass without comment.

He continued. "Amalthea wanted this to be an excursion with just her people. They proved they could defend against Han, but Zibanitu wanted someone from his House with you at all times. Amalthea knows better than to defy him, especially when she's waited so long to get in on some action."

"She said something similar to me. She *wants* to be dealing with this drama?"

Daniel smiled. "Strange, huh? But that's the truth. She's been sitting around here for who knows how long. She wants something exciting to happen. She wants to be involved in the politics among the three Houses who have yet to settle an age-old feud."

Dee sighed. More questions. She wondered if she should even try to figure out what he was talking about.

"Daniel, that's enough." Amalthea's voice was laced with warning. The pair didn't turn around to acknowledge her words, though Daniel bowed his head.

There was only silence after that.

25

Darkness bled from the earth as the sun fell below the trees, but the group continued forward. When the rolling, forested hills of Amalthea's estate turned to steeper terrain, Dee wondered just how far into the middle of nowhere they were going. She couldn't even guess how far they'd traveled, glad she'd kept up with the rest, who never called for a break.

An abrupt rise gave way to a level plateau. Dee found herself looking across a grassy knoll onto a three-story house carved directly into the mountainside. With a concave front and tall windows showing the brightly lit interior, the house was a beacon of modernity in the center of uninhabited land. A stone pathway, wide enough for three to walk abreast, meandered to the edge of a platform that dropped down into a sunk-in porch that ran the width of the house. The front door, nestled among the stone front of the structure, stood framed in narrow windows.

Dee stopped to gape at the incredible feat of architecture ahead.

Amalthea, pleased at her reaction, stopped next to her. "What do you think?"

"I've never seen anything like it. What's it doing way out here?"

"We all need our secret places." It was all the explanation Dee received before the Rishi moved on, Metis at her side.

Daniel lingered, eyes roaming the design with his own tight-lipped awe. Only when they were the last two did he gently push Dee forward with a hand at her back.

Expecting a cave-like quality to a house built into a mountain, Dee was pleased by the white oak flooring, bright lighting, and colorful paintings lining the walls. The lack of windows wasn't noticed under the track-lighting and high ceilings.

Disappointed she couldn't linger and gape, Dee hurried after Metis, who led her and Daniel up a broad set of stairs that curved past the second floor to the third. Every step screamed luxury and expense. Dee recalled Hamal's suggestion the Rishi's had enough money to colonize Mars. A house built into a mountain was nothing.

Leading them through a single door at the end of a long hall, Metis explained, "You'll sleep here. You'll stay here when not training, or when not with the Rishi." His voice allowed no argument.

-Just a more sophisticated prison.-

Any excitement she'd had about this new adventure disappeared. Dee looked back down the long hall they'd traveled, judging the isolation with new eyes. The space was a mark of security. Not knowing if it was security for her or from her dampened her mood further.

"Daniel is staying up here too?"

-That's the concern worth voicing?-

Metis pursed his lips. "Zibanitu wanted one of his people with you, so that's how it will be."

Daniel had turned his back on the conversation to study the room. She liked Daniel well enough but wasn't sure she trusted him sleeping in the same room as her.

Her eyes stayed on the Soldier's back, but her question was for Metis, "How long will we be here?"

"As long as it takes."

Dee took a breath to ask, *as long as what takes*, but Metis was already out the door.

Daniel continued to search the large room, pressing his hands into the walls in various places, then jumping lightly as if to test the floor. About to ask what he was doing, Dee was saved the trouble when he turned to explain, "This room is well secured. No windows. It's not even close to the exterior, so no one could consider coming through the walls. Amalthea is taking your security very seriously."

Ignoring the bout of claustrophobia that threatened her, Dee focused on another issue. "You're going to be sleeping in here?"

He met her eye straight on. "I bet Hamal would have come if he'd known this was how the sleeping arrangements would be."

Dee cocked an eyebrow, refusing to rise to the bait. She couldn't keep a blush from forming at her cheeks.

His chuckle turned to laughter. "Hopeless. But don't worry. I won't try to ravish you. Or kill you in your sleep?"

She turned away, walking towards a door she assumed was the bathroom. "I'm going to take a shower."

"Mmmmmmm."

She whirled at the hinting expression. "You stay out here."

He held his hands up in mock surrender. "Of course." He turned away. "Unless I think you're in danger."

She stared at his back, judging how safe it was to get naked behind a door that wouldn't keep him out if he didn't want to be kept out. But, what could she do? She wasn't going to skip bathing the whole time she was here. Or not change her clothes.

What was she even worried about? Daniel had taken a bullet for her. More than one. Because of her, he'd spent a night on Death's door.

-Truth is, you don't know who to trust or if any of them are really on your side. -

T he next day, having not been assaulted by Daniel who slept more like an infant than someone looking out for her, she followed the same group who'd accompanied her on the previous day's hike down a damp stone hallway. Curving steeply below a structure hidden even further in the forested hills than the house, she followed the others underground. The structure, which looked like an old mausoleum, hid the entrance to the stairs hadn't seemed too sketchy. After everything thrown at her, this was just par for the course.

As they continued to descend, the tight space lit by flickering bulbs, Dee's mind whirled with ideas about what she needed to see that couldn't be brought from this uber-secret location.

-*No one's going to find your body down here.*-

She refused to let her thoughts linger on the idea that she was being brought to her death. Instead, she focused on taking step after step, fighting vertigo, as the path drew her down, forever curving so she could never see what lay ahead.

Daniel was ahead of her, Metis behind, with Soldiers book-ending them. For a secured area, they were treating this as a dangerous place.

-*The things you don't know...*-

There was a lot she didn't know.

Dee's nerves were frayed by the time they moved into a large chamber, its vaulted ceiling lost beyond the shadowed light of sconces she wondered who had lit. The space was roughly twenty by thirty meters, bare of anything but dirt and spiders, who retreated from the newcomers with unnatural speed. Dee barely noticed, too busy peering through the dim space towards the iron, double door that lay on the opposite side of the room.

When that very door opened after a series of clangs from sliding bolt locks, she jumped. Metis' hand on her back sent her heart racing faster. When something beyond the door let out a moaning howl that echoed around them, a hand over her mouth was all that kept her yelp contained. Skin crawling from the noise, Dee barely noticed the emaciated figure scuffling towards them until the door was shut, erasing the awful sound. The figure stared straight down, and Dee wondered if he would run into them.

Amalthea stepped ahead to greet the figure, who stopped in front of her. The frail man bowed from the waist, his eyes never coming up from the floor. "Everything is as you asked, Rishi."

"Thank you, Waverly." She turned to catch Dee's eye, motioning her forward. With a gentle hand on her arm, she guided Dee towards the iron door, following closely behind Waverly as he led them back the way he'd come.

Thankfully, the moaning had quieted, so the group was greeted with silence when the door re-opened at Waverly's tug. Before Amalthea could make a move to follow the strange little man through, Metis was there, apologizing as he pushed ahead of her, Atkins close on his heels.

Dee watched Amalthea's face as the Soldiers carefully pushed her aside, waiting for some sign of anger or annoyance. The Rishi showed neither, merely allowing them to pass, an amused expression covering her face.

Noticing Dee's watchful glance, she smiled. "They think I'm an old lady, unable to take care of myself. I indulge them. It is what they have trained for, after all. They forget I could take all of them if I had a mind."

Dee believed her. A different kind of chill washed over her. She knew the Rishi wasn't just some middle-aged lady by the power that hummed in Dee's skull, but after being surrounded by both her and her Soldiers for so long, this warning system had become a dull hum she ignored.

When the all-clear was announced, Dee's stomach fluttered, wishing she'd asked precisely what it meant that Amalthea was going to *show* her. What was down here, hidden away, that the Soldiers wouldn't let them enter without first checking that it was safe? Hadn't the skinny man just come from here? Was he not what he seemed either?

The first thing to hit her was the noise. The howling had commenced as if cued by their entry. Now in the same room as the source of the sound, the volume overwhelmed her nervous system. She hunched in on herself, her steps slowing. Behind this howling, interlaced like some melody coined in Hell, were the growling snaps of some animal.

Looking at her feet, as if changing the direction of her sight might dampen the noise, Dee noted the floor strewn with straw. Curious by this, she allowed her gaze to dart around, glad for something to focus on other than the painful noise inundating the room. Too many smells vied for attention, plugging her sinuses. Antiseptic took first place and she clung to that rather than sift though the rest. She was sure she didn't want to know.

Much smaller than the cavern they'd just come from, the room was separated into six cells cordoned by metal bars. A center aisle from the door cut through the center of the room.

All thoughts blown from her mind by the incessant raging that filled the air, Dee didn't think to look at what might be in these cells until she heard Amalthea speak. "We'll start with the Burn, please, Waverly."

-Burn?-

Dee closed her eyes against the noise to better focus on Amalthea's words. When her eyes opened, she found Amalthea had moved to stand close to the bars of a cell where a human man lay on the stone floor. Thrashing and screaming, his movements cut his skin against the broken floor, so blood was smeared throughout the cell.

Horrified, Dee watched as the cuts healed, only to form anew when the intensity of his convulsions punched new wounds into his skin. Moving closer, her steps brought her next to the Rishi, though her mind screamed for her to flee the gruesome sight. As much as she tried to tear her stare away, her eyes seemed caught, unable.

"What's wrong with him?" Her voice was choked around the sob lodged in her throat.

Amalthea smiled sadly, turning to Waverly. "Do it now, please."

Waverly was ready with a hypodermic needle. His nod brought two Soldiers to the cell to grab the man's legs, pulling him towards the bars so Waverly could insert the needle into his thigh. The man never stopped his thrashing screams or made any sign he was aware of the group around him.

Dee shuddered, a tear falling from her eye. She didn't bother wiping it away.

When the plunger released the liquid into the Burn, he quickly fell silent, movements ceasing apart from an occasional twitch.

"Only a few of us are able to create Soldiers. None of us has ever truly figured out the why or how of it. Of all the Soldiers you will come across, only a handful have been with us since the beginning."

Dee continued to stare at the man in the cell, listening to Amalthea's words, trying to link what she'd seen in front of her with what the Rishi was telling her. "Not all who risk the change from human to Soldier survive. Most don't, and it is not something we ask of anyone lightly."

Dee nodded, remembering Daniel's perspective on this. "This man agreed to become a Soldier."

She stared harder, thinking of all the Soldiers she'd met. All who'd left their human lives to be enhanced through something they called Initiation.

"This is what happens to those who don't become Soldiers?" Dee's voice was steadier now that the room was quiet.

Amalthea turned her full attention to her guest. "Sometimes. What I mean to show you are all possible outcomes of the transition."

Dee turned, finally looking at what she'd ignored.

Across from the cell that held the Burn was something she recognized, and what accounted for the growled snarls she'd heard earlier.

"That's a Revenant." Dee took a step towards it, the flash of another snapping fangs in her face while she struggled against it clear in her mind.

Dee shuddered to think a person, agreeing to become something more, would wake up as one of these. She hoped there was no memory buried inside the snarling beast.

Amalthea nodded. "It is. There are varying levels of intelligence in these, but generally, they're animalistic creatures who hunt any warm-blooded thing."

Dee swallowed hard. Sadness morphed to anger at the thought that someone's life had been taken from them for a promise that might not have been real.

She couldn't keep the anger from her tone. "These things were sent after me. Who would use them for a targeted purpose if all they would do was kill anything in their path?"

"This is a question we are looking into."

Dee stared hard at Amalthea, attempting to judge if it was genuine ignorance of the situation, or if information was being purposefully withheld. Dee wasn't sure which was worse.

-The blind leading the blind here.-

The Revenant launched itself at the bars, hitting with enough force to show how well built each cage was, sending a spray of spit towards the pair. Dee stepped back, but Amalthea held her ground, looking pityingly at the creature.

The Rishi continued to stare at the enraged Revenant as she spoke. "Waverly is another. Sometimes, instead of enhancing the human form, the transition diminishes it. Most of these die soon after they wake, usually from some sickness they contract their bodies can no longer fight off. Waverly is one of the rare ones who has managed to survive this particular adaptation."

Dee watched Waverly as he moved between a string of monitors set up along the back wall. She wondered if he hated these Rishis who'd taken his life, even if he had agreed to it. Did he remember who he'd been, longing for a life he could never return to? Daniel had explained that most Soldiers began as exceptional humans. She wondered who Waverly had been before his change to the frail being he was now forced to suffer.

Amalthea had crossed back to the cell next to the Burn, where a girl seemed to sleep peacefully. "Some go to sleep and never wake, sometimes living in this comatose state for decades before finally fading away. None have ever woken, but we can't bring ourselves to kill them before they die on their own." Her voice dropped to a whisper. "You never know when that first one will rise."

The Rishi stared into the cell for a long time, and Dee wondered if the girl was someone Amalthea had been fond of. The idea made her think of something she hadn't asked. "How do you determine who will go through the process? How long do they get to decide if they should risk their lives to become—"

"More? Better? Raised up? Something greater?"

Dee nodded, not sure that's how she would have phrased her question. The odds that any of those things were met, rather than the horrifying changes she was seeing seemed low.

Rather than say so, she stared silently at the girl who seemed at peace in her dreams.

-*You think she dreams?*-

Dee didn't want to think about it. She asked the first thing that came to mind to distract from the tearing sadness of all she was shown. "How do you feed them? How do they live so long?"

Amalthea, eyes still focused far away, shrugged noncommittally. "It's as if they're in a state of timelessness. We never feed them, yet still, some live many, many years."

The Rishi turned again to move across the center of the room. Dee pushed herself to follow, ignoring the Revenant still attempting to force its way through the bars, its spitting ferocity unnerving. Already, the chaos of the noise was easier to handle.

The next cell contained a very awake, very conscious, very annoyed man sitting very straight on a cot at the far side.

Amalthea held the glare of the prisoner.

-*If looks could kill...*-

After a few tense seconds, the man spoke, his body rigid, words overly enunciated as if bracing himself in strict control. "Rishi, is all of this necessary?"

"You tell me, Pax."

Pax stood as if pulled by a rubber band, eyes drifting to look at Dee before returning to the one who'd imprisoned him here. "At least get me away from this frothing zombie. Please." He fell to his knees with the last word, hands gripping the bars in front of him, head bowing to look at the floor. While his body language suggested penance, his tone was full of hateful disregard.

Amalthea said nothing, inspecting the man as a mother who watches her child try to talk themselves out of a punishment they justly deserved.

The Revenant lunged at the shared bars, startling Dee's eyes from the man kneeling in front of her. Before her eyes had focused, her head was slammed into the iron that separated her and Pax. His act of contrition, with the help of the Revenant's convenient distraction, allowed the prisoner the opportunity to grab her, pulling her towards him with a quick jerk that left her face cracking against cold iron.

Dee barely registered the pain exploding across her face as she grabbed the man's hand in a wrist lock without opening her eyes. Twisting it, he fell back to his knees, screaming when she popped his wrist joint, so his fingers went slack. Her other arm came through the bars to grab him by the neck, fingers splaying around his throat, squeezing as she yanked his face into the bars.

As suddenly as it started, it was over. Two pairs of arms relocated her to a distance away from the cell to ensure it stayed ended.

Looking up to a blurry room through eyes filled with tears, she knew her nose was busted. She tasted blood. Licking her lips, she assessed the damage.

"You did good, kid." Atkins handed her a towel.

"Oh yeah? Maybe shouldn't have gotten close enough to get

my face bashed open." Talking brought more tears to her eyes, so she tightened her lips in a fine line.

Daniel stood next to Atkins, laughing tightly. "That's true, but I bet you'll never let it happen again."

Atkins dropped his chin in what might have been a nod. "No better teacher than experience."

Dee was too busy glaring across the room at Pax, who, she was glad to see, was holding his arm to his body, face bleeding from multiple cuts, throat red and bruising, to notice the genuine compliments handed her.

Daniel had another towel and was carefully brushing blood from her forehead. "Never a dull moment with you, is there?"

She smiled, an expression that morphed into a grimace as the movement of her lips re-split the cuts that were already healing. "It's not my fault. All this keeps happening because of you crazy —whatever you are."

He chuckled, eyes looking over her wounds. When he was sure she didn't need further attention, his gaze locked with hers. "Your face is going to turn a nice color of purple, then green, then yellow, not much different than it was a few days ago actually. It'll be a good story to tell."

"As long as we have that."

"Yes, we will have that." His gaze had taken on a heated edge she knew wasn't allowed, from his own mouth. She went rigid with surprise when his hand came up to her face to run a finger carefully down her nose. "How you do it... I understand Hamal better now."

She held his gaze as he back-stepped before turning smartly to assess what was happening in the room.

Did that just happen?

-Which part? Getting your face bashed in, or getting the moves put on you from the very one who said to keep it impersonal?-

Her face hurt too much for her to think about it. It was ridiculous. Why would Hamal or Daniel make their lives so difficult for her? It wasn't like she was the only girl around. There were plenty of female Soldiers who were way more badass than she was. Not to mention more accessible.

-You're the new girl. The notoriety will pass, and they'll forget you.-

Amalthea was moving towards her. Dee couldn't see into Pax's cell, now surrounded by so many Soldiers.

"My apologies, Desiree." Amalthea's hands rested on Dee's shoulders, eyes assessing her face for injuries of the spirit as well as the already-healing physical ones.

Dee's eyes flickered beyond the Rishi to Pax's cell. "Apparently, it was a learning moment for me."

Amalthea chuckled. "I do believe I just heard Atkins crack a smile. Well done." She winked before turning to the others. "We're done for today."

Four Soldiers stayed behind as she was flanked by Daniel, whose hand at her back pushed her along behind Metis, who followed Amalthea.

Dee turned her head to ask Daniel. "Who was Pax?"

"That's for Amalthea to tell." Daniel's answer was clipped. Not sure if it was his way of distancing himself from her, or if something else had ruffled his feathers, Dee was too ready to be away from the underground dungeon to cess it out.

26

Wrapped in a towel, Dee avoided glancing at Daniel, who perched in the corner, flipping through a book she could tell he wasn't actually reading. She'd evaded the shower for as long as she could, even after the Soldier had taken one of his own before brazenly meandering around the room stark naked, ignoring the look of awkward terror that had preceded Dee fleeing to the hallway.

"I can't guard you if you're hiding out there!" He'd called, but she'd refused to come in until he showed her he was clothed.

She could tell he was still laughing at her, even as he pretended to keep his attention on the book in his hands, one leg bent casually, the poster boy for unobtrusive.

She had planned to dress in the bathroom, but of course, she'd forgotten an essential element of her outfit. After staring at the door, she'd finally acknowledged there was no other way around her predicament except to come into the room with only a towel between her and prying eyes. It wasn't that she was a prude, there were just lines one shouldn't cross.

-Oh, really?-

"Amalthea asks that you join her for supper, with her sincerest apologies."

Dee jumped. Metis, standing just inside the door, had been overlooked in her distraction.

Heart thundering in her throat, she sent Daniel a silent curse that he hadn't warned her they had a visitor. She felt his silent laughter fill the room.

Focusing on Metis' invitation to circumvent her embarrassment, she wondered if her nerves could handle whatever else the Rishi might wish to show her. The bruises she'd sported on her face during the trip back healed, but that didn't mean she was eager to have them replaced so soon.

-It's not like you can turn her invitation down.-

She knew the Rishi genuinely felt guilty about Dee getting assaulted on her field-trip, but she also knew that wasn't the only reason for the invite. There was still much that hadn't been covered.

Dee forced words through a constricted throat. "Of course. When—"

"As soon as you're ready. I'll wait outside for you." Metis's eyes never left her face. Dee was grateful for his stale manner after the bemused attitudes of Hamal and Daniel.

She didn't move or speak until the door closed behind him. "He doesn't like me much."

Daniel tossed his book on a nearby table. "He doesn't like anyone much, though I think it's more that he's mastered the art of indifference. It's not his place to opinionate. He comes across like a dick, but really, he's pure neutrality."

"Hmmm." Dee turned from the door to shuffle through the clothes hanging in an armoire almost twice her height. The outfit she'd picked to lounge around in wasn't going to cut it for a meeting with the Rishi. That there were so many clothes, all in her size, was a point she accepted out of sheer exhaustion. There were too many questions that took priority over this detail.

-What does one wear to dinner with a Rishi in the middle of a forest in the center of nowhere inside a mountain?-

Daniel's arm reached over her shoulder, and she froze, heart thudding at his closeness, brain whirling that he'd moved from across the room without her noticing. She really needed to return to a more conscientious awareness of him. Of *all* of them. Especially with her internal radar she'd been ignoring.

"Wear this." He pulled out a green dress, sheer outer layer trimmed with a twilling of silver that gave the illusion of leaves blowing in a breeze.

Voice like steel, she sneered as she turned to look at what he'd chosen. "You're a fashionista, too?"

"I'm not sure *fashionista* is a word." He ignored her attitude, grinning with the laughter that hadn't faded since she'd fled from his nakedness.

The smile in his eyes helped loosen her own. "A female-fashion-guru, then?"

He let the laugh leak from his face until his expression was a blank mask. "I've picked up a few things here and there. I know what Amalthea likes, and she'll appreciate your homage to the green things she loves so much."

Dee nodded, taking the dress from him. "Thanks."

"My pleasure." He returned to his perch and the book he'd been flipping through.

She was staring at him, unaware she was doing it until his gaze rose to meet hers with a smile. "Regretting not staying around to check out the goods?"

Flame flashed over her face. She whirled, almost losing her towel again in the process.

Daniel's laugh rang out through the closed door.

Picture windows opened to the night allowed the mountain breeze to waft over them while an undisturbed sky full of stars flickered in the background.

Unfortunately, Dee was too distracted to appreciate the setting. It took all her energy to keep her voice calm. "I appreciate you showing me all of this, but I'm not sure I understand the context. What the Soldiers are, how they're made, that isn't what a Rishi is, is it?"

Amalthea smiled. If she sensed Desiree's mounting frustration, she didn't let on. "No, we are something else entirely. That, we will get to, I promise you. Just, not quite yet. I wanted you to know about the Soldiers because we feel you are some branch of them."

Dee stared off, the meal in front of her long cold. Her appetite had gone as soon as the conversation brought up memories she should have. The blank void in her past was where her answers lay. Her last lucid thought was of her and Steve standing in the kitchen of the tiny apartment they shared with Kim and Ray. Had they been cooking? It didn't matter. Steve had been about to tell her something, then Ray had banged through the door, filling the space with his overwhelming energy.

Then, nothing. Just heat and flames and confusion spilling together in a nonsensical jumble.

She shook her head to break free from the thoughts, bringing her attention back to Amalthea. "There's this huge chunk of time I don't remember. I was in my apartment with my roommates. Then I was outside some house in the middle of nowhere as it was burning to the ground."

Amalthea leaned forward. "Who took you to the house?"

Dee clenched her eyes shut as if the act might trigger an answer. "I don't remember. I'd never seen the house before. I don't even know if I would recognize it if someone showed me a picture. I only saw it engulfed in flames."

"No one was with you?"

She opened her eyes. "Just me."

"How long were you there?" These questions had already been asked, but the Rishi seemed to think some kernel of information might still filter through.

Dee's shrug told that this wasn't that time.

It was Amalthea's turn to look off. "It would be strange that you were given the Initiation in some unknown location. The

Rishis who transfer humans to Soldiers have specific space for this, and I know none was ever some house in the middle of nowhere. That one would try this in such a removed location, if that's what this was," her eyes came back to rest on Dee's face to emphasize this point, "suggests a Rishi we've never known to succeed in an Initiation has finally mastered the skill. That, or something entirely new has been discovered. If there was an accident, it might make sense that you got away. Maybe they thought you'd died in the fire. Maybe it took them this long to find you."

-Way too many maybes *for a conversation supposed to be making things clearer.-*

Dee sat forward, playing with the food in front of her as she mulled this over.

Amalthea had another question. "Where were you staying before you woke up at that house?"

"Where?" Dee glanced up from her plate.

"What part of the country? I assume you were still in the United States."

Dee nodded absently. "Northern California."

The Rishi received the bit of information as if it meant something to her, but changed the subject. "I showed you a Burn, a Coma, a Revenant, which I know you were already quite familiar with, and a Flawed. That was Pax."

"A Flawed?" Dee sat up in her seat, eager for some concrete information to sift into her meager file of data.

"Yes. One who survived the transition but with no augmentation occurring. They're extremely rare and are always given a position within the House. Pax grew bored with his assignments, so came to me with information on his former Master. He'd release the information to me if I gave him a more stimulating position."

"You imprisoned him because he's a traitor?"

"The timing was perfect to show him off to you." The Rishi smiled like the fortuitousness of the universe working in her favor was something she'd planned.

Dee rubbed her face. "He seemed stronger than a normal guy would be."

Amalthea shrugged. "Possibly, but not enough to pass the Soldier's test. Nor was his mind gifted to be used in any other capacity."

"His mind?"

"Another variance of the Initiated. Even Soldiers' minds are enhanced with their bodies. Sometimes the mind's enhancement overshadows the physical. These typically become Messengers, though their use has significantly decreased, as most Rishi's won't allow another House's messenger into their domain. No true Messenger has been seen in centuries, and only two remain."

Her eyes grew sad, turned inward, before noticing Dee's question-filled gaze.

"These Messengers' minds have been enhanced, so they possess some level of psychic ability which we train them to use in manipulation."

"Okaaay?"

Amalthea smiled kindly. "For example, a Messenger might have been sent to you so that you would agree to go with them to meet their Master. Barnard is one of the best Messengers ever to have been let out into the world. His talents, combined with a Soldier's training, have made his use most effective in the past."

Dee thought back to the day on the road when Barnard had held his hand out to her. There had been an active compulsion to go with him. Was that this Messenger trick, or just her wanting to explore all her options?

Amalthea smiled as if sensing what she was thinking of. "Yes, I imagine he used his skill on you then. You are either stronger than most, or he was gentle, unsure how your brain might react."

Dee looked up. "What could have happened?"

"Lesser humans have become enthralled, another reason the use of Messengers has fallen out of practice. Some have been known to start cults of fanatic followers."

Dee shuddered at the idea, wondering how horrific the time

when Messengers were slaughtered. Based on Amalthea's reaction to their explanation, that only two remained, she was sure some terrible story surrounded this explanation.

"Okay, so," Dee counted on her fingers. "Waverly."

"Pallid."

-Really, with these titles?-

"Right. Pallids, Comas, Burns, the Flawed, Messengers, Soldiers, Revenants. Seven possible outcomes when someone decides to be Initiated."

"Death is another possible outcome."

"Of course." Dee let out a flustered breath. "Eight outcomes then. And the running theory is that I'm a Soldier."

Amalthea nodded hesitantly.

"You don't think so?"

The Rishi smiled, the motherly warmth that flooded her demeanor wrapping Dee in comfort. "I am loath to say what I think at this point."

Dee sighed. "Will you tell me about the Rishis?"

"No, but others will. We will visit them soon. It is their skill to tell stories, where it is my way to show. The past is difficult to present in tangible terms, so I leave it to others who are better suited for such things."

"Another field trip?"

"Yes. One I promise to be much less violent."

Dee laughed, touching her healed face, even while her insides screamed in frustration.

27

Dee was distracted, mulling over the lack of information she'd gotten from Amalthea. Distracted enough, she almost missed Daniel's question. "Learn anything useful?"

Her distracted answer of *maybe* drew a laugh from him. "You're fitting right in."

"Hmm? Oh? Oh, right." She grinned. "Yeah, sorry, but really. There's not a lot of actual answers going around."

He nodded, pacing quietly at her side while her thoughts returned to their spinning.

-Amalthea doesn't think you're a Soldier, implying you're more. If you were less, she wouldn't be so interested.-

It wasn't a fact, but it was a possibility. If she were more than a Soldier, there were still things inside her she hadn't tapped into. The notion made her buzz with excitement.

"Daniel? You think we can go for a hike?"

"A hike? It's dark."

"Don't tell me you're afraid of the dark."

He grinned. "You know better than that, but I don't think it would go over well if we went traipsing through the woods when you're supposed to be under heavy guard."

"Is there really anything to worry about out here?"

"I couldn't say. And even if I could say, I wouldn't."

She pouted for a few steps before another idea came to her. "You think anyone would be up for some training?"

He smiled broadly. "Of course they would. We were, literally, created for fighting. There's not one of us who doesn't hate to stand around waiting for something to happen."

———

A half-hour later, every Soldier on this field-trip, other than those on some security detail, were gathered in front of the house where just enough space allotted a training area before the plateau plummeted steeply down the mountain. Dee was surprised how many more were there than had hiked up with her.

"Restless already, Noob?"

Dee laughed. Apparently, Daniel had told someone about her *noob* comment, and she'd found herself with a new nickname. It sounded like Vali, but she couldn't be sure. It didn't seem like him to make a joke.

"Something like that."

-Let's kick their asses.-

She felt the excitement of her inner-voice, finally loosed from its shackles by her expanding perspective of what she might be. Willing to believe she was something more, it was exhilarated at the opportunity to let itself out of its cage.

Stepping to the center of the half-circle of Soldiers, wielding a practice sword, Dee waited to see who would be the first to join her. Surprisingly, it was Atkins, whom she'd barely seen since he'd held her hostage her first day at Amaltheum.

She'd heard the rumors, seen the way the others looked up to him. Nodding to the voice in her head, she analyzed the way Atkins felt, attempting to differentiate what made him more than the others through the way he hummed in her skull. The warrior nodded back, thinking the gesture had been for him, which was fine. It was an appropriate greeting for the sparring ring.

Atkins moved forward quickly, but not so fast as to overwhelm her. She knew he was going easy on her, testing her. His attack was styled differently than anything she'd seen from the others. Rather than engage, she flowed smoothly away, allowing time to read his movements before coming up with a plan of attack.

Atkins smiled at her evasiveness. "Well played, Ms. Galen. Learn first. Engage when ready."

They were still moving around each other, Atkins continuing his probing attacks while Dee eluded them. "What if I'm never ready?"

"Then, your opponent will slaughter you." His voice was conversational, instructing.

"Should I run?"

His eyes flicked to her face before returning to her movements. "Sometimes that is the right decision. Sometimes, it is just another way to die."

She knew he still hadn't begun to show her the magnitude of what he was capable of. Remembering Daniel's words about not being afraid to be embarrassed because one couldn't learn without putting yourself on the line, she engaged, moving as fast as she ever had.

FEEL.

It was like her consciousness coursed from her brain to extend through every cell of her body. She anticipated his movements, forced him to move further into the best of himself as she drifted around his attacks, blocking when necessary.

Press.

Another calibration of senses and she was pressing forward, forcing the greatest of opponents to defend himself against her blur of offense.

Flow.

No longer were the words in her head but rather a song that hummed through every synapse, sparking inside her blood. She sensed and obeyed, saw and reacted until she was proceeding with a surge that made it impossible for her to be hit.

Atkins' amazement was palpable, so heavy that it rang against her thoughts, wrestling her from her heightened state until she was forced back into defense. The loud crack of their practice swords rang out to echo back at them from the hills.

Dee laughed at the sound, enjoying it so much she purpose-fully matched him strike for strike, so their fight became a song of percussions. Then, as if given some cue only the two could hear, they came to a stop, panting breathlessly.

Blinking from the trance of the fight, Dee looked around at the semi-circle of staring faces whose expressions told all she needed to know.

Daniel's voice broke the silence. "Curiouser and curiouser."

She remembered him saying the same thing when they'd first met. Finding his face amount the others, she held his gaze and smiled.

Ainn approaching the pair drew Dee's attention. "A sudden growth in your skill seems..."

The Soldier didn't finish her sentence, so Dee did for her. "... like I've been hiding it all along?"

The Soldier said nothing, but the distrust was apparent on her face.

Dee sighed. "I might think the same if our positions were reversed, but, please, believe me, that's not the case. *You* did this. You and Ellie and Daniel. You said my lack-of-belief in what I can do might be holding me back. Something Amalthea said earlier made me wonder if there wasn't more I could find."

Ainn stared at her with blank eyes, studying her student's face for any sign of deceit. Dee met her gaze, reading the mistrust that lay within. "Is there any way for me to prove this to you?"

"No." There was no hesitation in the response.

Two steps forward, three steps back.

She'd found her confidence among her betters. She'd found they weren't better and along with that, found a piece of herself

C.M. MARTENS

she hand't known to look for. But in that, she'd isolated herself even more. Looking around at the group who'd maintained their positions in the semi-circle, postures denoting their readiness for a fight despite their blank faces, Dee suppressed a sigh.

"I think we're done for the night," Ainn decreed. No one contradicted her, though Dee felt the disappointment in many of the Soldiers who hadn't gotten the opportunity to cross weapons with her.

As the others dispersed, Daniel moved towards Dee, eyes on Atkins. "A fine display, Atkins."

In spite of the somber tone, Atkins' attitude wasn't affected. In fact, he seemed as jovial as Dee had ever seen him. "My thanks, Daniel. It has been a long time since I've played." He smiled a full mien that lit up his face. "It was fun."

Dee smiled too, something inside her loosening that Ainn's examination of the event wasn't reciprocated by him. "Yes, it really was."

"I think you call it a rematch? I'll ask for one soon."

Her smile broadened. "Sounds good to me."

She and Daniel watched the Soldier walk away until they were the last two outside. When all was quiet, Daniel turned to her. "You understand what you just did, right? Why everyone is so freaked out?"

She shrugged. "Atkins is really good."

Daniel laughed. "That's putting it mildly. He's one of the best of us. In any House. He might even be able to beat Castor."

"Who's Castor?"

He laughed. "Oh, there's still so much for you to learn."

"Yeah, no kidding. Maybe you could tell me some things."

His laughter stopped. He turned to study her the pout on her face, his voice a whisper. "Don't do that."

"Don't do what?" She wasn't looking at him.

"Don't get mad. Especially don't get mad at me. We're all bound in some way. Some more than others."

"Sure, sure." She started walking towards the house, ready for another shower. Maybe even a hot bath in the deep tub she'd been eyeing since arriving.

Daniel grabbed her hand, pulling her back to him, so she tripped, hand landing flat on his chest reactively to stop her forward momentum. She looked up into angry eyes. Eyes that made her sad, rather than frighten her. "I'm not mad at you. Relax."

She shifted to pull away, but he caught her hand to his chest, holding her there.

His voice was low, eyes peering through her. "Don't be angry at all. Not at this. Be angry that they'll take you, cut you off from your life, even as they suggest you asked for it. Even as they suggest you couldn't survive without them."

His words froze her, her attention moving from the heat of his hand over hers to the pressure behind his gaze. Running his words over in her head, she remained motionless against him, staring up into the lightest green eyes she'd ever seen. "Your eyes. I never noticed their color before."

He let her go so abruptly she stumbled. He was already half-way to the house when she turned. "I'll have food brought up for you." His words were clipped.

-*What?*-

"Umm, okay. Sure."

She stared at his retreating form, continuing to wait for some explanation even after he stopped just outside the door. Holding it open, avoiding her look, he lingered like a good bodyguard.

With a loud sigh, she moved to the house.

28

His raging garnered so much attention that he found himself face-to-face with Zibanitu himself. The Rishi's stare studied the human's face as they stood eye-to-eye in front of the lenses that projected them to each other.

Hearing Amalthea had taken Dee to see the Twins was enraging enough. Hearing Zi's people had been barred from going sent Hamal over the edge. It was bad enough he'd been unable to watch over or guide her once they'd reached Amaltheum. He'd pulled away when told to be careful where his human senselessness was leading him. That was what Amalthea's speech had told him the night he'd gone with Desiree to her room.

He could have lived with distance, if at least able to keep an eye on her. Having her taken entirely from his sights was maddening.

For three minutes, Zibanitu studied Hamal, whose skill at remaining passive under such scrutiny was pushed to its limit.

Hamal counted the seconds in his head to keep from saying something out of line, which, on this matter, would have been anything he had to say. His mission was complete. The only reason he was still here was a matter of security. No one was being moved from this location at this time. That he was facing the Rishi was both a relief and an embarrassment.

Hamal's eyes snapped to the Rishi's face when Zibanitu finally broke the silence. "I understand you have concerns about the girl."

So, she was still just *the girl*. Hamal didn't like what that might mean. If she was still nameless, she still wasn't significant enough to fight for if something went wrong.

"It's not my place to have concerns."

Zi actually laughed, teeth showing white against deep bronze skin patched with pale creams. His skin exactly resembled vitiligo, its appearance so similar as not to need its own description. As far as Hamal knew, he was the only Rishi to exhibit a skin coloring other than the unmarred bronze of the others.

Hamal's eyes widened in surprise at the reaction, gaze forced downward so his expression might not show, lips pressed together in concern. He couldn't recall a time when he'd ever seen the Rishi appear to indulge in delight. He was at a loss.

"You speak truth, Hamal, yet it has come to my attention that you'd risk us all for erroneous attachments."

A slow inhale kept his displeasure of the Rishi's words off his face. Biting his tongue kept his words to himself.

Zibanitu wasn't content with silence this time. "Are these concerns correct? Or has my time been wasted with inaccurate gossip?"

Hamal didn't have to look up to know the smile that had been on the Rishi's face was gone, replaced by annoyance that bordered on anger. Hamal had managed never to have this anger pointed at him, and he wasn't about to let this be the first time. "You sent me to watch her, then to protect her. I—"

"Protecting her was your own decision. An unsolicited conclusion drawn outside the scope of your mission parameters."

Hamal took a breath. Believing his words, his voice remained even. "Your parameters were crap, and you know it. You sent me to handle it exactly the way I did. You sent me because I was the only one who could have handled it this way. She'd be in The Ophiuchus' hands right now if not for my interference."

Zibanitu studied Hamal again, maddening the human with his inscrutability. Hamal had seen Zi hand out a death sentence in the same breath as praise and wondered if that might not be his fate now. He wasn't helping his position by mouthing off to the one referred to as the Air God. He hoped his unique relationship with the Rishi, one that resembled uncle and favored nephew, would help his case here. But even Michael Corleone had his own brother killed.

"Your interference did save the girl from his hands. We would never have regained the opportunity to figure out what she is if that had come to pass. Your decision-making skills under pressure have always been excellent."

Hamal held his breath, waiting for the shoe to drop, eyes peering at the screen that showed Zibanitu's face. "It's your decision to call on another House that has me second-guessing your motives."

Hamal laughed, a burst of sound too loud. He cut off the noise before it could grow to fullness. "You aren't second-guessing my decision. If that were true, we'd have spoken long before now. It was the right call, and you know it. You even sent Dimitri and Daniel to help us. It's my decision-making abilities at this exact moment you're questioning because you've heard rumors about me having feelings for this girl. This girl who's so important that no one will call her by name, or risk their asses to help."

He clenched his hands, fingernails pressing into his palms. That hadn't come out like he'd wanted. There were too many words that illuminated the lie he'd been telling himself. He didn't have to meet the Rishi's eye to know he'd over-explained the truth of the problem and, in doing so, given away another fact of the matter.

Surprising Hamal again, the Rishi chuckled softly. The sound was almost kind, pulling Hamal's eyes to the face broadcasted through the large screen. "Sometimes, there are things we can't plan for. Sometimes, things happen outside the design that makes the pattern, itself, better."

Zibanitu lowered his chin in a more relaxed posture as Hamal thought on his words, not sure he should believe their implication.

The Rishi spoke before Hamal could decipher what the implication was. "Hamal, it's important to me that you know I understand. I also need you to understand that it matters not. However this had gone, there would have been nothing you could have done to help her. No manner of interference from me would have kept her away from the others. Calm your anger. Sit tight. She'll be back to you in a matter of days. I won't interfere with you resuming your shadowing of her, but, for your own sake, until we know what she is, keep some distance."

Hamal's fists clenched tighter. His elation that he be allowed to stay at her side squashed. Still, this stipulation wasn't as bad as the realization that he was in over his head even farther than he'd considered. What could he do to help her against superior beings? He reminded himself that Zibanitu's rules were to protect him, not cause him pain.

Despite this, the words still came out of his mouth. "I don't think I can do that."

Zibanitu's eyebrows shot up, shocked to be so blatantly contradicted. "What do you think you will do?"

His tone was part mocking, part warning. Hamal ignored both. "I'll continue the mission you put me on."

"Gather information? I have better spies than you on the job now."

Hamal knew the only reason the Rishi allowed the conversation to continue was a morbid curiosity about what the human would say to justify his self-destructive attitude.

"I can watch out for her. Keep her safe. Teach her."

They both knew he couldn't keep her safe, and others could teach her much more efficiently. Still, the point was used for argument's sake.

"Teaching?"

Surprised he was allowed to continue, excitement bolstered his words, so he forgot the inherent lie in them. "You expect her to navigate your world, but she has no idea what's going on. She needs someone to explain it to her."

"She is being told what she needs to know. It is not your place to tell of things you do not understand."

Hamal held Zibanitu's gaze, knowing he was pushing his luck well beyond a place he'd ever been but unable to hold back now. His stare dared the Rishi to stop him.

This challenge sat the Rishi up straighter. "Hamal? What are you asking of me?"

"I don't know exactly. I didn't know I'd be making this argument. I didn't know I wouldn't want to give her up. My plan was to ask to come home." He clamped his mouth shut against the words that tumbled from his mouth. Vulnerability was not something he shared with Zibanitu. Not anymore. Not since he'd been a child.

"Maybe coming home is exactly what you need." The Rishi's voice was quiet, soothing.

Hamal said nothing, hearing the truth in those simple words, but not wanting to admit it to himself or otherwise.

Silence stretched between them.

"There is another way."

Hamal barely caught the words, so softly were they spoken. His eyes shot up, surprise covering his face. It had been in his mind to ask, but he didn't know how. That the Rishi would bring it up without Hamal's direct prompting said much.

Still, Hamal needed to know what had initiated the sudden change in the direction of the conversation. "Why now?"

Zibanitu looked away, staring at something off-screen. Hamal thought he caught a glimpse of real emotion shadowed in the look, but it was gone before Hamal could be sure. "I would not risk you, but neither can I stop you from following your path."

Hamal was quiet, swirling the words around in his head. Zibanitu could very well stop him. It was the Rishi's way, to control what he could. That he'd used this phrasing meant Hamal was being offered a gift only a rare few ever received. He was being offered the ability to choose.

Zi let him have his moment of thought before continuing. "Be sure. Surer then you've ever been. There are many ways her path may lead. Even I am not sure of their direction. You might not get what you desire if you choose the dangerous path. In patience, you may. Coming home does not mean erasing yourself from her life, or that you can't revisit this decision at a later time. You will always be the first who made contact with her. You will always be a part of her story."

"If I survive."

The barest flinch of a nod validated Hamal's point. "Even if you do not, those things will still be. If you survive, if you successfully achieve what you are suggesting, you may still be too far from her. If you manage to be by her side, you may be farther away than you are now."

It was a fair point. A point he hadn't considered. Could he watch her, be by her side, forever on the sidelines as her shadow? Always watching but never able to touch?

"I could wait."

"You could wait."

Hamal smiled at Zibanitu repeating his words, as Dee was prone to do. She did it to assist her in learning. Zi did it to emphasize that which he wanted someone else to learn.

"I could wait." Repeating it, the words didn't sit right. He was already going crazy, not knowing what was going on with her. Could he wait longer? Could he remove himself entirely before coming back with a clearer head?

If he decided on taking the Initiation, he might be out of commission for weeks. He might be out of commission forever.

But, if he stayed as he was, he was guaranteed to be out of commission as far as her life was concerned.

"Why did you agree to let her meet the Twins?" The words slipped out while his brain was distracted by other things.

Surprising him, Zibanitu answered. "The Ophiuchus was close to breaching Amaltheum's security. We needed the girl out of there. Amalthea wants the Twins to tell our story. It was the perfect cover and the perfect place to go while a military of this might closed in."

Hamal looked up, worry-turned-anger burning in his eyes. "The Twins don't have a military. It's just the two of them! They won't be able to stop him if he attacks there."

"There are a few more than just the two of them. Besides, don't underestimate them. Not that it will matter. By the time the Ophiuchus knows where we've sent her, she'll be on her way back to a reinforced compound."

"You need to—"

Zi cut him off, the fatherly figure morphing to the Rishi Hamal knew to be wary of. "Careful, human. You are dear to me, but not so much that you may throw your judgment around so flippantly. You've been given enough liberties with this as it is. Porrima would seek your skin if she heard even a portion of this conversation."

Hamal stood motionless, afraid to even blink. He'd forgotten himself and hoped he wouldn't pay dearly for it.

PART 3

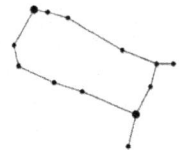

29

The city sprawled as far as the eye could see. She'd never seen anything like it. An enormous contrast to the small town she'd spent most of her life, Dee found São Paulo unreal.

Her face pressed to the window of the private plane, eyes straining to see past the aircraft's wing as she swung her gaze from side to side. She stared across an endless sea of buildings, patches of trees as lakes of life in the topography of cement and steel. Single story buildings, a sandbar along the taller skyscrapers, were a dense layer of residency she couldn't imagine living in, their squalor a harsh juxtaposition from the towers of mirrored glass rising around them. Her house in the woods, so much open air surrounding it, would be alien in this place.

Excited by the news of traveling, Dee'd held the emotion back, afraid she'd be sequestered away in some deep, hidden fortress, surrounded by security. Still, she allowed herself indulgent ideas of sightseeing as the plane coasted over the new city on its landing path.

As they touched down, it occurred to her that not only was the urban landscape far removed from her father's house where she'd grown up, it was also the opposite of what Amalthea called home.

This brought up more questions about the Rishis. Obviously, they weren't all the same.

The idea made her more nervous.

The chatter of Alnath, the female Soldier assigned as her personal guard for this trip, citing facts about the city they soared above, became a hum in the background of her thoughts. She'd let Amalthea's motherly nature calm her to a sense of safety that might not exist. Hadn't her promise of protection proven untrue when she'd visited the cold underground where Dee had been shown the risks of Initiation? What new danger might she run into here? And why had it taken until their arrival for her to consider it?

-Maybe your lack of control over anything going on? You stopped paying attention.-

Dee closed her eyes against the memories of The Ophiuchus' roadside attack that had left one of those sent to protect her dead, and two others near death. Was a similar ambush waiting here?

Or, what if the Twins she was about to meet decided they didn't like her? What if she didn't like them? What if they thought she should die? Would Amalthea's people be able to stop them?

She closed her eyes, swallowing around the tightening of her throat. Breathing slowly, she turned from the window to face Alnath, whose replacement of Daniel was taking some adjustment. Zibanitu's people had been forbidden into the Twins' territory. As Amalthea had seemed unconcerned by this, neither had Dee, until now, when questions she should have thought of earlier cluttered her mind.

"...it the New York of Latin American."

Dee nodded politely to the well-muscled woman whose long hair was pulled back in a tight ponytail. Alnath noticed the distracted look and stopped talking, deducing, "You're nervous."

"That obvious?"

Alnath nodded. "Only because of the change in you from three minutes ago. You were excited. Now, you're not."

Dee's eyes skimmed over the plane's occupants. "What if they try something? Do we have enough people to keep me safe?"

"Keep you safe from the Twins?" The Soldier chuckled. "All of Amalthea's people combined couldn't keep you safe from the Twins. Even The Ophiuchus won't try something against those two."

Dee's nervousness turned to panic.

The guard lowered her voice. "I think that's part of the reason the Rishi was eager to get you here. Apparently, she trusts the Twins enough to risk their fickle nature, knowing it wouldn't be much longer before The Ophiuchus was pushing against her walls."

-Nice to find one of them so eager to explain what's going on.-

Dee barely registered the plane landing as her thoughts turned to the specifics of her security none bothered to explain until now. While she'd remained inside, convincing herself things were going to be alright, danger had pressed closer.

-I think we've left the eye of the storm.-

Dee gulped. If that were true, they were walking into catastrophe.

Coming out of the plane to two sleek limos waiting on the tarmac, Dee was held back by Alnath. They watched as their luggage, and most of their entourage, piled into the two cars. When the pair of limos pulled away, Alnath led Dee, with Amalthea, Metis, and Atkins, to a third limo that had pulled up in the others' wake.

Alnath held the door open for Dee. "This will take us to our transportation."

-This isn't transportation?-

Dee climbed into the luxurious car ahead of the rest, noting Amalthea's uncharacteristic quiet. She'd left Dee to her thoughts for most of the flight. Was it that she understood the girl needed space rather than oppressive overlooking, or was something bothering her?

It was just another thing to make Dee nervous.

When the car came to a stop, still on airport property, near a helicopter, Dee understood what transportation Alnath had spoken of about. The whistling blades of the aircraft erased Dee's long-assumed notion that all helicopters were loud, annoying beasts. A red carpet set a clear path to the open door of the metallic bird from the limo.

Dee had never been in a helicopter, and her body thrummed with nervous excitement. The sleek, long-nosed design was far removed from the egg-shaped metal bin she would have pictured, its size clearly able to hold their entourage with room to spare. This wasn't a craft to pack passengers in like sardines.

Climbing inside, her chin hit the floor.

-Who knew there was a market for luxury helicopters?-

White leather covered two large swivel chairs, and an L-shaped couch stationed behind the pilot's seat, so its short end was to her left spilled around to the far side. Following Amalthea's direction, she took the bucket seat to her right, across from the Rishi. The Soldiers perched themselves on the couch.

Dee looked around, stunned at the space available inside the machine. This rivaled the comfort of the private plane she'd spent the previous ten hours in.

"This is yours?" Dee couldn't help but ask.

Amalthea smiled, enjoying the girl's wonderment. "No. The Twins sent it for us. Traffic through the city is impossible. Helicopters have taken over as the chosen means of travel. For those who can afford it anyway."

Alnath added her two-cents. "And for those who can afford it, these birds are so quiet, there's no longer need for us to wear head-sets to talk to each other. Technology is wonderful."

Dee stared at the ground as the helicopter took off. How the pilot knew where to go was a mystery. From above the city, everything looked the same to her. Noting the streets jammed with unmoving cars, she was glad for the use of the helicopter. Hours in a car to go a few miles didn't seem enjoyable, especially after having sat on a plane for most of the day. She wondered how the others, forced to travel in the limos on the ground, were faring.

Amalthea's voice pulled her attention from the passing view. "We'll be landing soon. There will be plenty of time to freshen up before making our dinner reservation. I thought a relaxing evening for us might be nice before you meet the Twins tomorrow."

Dee relaxed, ecstatic not to be headed directly to meet a pair of powerful beings who may, or may not, have tried to kill her.

D ee enjoyed a quiet shower in a lavish suite she assumed was the penthouse of an opulent hotel.

Coming in from the rooftop, she had yet to descend below the top floors. She understood how easy it might be for one living so far from the rest of a population to grow disconnected from the rest of the world. Looking out from her lofty height, she almost forgot her own troubles.

Pressing her forehead to the glass that ran from floor to ceiling, she shouted in her mind, -*I'm the king of the world!*-

Abandoning the lofty view, she made her way into the living area of the suite. Nodding a greeting to Alnath, who remained positioned by the main doors, Dee made a slow spin, taking in the room she hadn't bothered to examine upon entering. Everything was trimmed in gold. Walls, floors, and ceilings, highlighted with cherry wood furnishings told of a price tag even Dee's fortune would have balked at paying. Surrounded by white carpet, Dee was afraid to walk through the room for fear of leaving a trace of dirt.

A quiet knock on the door revealed the presence of Paige, who Dee hadn't seen since she'd left for the mausoleum of frightening Initiates. Dee smiled a warm greeting, surprised how much she was glad the girl was here, even as she wondered about how the child's life worked.

-Don't overcomplicate your life. Worry about child labor issues after you've secured your own position.-

Paige all but ignored Alnath, who'd opened the door to let her in after a complicated exchange of passwords.

-Are they always so paranoid, or is there something we don't know?-

There were so many things she didn't know, Dee didn't let this one add to her stress, instead focusing on the girl who'd entered the room. "Paige, it is great to see you."

The girl blushed. "Rishi said you would need help preparing for supper." The child looked Dee up and down, frowning at the towel wrapped around her head, the too-big robe barely held on by a hastily tied loop.

-Supper? No room service then?-

Dee sighed, disappointed she'd have to wait even longer to eat. She was sure by the time food was placed in front of her, her stomach might have eaten itself, and it would all be for nothing.

Following the girl to the bedroom, Dee allowed herself to be primped for an evening she hadn't anticipated. Paige surprised Dee with her expert hands, watching as the girl's tiny fingers folded and pinned her shaggy mess of hair to elegance. Perfectly applied makeup turned her features up, so she barely recognized herself.

"Paige, why all of this? What's happening tonight?"

"Just supper downstairs."

Dee raised a manicured eyebrow. "All this just for dinner?"

Paige shrugged, showing no sign of a hidden agenda. At least not one she was privy to. Dee sighed. There was still so much to understand. Learning about the Soldier's Initiation was interesting, but it didn't really help her figure out what was going on, or what her link to all this was.

She closed her eyes as Paige finished her makeup, forcing her memory to those painful moments of blazing fire. The information they were looking for was there, she was sure of it, but how might she remember?

"Time to get dressed." Paige's quiet voice pulled Dee back to the room, her growling stomach reminding her how long it had been since she'd eaten.

Dee stood mechanically, opening her eyes as she turned away from the mirror to watch Paige unzip a garment bag lying across the bed. A brilliant blue dress, a perfect match to the color of her eyes, was hidden within.

Sliding the dress over her head, a strapless silver bust line fell away in layers of blue material to her feet. She twirled in front of the mirror, unable to help herself, noting how the dress highlighted her toned shoulders and arms. The intimidation she'd felt amidst all this glamour fell away, as it turned to intoxication. She could get used to this. For once, she didn't feel like a stranger in a strange land. She didn't feel an imposter. She felt she could find a way to fit in.

Paige held out a pair of silver heels and doubt crashed back around her.

"I don't think I'll be able to walk in those."

Paige's look told Dee the shoes were non-negotiable.

The shoes strapped around her ankles in crisscrossing hatches, the six inches of spike at her heel scaring her more than meeting any Revenant in the woods ever had. Taking Paige's hand skeptically, Dee was shocked to find she had no issue walking. Her intense training with the Soldiers must have some alternative benefits.

Dee stared at herself in the mirror. "Wow, Paige. You're an artist."

Paige's face lit with appreciation, and Dee continued to stare, unable to stop herself from twisting her hips back and forth to watch the layers of fabric on her skirt sway around her.

When a knock came at the door, she froze, all her confidence forgotten. She had no business meeting a timeless being. No business being paraded around.

She took a breath.

Whether she was ready or not, this was happening. She reminded herself she wouldn't meet the Twins until tomorrow. This was only a meal with Amalthea who'd shown her nothing but kindness.

Taking a last look at herself, she squared her shoulders and stepped towards the door.

30

Vali joined Alnath as her escorts, both dressed to impress in stunning evening wear. Dee wondered at the practicality of their outfits, even as she hoped she wouldn't need the extra protection.

Alnath noticed Dee frowning at her shoes and laughed. "Don't worry. They're really not a hindrance. When I was human, you wouldn't catch me dead in heels. Now, I don't even notice the difference between them and regular shoes."

Dee might have doubted her, except for her own comfort in heels three-times the height of her guard's.

Moving through the hotel, Dee wondered who the staff thought she was. Judging by their prostrating, they seemed to think her some kind of royalty. Or maybe that's just how those who could afford such posh living were treated. No wonder there was such a disconnect among tax-brackets.

Surprised to be led all the way to the street, then out to a waiting car, she didn't think to check out details of her surroundings until the car was speeding through the streets. The city lights were dazzling, though not so different as any other metropolis from this vantage. She sat between her guards, the traffic much easier to navigate at night than during the day, so they moved smoothly to their destination.

Entering the restaurant, Dee saw that an entire section was cleared around the table Amalthea sat at, her guards positioned subtly throughout to blend in with the wait staff and other diners. Metis and Atkins sat at the nearest table behind Amalthea, who stood to hug Dee warmly as she approached. "You look beautiful."

"Thank you. The dress is beautiful, and Paige's skills are magnificent."

The words were like a spell casting a bubble of surrealism over her. Here she was in São Paulo, scheduled to meet another pair of Rishis, to be further incapsulated in this strange underground subculture, and they were making smalltalk about clothes.

Amalthea smiled as if the compliment was hers to accept, allowing Metis to hold her chair while she sat. Vali did the same for Dee before moving to his place nearby with Alnath. As Vali walked away, Dee allowed herself to look at him. So concerned until now with everything else distracting her attention, she'd barely noticed this second addition to her personal guard.

She remembered him, vaguely, from her rescue at Roadside, and had seen him among the faces who'd watched her on the training grounds, though she had never sparred with him. His blue eyes, lighter than her own, pierced the room with no hint of the mirth or mischievousness Hamal and Daniel shared. A small scar marred his top lip, setting his mouth in a constant sneer. Dee got the impression this sneer would have been a part of his expression with or without that scar. While Hamal's arrogance carried welcome, Vali's revealed unmasked contempt. Or maybe he just wasn't a fan of guard duty.

A waiter appeared to pour Dee a glass of wine. She tasted the liquid around the tightening of her stomach. Even around her nervousness, she appreciated the wine's flavor. Things really were better in luxury. She'd have to learn how to spend her money.

Amalthea appeared to enjoy watching Dee take delight in this

C.M. MARTENS

new experience. If she sensed the girl's unease, she didn't mention it. "Coming to the city is not usually an idea I back, but, since it seemed the right call, I thought we'd at least take our time to enjoy it. Tomorrow I'll introduce you to the Twins. Who knows how long they'll draw out their telling. Or, if they're in a foul mood, we might not get a story at all." She twirled her glass of wine. "However we find them, our time here will not be wasted."

Dee's shoulders tensed. Amalthea gave a smile meant to relax her. "There's nothing to be nervous about, child. The Twins have managed to hold their own House under circumstances that suggested impossibility. They will not risk another tribulation, regardless of how interesting they might find you."

Dee knew better than to overthink the Rishi's words. Amalthea trusted where they were, so Dee should too.

-*Right, because we trust those who're giving us advice on who to trust?*-

Continuing to wrap herself further in this impossible situation, Dee allowed herself a genuine smile. At least for the evening, there would be nothing to worry about. She took a breath, forcing the tension out of her shoulders, ignoring the impulse to roll her neck.

"I would like to apologize that Hamal or Daniel weren't able to accompany us. We all see how fond of them you've grown. It was the Twins' express wish that none from any House but my own join us."

Placing her wine glass on the table, knowing getting drunk would not be a good idea, Dee smiled courteously. "Alnath has been great company. And Vali seems more than competent. I don't know that I'd have been better off with Zi's people here."

Amalthea laughed, a heartfelt sound that, at first, set Dee's nerves ablaze before she realized it wasn't mockery. "I'm sure Vali appreciates your sense of his competency." She even winked.

Dee reached for her glass, hoping no one noticed the tremble in her fingers.

Settling back in her chair, the Rishi nodded, moving backward in the conversation. "It would reflect badly on them if something romantic were to happen, but I think sometimes we forget the value of such things. As long as they're valued for their own sake, of course, and not used to confuse the mind."

Dee blinked stupidly.

-Is she suggesting you have sex with them as long as you don't allow it to turn into a relationship?-

She thought that's precisely what the Rishi was suggesting. Her blush brought more gentle laughter from across the table. It was the last thing she'd expected to hear. It was the last thing she wanted to talk about. Boys were the last thing she needed to be concerned with when the state of her life was still up in the air.

Trying to think of a way to change the subject, her mouth was speaking before her brain caught up to what she was saying. "Daniel said such a thing was forbidden."

"Forbidden? Did he use that word?"

Dee tried to remember exactly what he'd said. "No. He said if I had feelings, to forget them."

Amalthea nodded. "Yes, feelings cloud things, but a physical act is not the same as feeling from the heart."

Dee understood the point but didn't have much experience with it.

A wash of power flooded her senses, overshadowing whatever else Amalthea said. Dee searched the room, eyes wide, searching for the source. She gripped the side of the table to keep her from sliding beneath it to hide. Her eyes moved to her guards to see if they'd picked up the source of this new power.

Dee had grown so accustomed to the tingling of energy in her head from so much time around Amalthea and the members of her House that her radar had been repressed. It was because of the *newness* of what she felt that it filtered through. Someone, or some*thing*, she hadn't yet come across drew near. Someone powerful enough to be Master of their own House.

Amalthea watched one of her people, a Soldier Dee hadn't noticed planted near the front of the restaurant, move to the lobby. Another followed. This second Soldier re-appeared after seconds, looking first to Metis, then Amalthea, hand gestures explaining what was going on.

Dee barely caught the exchange, not knowing the secret language. Her attention remained on the entrance.

Amalthea rose from her seat. "It looks like we will be having company."

Dee's breath froze in her lungs. Three Rishis in the same place?

Vali moved up to take a seat at the table next to Dee while Amalthea, escorted by Atkins, moved off.

Vali's eyes scanned the room, never ceasing their search for danger, even when he spoke to her. "Remain seated. The Rishi will greet them. Rise when they come to the table."

Dee dropped her chin in curt acknowledgment, panic continuing to wrench the breath from her.

Could she escape? Her eyes flew around the space, realizing she had no idea where to go even if she survived the restaurant. There was no chance she'd find her way to safety.

The suspense of waiting pushed against her.

The world paused in shared suspense as two of the tallest, most striking men Dee had ever seen glided into the dining area. They resembled Dee so closely, she was nervous they were here to tell her she was their long-lost sister. Long dark hair flowed around their shoulders, accenting deep blue eyes set into clear skin—skin much lighter than the other old-ones she'd encountered, though still maintaining a hint of the unique copper-hue they all shared.

Their power cascaded over her as they moved closer, and if Dee hadn't been so mesmerized by the sight of them, she might have curled up in fear.

They greeted Amalthea with warm hugs, enfolding her shorter stature even as both pairs of eyes searched out the anomaly they'd come to see.

Amalthea smiled encouragingly at Dee as she led the pair back to the table, her guards spreading quietly back to their posts, noticeably more uptight than before. Dee noted the Twins' lack of bodyguards.

As they approached, she stood, remembering Vali's instructions.

Amalthea smiled, enjoying her opportunity to introduce them all. "Desiree, meet Castor…"

The twin to Dee's left stepped forward, bowing gracefully from a height over a foot taller than her, taking her hand gently to lay the barest trace of a kiss.

Amalthea continued. "…and Pollux."

The second twin bowed, stepping closer to the girl than his brother, meeting her eyes with a penetrating gaze she couldn't decipher.

-A warrior's appraisal or a suitor's lust?-

"We are very excited to have you here, Ms. Galen." Pollux's voice barely penetrated the ambient sound of the surrounding tables, most of which continued to stare at the distinguished group. He took her hand as well, laying a kiss into her open palm, a surprisingly intimate gesture that washed the tension from her stomach.

Dee looked away from his gaze, not sure if she held the polite smile she was attempting, or if it morphed into a grimace.

Castor cocked an eyebrow at his brother.

Dee's eyes were drawn to Castor's face, curious about his reaction, but there was too much going on for her to linger on the question.

Metis had moved to stand behind Amalthea's vacant chair, tension showing in his grip on the fine detail of the seat though his face was nothing but a mask of calm. The Twins' charm had alleviated some of Dee's panic, but seeing Metis' reaction brought it soaring back.

Vali, clearing his throat behind her brought her attention to the table. Pollux waited for her to sit, his hand on her chair, an expression of patient mirth on his face. Embarrassed, Dee sat quickly, wishing she could slide under the table and hide.

-Nice. They're all laughing at you. Castor thinks you're a naive little girl and Pollux thinks you're daft.-

Dee mentally rolled her eyes, wondering if maybe this wasn't how she wanted everyone to view her. Might they let her go if she seemed too ditzy to pose a threat, or whatever it was they worried about?

"Your message suggested you wouldn't be available this evening." Amalthea leaned into the table as she spoke, not in the least put out by the unannounced change in plans.

Pollux leaned back, swirling the wine that had been poured, allowing his brother to run the conversation while he continued to study Dee.

Castor's voice was smooth, suggesting perfect control. "It was necessary to judge the merit of your request."

Amalthea frowned, sending an alarm through Dee's internal system.

The Rishi's voice remained even, though her usual warm tone faded. "The *merit* of my request might have been considered before we came all this way."

Pollux smiled as if from some private joke, monitoring Amalthea for a moment, whose eyes blazed as she stared his brother down.

The silent brother leaned Dee's way, still swirling his wine, whispering so only she could hear. "My brother knows how to push her buttons. Sometimes, I'm not sure he even means to do it. She'll either explode in a rage or relax in motherly patience." He raised his glass to point to the pair glowering at each other across from them. "Just watch."

Dee followed his gesture, noting Amalthea's frown challenging Castor's calm until Castor's face morphed to laughter. "Oh, Amalthea, you're too easy. I'm shocked you weren't prepared for us."

Amalthea's lips pursed, not amused. "Assumption, my boy. *Ass*umption."

Now Pollux laughed. "And the ass you typically are, brother."

Castor feigned a frown, shooting it his brother's way. "Right, I'm the one known as the ass." He shook his head, turning his attention to Dee. "Ms. Galen, you're proceeded by an extraordinary reputation."

Dee stared back at Castor with a blank expression. "Oh?"

He turned back to Amalthea. "Eloquent."

Amalthea laughed gently, chiding the twin. "Give her a chance, Castor. Until a few weeks ago, she was living as a modern girl from a small town in the United States. No one's ever taught her eloquence, or communication, or anything really." She shot Dee an apologetic glance. "No offense, Desiree. It's not your fault."

Dee drained her glass, fighting to keep her expression blank.

Don't be embarrassed for what you've never learned. Daniel's words echoed in her head. She sat up straighter. She wouldn't let them bother her, especially if that's what their goal was.

The Twins shared a look Dee didn't understand. Then Castor spoke to her again. "Amalthea's brought you to hear our story, but first, I would ask to hear yours."

Dee looked at Amalthea, frantic pleading in her eyes.

Amalthea attempted a rescue. "Her memory is gone, her story lost even to herself."

"As you've said, but still, I wish to hear it from her." Castor's eyes never left Dee's face as he communicated with Amalthea. Pollux leaned back.

She looked to Amalthea, but there was no help to be had there. She was going to have to explain to this group what she remembered, even if it wasn't much.

Not sure where to start, Dee took a breath. She'd always hid pieces of the story, never sure how the listener would react. Here, she decided to just tell the story as she remembered. Maybe it would even help jog her memory.

-Maybe these aren't the guys to be remembering for.-

She was afraid of this, but she needed to move forward, rather than continue to play this game of circles.

She was looking at her hands, clasped on the table as she debated how to handle this. "Six or seven years ago—"

"Six? Or seven?" Castor interrupted.

She took a breath, closing her eyes to count the time.

Her father died in November. She lasted in his house until the following summer when she'd bolted for the other side of the country. For three years, she'd moved around with Kim, then Steve and Ray. When Mike found her, half-dead on his porch, it'd been two years since he'd last heard from her. That was almost two years ago now.

She choked back a sob, realizing just how much time she'd lost in whatever game she'd been pulled into. Locked away with all her other memories, she'd never let herself think of the details that might strip her of the precarious hold she maintained on her sanity.

When she opened her eyes, only a sheen of tears glimmered. She was proud when no trace of warble was in her voice. "Two years. I can't remember two years. But it was seven years ago I moved to California.

"I lived with friends. We'd been moving around together for about a year and a half, finding jobs that paid just enough to pay the rent, and still keep us regulars at the local clubs. That was why we lived, to drink, and dance, and forget the world."

She half-smiled, remembering Kim and Ray, then Steve's face as they'd looked in the syncopated strobe of the club lights, all sound drowned out by the deep thrumming of house music. Nostalgia made those days seem glamorous in her memory, rather than the stressful, avoidance-ridden reality they'd been.

"I remember being home with Steve when Ray came in. I don't remember where Kim was. Maybe at work?" She chuckled. "That's a shocker, but it must have been where she was."

Dee closed her eyes, fighting against the blank gap that came next. "Then, the heat of the fire. Waking up in the grass, in the backyard of some house I didn't recognize. I sat there for a long time. I think it was a long time. Just staring at the flames. Eventually, I got up and started walking, coming to a town where I stayed until I was attacked."

Amalthea's head perked at this. It was a detail Dee'd always left out. That she'd been nothing more than a bum living on the streets never seemed relevant. She wasn't even sure it was true.

"I don't remember the specifics of that either. I remember being attacked, something coming at me from behind. Then, it was gone." She closed her eyes in the hopes the memory would be clearer. "No, that's not right. I don't know. An attack. Of that I'm sure. Then I'm home. Well, not home, exactly, but the place I was staying. I don't know what happened to my attacker. I don't know how I got from the street to my bed. I was hurt pretty badly. A lot of blood from scratches all over me."

She paused for a moment, collecting herself. It was the first time she'd ever talked about it. It was the first time she'd remembered sitting in that grungy room, bleeding, not knowing who to call or where to go. How long did she sit there before she decided to make her way back to Mike's? How long did she travel before she made it back to her hometown?

Something tugged at her memory, but like a word on the tip of her tongue, the more she chased it, the less clear it became. "I figured they'd all died in the fire." She regressed, not sure why this part seemed important. "Ray's truck was in the driveway. I remember that. We went everywhere in that beat-up truck. The four of us barely fit, but we did it. The four of us went everywhere together. If I was there, and the truck was there, we were all there."

She smiled as a memory of her sitting on Ray's lap, Kim trying to keep her legs out of the way so Steve could shift gears was conjured in her mind. Ray had tried copping a feel like he always did. It was his game, trying to get the girls in bed with him. Sometimes it was endearing. Mostly, it had been annoying. She remembered she'd *accidentally* jabbed him in the throat with an elbow.

"Mike says I showed up half-dead on the doorstep. That was last summer. No. The summer before."

Hamal trained her this past summer. It was already February.

Castor looked at Amalthea as if to ask if that was all she knew. Amalthea's look must have assured him it was, since he asked nothing. The brothers matching postures reclined in their chairs, swirling their drinks as if of one mind.

Dee forced her eyes to dance around the grand restaurant while she waited for someone to comment on her story.

Castor spoke softly. "How did you get to Mike's?"

Her stomach flopped. She'd just been thinking about how she couldn't remember this.

He noted the confusion in her face, pressing her with a flippant tone. "Did you drive? Walk? Hitchhike?"

"I really don't remember." Then, more to herself, "Why don't I remember that?"

"You started in Northern California, then made it to Upstate New York with almost no memory of any traveling. You remember seeing Ray's truck in the driveway, though you say you woke up in the backyard."

Dee shook her head, eyes staring into the past, tears glimmering in her eyes. The shock of all that happened had been repressed for so long that talking about it took a toll on her. It was definitely not the time to be succumbing to a loss of her senses, not when surrounded by these ancient beings.

"Where did you stay between the fire and your return home?" Castor's voice was quieter, more soothing as if he knew she was on the brink of losing it.

"I only remember that dirty room. I slept all the time. Sometimes I left to get food. I have no idea where I was. I cried about my friends. I cried because I was so confused about what had happened."

"Explain." Castor swirled his wine. Pollux had put his glass down, leaning forward towards her.

"Explain?"

"Yes, explain what you were feeling. You woke up outside of a burning house you suspected your friends were killed in, then you walked to the nearest town after no one came to put out the fire, and you never told anyone. You stayed in a place you didn't know. You must have talked to someone in order to have a place to stay. How did you pay for it? For food?"

She hadn't called anyone. Hadn't told anyone. Were her friends' families still wondering what had happened to them? Had anyone ever found that house with the three sets of burnt bones lying beneath the rubble?

Her stomach was sick with grief and regret. "Oh my god. I never thought to tell anyone. I didn't know what to say, so I never did."

"Explain your feelings of confusion."

"My feelings?" She caught herself from letting out a hysterical sob. Tired of talking about things she had never wanted to think about, she managed to find a response besides *go to hell*. "I was confused. Lost." She took a breath, closed her eyes to immerse herself in the memories, forgetting her surroundings. Forgetting even Pollux's weighted gaze on her.

"So tired." She whispered. "Afraid. I don't know what of. Maybe that someone would find me and think I had something to do with the fire. Was that why I didn't tell anyone?" Her words were for herself now, questions she should have asked long ago finding an outlet.

Her eyes remained closed. Tilting her head, she continued to analyze thoughts she'd avoided. "Sleep. Dreams of—someone, standing over me. Watching me. Tired. Lonely."

She took a frustrated breath before opening her eyes. "That's all I remember. Being tired was the highlight. So tired, I didn't get out of bed for days at a time."

"And you never saw what attacked you?"

She shook her head.

"Could it have been a Revenant?"

It wasn't the first time the thought had occurred to her. "Maybe."

"If it was, then whoever found you in New York had most likely found you before. I'm not sure what it means that it took them so long to re-discover you, but it does add more weight to the idea that one of us was with you at that house that burned. That one of us was doing something they shouldn't have."

Castor looked at Amalthea, who returned his gaze. The two stared at each other for a moment, and Dee wondered if maybe they were speaking telepathically.

Pollux continued to study her, while Dee sipped at her refilled glass to give her something to do other than squirm under his gaze. When he stood with a hand out for Dee, she didn't bother to hide her surprise. His words surprised her even further.

"Desiree, would you care to honor me with a dance?"

Dee looked around. There was no one else dancing. The classical music playing was loud enough to hear, but nothing to inspire dancing. She was sure the activity would bring more attention to their group. She glanced at Amalthea, but she and Castor seemed locked in some silent conversation.

Pulled to her feet by the less disparaging of the brothers, Dee stood. She matched Pollux's steps away from the table. Nervousness replaced her annoyance.

Pollux seemed to read her hesitancy. "When you spend money like we do, they allow you certain indulgences. No one will mind watching such a handsome couple dance between the empty tables."

Taking Pollux's hand, he guided her with graceful steps to an empty space. A maître d' motioned for staff to take the closest table away to allow them this impromptu dance floor. Pollux didn't seem aware of the activity. He wrapped his arm around her waist, his light touch respectful. His towering height forced Dee to either stare into his chest or crane her head backwards to see his face.

He was a fantastic dancer, leading her around the space as if a seasoned pro.

As the song blended into another, Dee allowed her fears and apprehensions to fall away.

"You move like a trained killer."

His words startled her. She looked up, allowing him to catch her eye.

He laughed at the shock in her face. "This is the greatest of compliments, Desiree. My brother and I were trained for killing. Somewhere along the way, we discovered that the best killers are also the best dancers."

Dee couldn't help but grin.

Daniel's words flashed through her head: *You realize what you just did? He might be as good as Castor.*

In conversation about the best, the Twins were the ones to beat.

She thought about how skilled a warrior he must be and if she could feel that in the way he moved now—the arm around her, the grace that led her—even as she remembered her manners by accepting his compliment. "Thank you, but I'm not sure I'm deserving of such a high compliment."

"No? Why not?" He spun her in a clean turn before pulling her back to enfold her in his arms. The movement took her breath.

-Really? You're going to get all hormonal with another one of these guys?-

She couldn't keep the frown from her face and hoped Pollux wouldn't notice. In the next step, she was twirling out, then back to their original posture.

"I've only just begun to train. I haven't even begun to learn."

He smiled. "Maybe not, but I've seen you. Your battle with Atkins was magnificent."

The look on her face asked the question as her stomach flip-flopped.

He laughed gently. "No worries, Ms. Galen. Amalthea has

been keeping a close eye on her charge. She sent a video for us to view when she appealed to us to help you."

Dee didn't feel much better knowing she'd been being watched so closely, especially knowing that a video of her had been handed out. Who else had Amalthea been sending updates?

-Zibanitu, for sure.-

The smile left her face. "Why did Amalthea *appeal* to you?"

"She thinks we might help you understand what you are by explaining what we are."

Dee's brow furrowed. "She already showed me the Initiates."

Pollux chuckled. "Yes. But they are not what we are."

She paused for a moment, thinking about his words. "You think I'm like you? Not the Initiates?"

He shrugged.

"What are you?"

"You will have to wait for that. I will say, now, there is not a word for our race in your language. Or any language still known. antediluvian covers it, but is more a general term than one that pertains to just us. *Us* is not widely known, so language hasn't needed to encompass our existence. Your scientists throw out any evidence that suggests a race as old as us is possible. How could there not be extensive archeological evidence, they ask. We are fine with these delusions."

The scope of time he was talking about made her head ache. How did one live so long and not go mad? Two-hundred thousand years since the birth of homo sapiens? Was that right? The Rishi's were older than that?

And he'd mentioned antediluvian. Before the flood? *The* Flood? She recalled that every culture's origins had a story of a great flood that wiped out the Earth so life could start anew.

Her head spun.

Holding out her chair before taking his own, Pollux's thanks for the dance brought her from her thoughts. She forced a smile to mask her face, surprised to find the truth in her words, "I should thank you. I didn't even know I could dance like that. It was—nice."

He smiled, grinning wider when his brother threw him a look. "Brother, relax. It was your boring conversation that sent us away."

"Boring conversation? We might be looking at the first flare of war in centuries."

Rather than cast a pall over the table, the news seemed to excite the dancing twin.

Amalthea shook her head. "Boys, let's not anticipate the worst."

"If The Ophiuchus is moving on others, especially against those who have never played at war, the rest of us will be there to stop him." Castor was adamant.

"I thank you for your chivalry, but let's keep talk of war for another day." Amalthea's voice was firm. Dee wondered if she caught a hint of sarcasm there as well.

Food was served, and Dee gratefully dove into her plate. After a few bites, she felt brave enough to join the conversation. "War? Because of me?"

Castor played with the food in front of him. "Curiosity is a tantalizing thing to those like us who find the repetitive patterns of man exhausting. You are a curiosity never seen."

-Anomaly.-

"So, basically, you'll be fighting over possession of me?" Dee didn't have the knack of keeping her voice conversational when she was angry.

The three looked uncomfortable at her choice of words, though none made a correction. She put down her fork. "If I had gone with Barnard, none of you would have even known about me, would you? Only Zibanitu, who wouldn't have risked sending anyone after me."

Pollux sat up straighter, looking to Amalthea for confirmation.

The matriarch nodded solemnly. "Only because Hamal called Atkins did I find out. If you'd never come to me, I may not have believed your existence." She turned to the Twins. "Barnard was sent to acquire Dee in New York, but Hamal had already called Atkins in to help. Atkins told me, I called Zibanitu. Zibanitu sent Daniel and Dimitri, and here we are."

Pollux's voice was thoughtful. "We knew Barnard was with the team to take her on the road, but we hadn't been told about this earlier visit." His attention turned to Dee. "What did Barnard say to you? Why didn't you go with him?"

Dee shrugged. "It never occurred to me Barnard wasn't there to kill me in New York, so I attacked him. Atkins showed up before he could tell me why he was there. When he came to me on the road, I thought about going with him. I wondered if it would stop all the fighting." She frowned. "I guess maybe I should have gone with him."

"But, you didn't."

She shook her head, thinking, *I'm here, aren't I?*

Pollux's stare was intense, when he asked, "Would you if he caught up to you again?"

"Not if it wouldn't stop the fighting."

Pollux smiled wickedly. "That time has passed."

31

S he wasn't sure what she expected, but it wasn't this. Walking into an ancient Roman theatre nestled within a sleek, modern skyscraper was the last thing she'd anticipated.

Another helicopter ride over the city brought them to the Twins' home, and Dee wasn't ashamed to admit how surprised she was that their center of operations was in the heart of such a major metropolis. Her idea of the Rishis all hiding themselves away in remote corners of the world was obviously incorrect. São Paulo was hardly a quiet place to be reclusive.

She was chaperoned on one side by Atkins and on the other by one of the Twins' own Soldiers, Leda, whose five-foot-ten managed more intimidation than Atkins' six-foot-plus. Her blue-black hair and impressive muscularity had Dee wondering if maybe Wonder Woman wasn't based off this being next to her.

Following her from the elevator, Dee's eyes looked up to a ceiling that stretched twenty meters over them. Ten meters ahead, the floor sloped downward, thick steps sculpted from smooth stone holding dual-purpose as both stairs and seating which leveled off at an orchestra pit that took up the half-circle before the stage. Stretching the width of the room, at least forty meters, the stage yawned, its stone design matching the rest of the room as if carved from a single, gigantic boulder. Rising up from the stage were eight columns that held the high ceilings from tumbling on the visitors. The stonework was threaded with thin veins of silver and gold that sparkled in the light that had no source Dee could find.

Atkins' gentle push at her lower back got her moving. She wasn't sure how long they'd let her stand there, gapping with her chin to her knees, blocking their entry into the grand room, but it was long enough that Leda had stopped to wait for her.

In Dee's first few steps, she noticed the blackness of the stone and the many-size pockmarks that covered it. It reminded her of lava rock she'd seen once, though that had been anything but smooth.

Amalthea and Metis stepped past her, unimpressed by the sights. That, or their sense of propriety wouldn't allow such blatant expressions of awe. Either way, Dee found herself stepping slowly, eyes unable to stray from the grandness surrounding her. So much was her attention taken, Atkins finally placed a steady hand on her elbow when she almost fell for a third time. The thickness of the steps was hard enough to manage without roving eyes making her clumsy.

Three-quarters of the way down to the stage, Dee stopped, mirroring Amalthea as the Rishi chose a seat. Pillows had been stacked and arranged for them, and Dee wondered just what sort of storytelling she was about to witness. Her attention settled on the stage, imagining how grand a production would look in this venue.

Dee noted how Amalthea lounged in the fashion of old Rome. Too out of her element to get so comfortable, Dee sat forward, resting elbows on her knees.

Atkins and Leda moved away to stand just above and to each side of Dee, so the guest of honor was sitting alone in a sea of black rock.

Invited by the silence, Dee said, more to herself, "I can't

believe this place is hidden inside a skyscraper in the middle of the city."

Amalthea nodded. "Things are easily hidden when no one knows to look."

-*What else is hidden in plain sight we've been missing?*-

Dee didn't have time to wonder. The lights dimmed. Two stage lights burst to life to shine on the pair who seemed to materialize on stage.

As if a reflection of each other, the Twins stepped forward, movements so synced Dee's brain was legitimately convinced she was watching one person and the mirror of that person, rather than two separate beings.

The doppelgängers stopped at the edge of the stage, attention turned to Amalthea. They bowed low, their movements slow, before rising in uncanny synchronization to turn their full attention on Dee.

She couldn't look away, feeling the dual weight of that ancient experience press against her, long, dark hair framing bright faces, large, blue eyes staring piercingly into her. They had a strange beauty, humming with underlying notes of violence momentarily calmed.

Dee shivered as another second stretched.

In these moments, the giant room, already silent, seemed sucked of sound. Her breath held, heart hammering as she waited for what would come.

When the Twins spoke, her skin rippled with goosebumps, their voices blending together as one, maintaining the eerie illusion that they were one being temporarily split into two.

"Forgetting and remembering. Two sides of the same coin. Linked passages in the brain that obliterate self, sense, being."

Dee swallowed, panicked she might make too much noise, unable to look away from the pair of eyes that held her trapped. She fidgeted in her seat, leaning backward as if the greater distance would render her safe.

She realized she was wringing her hands. She clutched them

together before wiping her palms across her thighs. Breathing was difficult. Had she blinked? She did now.

Silence stretched again.

In this silence, their words echoed in her head, so she postulated their meaning.

Forgetting and remembering; the same?

She understood forgetting. Would remembering be the same? How could it?

"In forgetting, how does one not change? In forgetting, how does one not lose all they were? Do we become something else in the forgetting? Is who we were lost, pulled away by those things departed?"

Again, their voices blended as one, inciting more goosebumps. This time, Dee found she could relax, allowing the strange monologue its place in her thoughts. Her eyes lost their startled glaze, her posture loosened, so her attention focused on what was told.

"Remembering adds, morphing self to something else. Changing it. In both, there is alteration."

Another pause.

Then, the images came, implanted in her mind from some unknown source. Her eyes darted to Amalthea to see if she saw the same. The Rishi's eyes met hers for a moment, face unreadable before she smiled a gentle smile, a look that told Dee all was well.

Dee relaxed into the visions, even as she continued looking at the Twins on stage. Curiosity won out over her fear.

The story unfurled with no more interruptions.

The theatre was gone. There was only the past unfolding in her mind's eye.

She saw an Earth spread with green, thick-leaved plants, taller, more massive than any she'd ever seen. Even the green seemed different, each abundant shade more vibrant than the colors she was used to.

Placed among the landscape, a great city sprawled high, thin skyscrapers sectioned at junctures where wide platforms connected them to others. Long, bracing legs reached the ground where gardens and forests lay unaffected by the metropolis sprawling around it. Here was a city in symbiosis with the land.

There were people, all with the bronze skin shared by the ancients she'd met. They were happy. There was peace.

Something in her vision shifted, the peace threatened, though she couldn't explain what had changed to shatter the bliss. She saw a figure, away from the cities, arms raised to the sky, others flocking towards him.

This was Sabik Han. The Ophiuchus.

A part of her thought to be angry at him, but that was the influence of past conversations. The Sabik Han she saw now was another version of him. A version whose curiosity, whose thirst to know, whose desire to look in, rather than out, ruled him. The Sabik Han before the hate of the others crashed around him.

Another was there. This one's skin spotted with splotches of paleness. Zibanitu had spoken for the others even then.

Their conversation turned to argument. Han didn't agree with Zibanitu. He left the cities. He left them all to search on his own for that which he felt in his heart was there to find.

Bliss returned, though an undercurrent of violence threatened. That was the Twins watching, searching for what Han might do, even as the others pretended all was well.

Dee felt herself smiling as she watched these mental pictures of an ancient time. Even before they found immortality, they were long-lived.

Her mind had wandered. A spike in her heart rate hit her before her mind comprehended what was changing.

War.

It came quickly to those who weren't privy to the politics, but to the few who watched the path unfold, it was no surprise.

She saw the Twins in their glory.

Standing at the front of armies, they were the generals trained to lead warriors and fulfill the plan set by the Council, who'd chosen this route to combat The Ophiuchus' moves.

Dee's mind raced. What had Sabik done? Had she missed something? Had they skipped a part of the story?

She watched as armies clashed. Millions died, yet the fighting did not stop. Years. Decades. Still, war waged.

Tears fell down Dee's cheeks as her heart ached from the losses. Choked sobs caught in her throat as she was pulled through a time she'd never imagined yet was emotionally tied to in a way she'd never felt in her own life.

Dee watched two events unfold. First, great weapons were loosed, rocketing the Earth to charred ruin. Nothing remained but pits of molten rock, charred landscapes, and scarred ground. An entire planet scorched to nothing.

In this other scene, Dee watched Han, standing naked, arms reaching over him in a large Y, his powerful form exuding a calm serenity that juxtaposed the thrumming energy building around him.

They will make us forget. We should not forget.

It was a voice she didn't recognize but knew. It was the voice that had spoken to her through Barnard's welcoming hand, offering her a home.

His mouth opened to let out a chant which created a strange reverberating melody through the rhyming cadence of a language Dee didn't recognize.

She didn't need to understand the words, his intent penetrating her mind from the word-spell the Twins weaved.

Tying himself to the Earth. Never to forget. Never allowing their technology to supersede what they were, what they could be. For what he believed, he would force the others to see what he intuitively understood. He would force this connectivity through them all, tying them directly to the heartbeat of the universe. He was sure that would bring lasting peace to his people.

But the bombs were already going off, counteracting his mission. Weapons that stripped all evidence of their great technologies, sending all his people had built to smoldering dust. Nothing could survive what this war had wrought.

Despite the destruction that obliterated all, a small island of hope remained where Han stood. The others converged there, staying just ahead of the blasts erasing everything they had built and loved.

Han's chanting grew incensed, the power crackling in the air, so Dee was sure gravity had lost hold on her hair where she sat. Whatever magic, or science, Han worked took on a power of its own.

Commotion flooded Dee's senses. There was no understanding the source, her eyes searching the space beyond Sabik Han for insight into what was happening.

The Twins were there, facing the still-naked sorcerer. Time had skipped, so Dee wasn't sure how they'd arrived. There were others, many, many others, behind the pair, but she couldn't see them, only feel them in the memory of the story.

Few words were spoken, though Dee sensed communication happening in the long stares the trio gave each other.

Then there was fighting.

Fluid agility whirled as the Twins fought to take out The Ophiuchus before this last piece of Earth was ground to dust.

A mortal blow put Castor on the ground, Pollux now fighting to keep Han from finishing his brother, rather than kill the one who'd doomed them all. One brother alone could not best Han, and they all knew it. Only as one had the brothers had a chance to end this.

Dee felt more tears. They were Pollux's emotion made tangible. The emotion overwhelmed her as Pollux's frustration turned to fear that his brother would die. She choked on this fear, *his* fear. She came to her feet, so wrapped in what she was seeing and feeling.

As the Twins had appeared, so too were others suddenly there. Ten bodies, six females, one Dee recognized as Amalthea, and four males circled Han, who stopped. He was so still Dee was sure he'd been trapped somehow.

A moment before the spell hit, the leader with the marbled skin turned, yelling a command. But it was too late.

Those caught in the spell's radius were brought to the ground, forcefully pressed tightly to the Earth.

Those outside the spell were caught in the blast of the atomizing bomb released by the leader's last command. As the blinding flash lit the world in bright oblivion, those pressed to the Earth were saved.

Saved from death but forever forced to live with what they had wrought.

Dee's awareness came back to the theatre, eyelids stuttering.

She was standing, Atkins at her elbow, ready to assist if she moved to fall. As her brain acknowledged this, her legs collapsed, the stone seat catching her while her eyes continued to blink, clearing the overflow of emotion from all she'd been shown.

Remembering Castor bleeding out on the ground, her eyes darted to the stage, where the Twins remained, watching her, waiting for her senses to fully release her back to the present. She held Castor's gaze then raked her eyes over his form as if something in the way he stood might explain his survival.

Remembering Pollux's pain, her eyes turned to him, and they shared a relieved smile of shared experience.

Blinking again, she took a breath, then another, recalibrating back to her own skin.

Finally, she turned to Amalthea. "I see why you wanted them to tell this story. That was—incredible."

Amalthea nodded, a weight to her look that set Dee's radar screaming. "What is it?"

"Their storytelling was in the nature that we can speak to one another. Only those of us who've survived since that day can use this telepathic speech. None of those we've created has ever had this ability."

Dee frowned.

-She's telling you you shouldn't have been able to see the story.-

Dee looked at Amalthea, fear shining from her eyes, even as she attempted to keep it hidden behind a mask of contemplation.

Amalthea opened her mouth to comfort the girl, just as Pollux stepped from the stage to offer reassurance. Both stopped when the elevator door opened, its motorized function echoing in the stillness of the room. Not turning to the sound, still too dazed, Dee felt, rather than heard, the frantic approach of one of the Twins' people.

"Zosma—"

The word, a name, filled the room.

Pollux leaped to action, as Castor shouted a command to hidden guards, cutting off the rest of the message.

But there wasn't enough time. Soldiers surrounded them, rappelling from the ceiling as others moved in from hidden doorways near the stage and around the perimeter above and behind them.

It happened so fast, Dee hadn't thought to move.

"I think you have what is mine." A deep, booming voice filled the room, cutting through the chaos of so much motion. The stillness held for a breath before erupting in anxious calamity.

-Are we being overrun? Seriously?-

Dee turned to the voice that rose from the shadows, a voice that claimed her as his own.

His red hair was neat, while large eyes flashed arrogantly on an attractive face. He was thin, but the command that blazed around him had Dee wondering if that thinness wasn't a disguise his clothing offered and underneath was nothing but hard, sinewy muscle waiting to be released.

The implication of his words infused her shocked brain, and her attention on him changed to wide-eyed surprise. Was he someone who actually knew the answers to her questions?

-Wouldn't that make him the one who did this to you?-

She stared up at this new Rishi with adrenaline spiking through her veins. How was she supposed to react? Was it time to run? To fight? Part of her wanted to step forward and barrage him with questions.

The Twins had pulled weapons, moving to stand between Amalthea and Desiree, Pollux close enough to Dee that he could protect her if necessary. Atkins stood just ahead of her, blocking her view of Zosma, who towered over them all from his vantage at the top of the steps.

Amalthea's fierceness met him with challenge. "You have no right to be here. Zibanitu will end you for this."

Zosma laughed at the threat. "Zibanitu can do what he likes, but he won't be able to fault me in this when I show him the truth to my claim."

Seeming to float up the steps, defying the girth of her frame, Amalthea spit her next words. So venomous were they Dee wondered if there weren't some long-standing feud between the two. "Your claim means nothing. If your claim were so polished, she wouldn't have come to me!"

"Careful your temper doesn't get you into more trouble than you can get out of. You may have fallen across this bit of drama, but don't think it means you're worth any more than you ever were."

Not even Metis' hold could stop the matron's fury. Castor called out to her just as she reached the top landing where the newcomer stood, but she was too far gone.

Dee hadn't realized Amalthea carried a weapon. It was out, slicing downward with incredible speed that further revealed the power hiding beneath her matronly frame.

Flinching at the blow she was sure would land across Zosma's face, he managed to block and parry the onslaught. Castor and Pollux, waiting to see how the lady would fair, were suddenly on the landing with her, three to Zosma's one.

Showing the agility he possessed, Zosma vaulted backward to surround himself with his own Soldiers whose weapons were aimed and ready.

Despite the ample space, it was crowded as more Soldiers

from contending sides faced off. A barely contained potential energy charged the room with an almost audible hum, and Dee's hand itched for a weapon. She cursed the decision that she not be allowed one, and held out a hand to Atkins.

Not bothering to comment, the Soldier handed over a long knife Dee hoped would be enough. She shifted the weapon in her hand, getting a feel for the grip before settling it firmly in her palm.

Amalthea continued to seethe at the group of invaders. Still flanked by the Twins, all locked in this moment of decision.

It was Castor who broke the silence. "If you leave now, there will be no harm done."

Pollux shot a hard look at his brother. "No! Harm has been done. We can not let it lie!"

He stepped forward to begin an attack, but a stern, clipped syllable from Castor stopped him. "Just a moment, brother." Castor's voice echoed through the cavernous room. She noted Zosma's eyebrows rise in barely masked contempt. "We should at least offer the intruder the chance to explain his breach of our laws."

Pollux turned his attention on his brother with a smirk. If Dee didn't know any better, she might think the Twins were baiting Zosma.

Castor continued, speaking directly at Zosma through the wall of Soldiers who'd lined up between the Rishis. "What is yours, as you claim we have, that has allowed you to risk war by breaking into our space?"

Zosma met Amalthea's smile, then held each of the Twins' eyes. He raised an arm, single finger pointing through the crowd to Dee.

All attention turned to her.

He didn't wait. Zosma sprung, vaulting towards the trio, his own Soldiers moving with him to clash with the army waiting to defend their Masters.

Dee found her feet leaving the ground, just as she noted Atkins, Leda, and Vali crossing swords with Zosma.

How had he gotten so close? How had he gotten through Amalthea, and the Twins, and the guards?

Carried like a sack of bones, she struggled to get free, until Pollux's command stilled her fight. The world spun by in her upside-down position, preventing her from checking on the condition of the others. Amalthea's shout convinced Dee the Rishi was still okay.

Gunfire erupted.

Dee squeezed her eyes, body clenched in anticipation of getting shot.

-Well done. If you can't see, the bullets can't hit you, is that it? Maybe wish hard enough, and you'll teleport right out of here and into Mike's living room. Click your heels three times...-

But there was nothing else she could do. Pollux carrying her off had negated any ability she might have of assisting in her own escape.

-You could tell him to put you down. You could fight him. Maybe you should kill him like you should have killed Hamal.-

---

Amalthea whirled on Castor as gunfire filled the room. "Where is he taking her?!"

Castor glanced at the Rishi, whose rage pushed against him. "My brother is prone to overreaction. She'll be fine. He'll keep her safe."

Amalthea seethed, ducking around the flurry of projectiles, even as Metis was there to ensure her safety. Glaring at the spot she'd last seen Desiree, she gathered control of her anger. Matching her speed to the frenzy of activity around her, she turned to the fight, thoughts still on the girl she'd promised safety.

Castor moved through the chaos, following, albeit much more

slowly, the path his brother had taken with Dee. The secrets buried within this building were vast, security in their own right, though the fact that Zosma had managed to infiltrate left her afraid it wouldn't be enough.

32

"**K**eep your feet."

Dee barely interpreted the words before she was spun from Pollux's shoulder, managing to stay upright as her feet met the ground, their speed never slowing.

She hadn't seen much of where they traveled but guessed they'd ventured down several secret passages leading through mostly unused portions of the building. Whether or not she'd find herself hiding out in a hidden corner of São Paulo, or somewhere new, she would have to wait to find out once their frantic retreat came to an end.

Using that skill that allowed her to know when they were near, Dee was alerted to Zosma's approach. He'd caught up to them, despite Pollux's hidden doors and switch-backing escape.

Assuming Pollux was aware of the approaching Rishi, she kept the knowledge to herself. When he didn't appear to change speed or direction or do anything that might stop the invader from catching them, she called out her insight.

He looked back without slowing, head cocked over his shoulder so she could see the incredulous smirk on his face.

She frowned. He didn't believe her.

Stopping abruptly in the stone passage got his attention.

Forced to stop, or leave her behind, he whirled. Her backpedaling was the only reason he didn't scoop her back onto his shoulder. Seeing she wasn't backing down, he stopped coming after her. "You're serious."

Dee was too relieved to be mad. "Yeah, I'm serious. He's behind us, catching up."

He studied her face a moment longer before shrugging. "Very well."

Pulling his sword in his right hand, a long knife in the other, he paced past Dee, waiting for their pursuer.

Somewhere along the route, Dee had lost the weapon Atkins had given her. She cursed her uselessness. After so much time being trained by the best, even showing the best she could hold her own, she continued to be the damsel.

Her inner-voice was cut off before it continued her self-rebuke when Zosma appeared. His raging energy surprised her. His seriousness about getting her was not what she expected, as she hadn't expected on of them to claim her.

A sword materialized in Zosma's hand. He stalked forward, halting ten meter from his quarry. "Pollux, you served me once. Would you really try to take my life now, over some girl none of us know?"

Pollux's voice was icy calm. "You claim to know her."

Dee's muscles tensed in anticipation of his answer.

The intruder tried a different tact. "I'm not sure I understand this play of yours to whisk the girl away. Your brother seemed surprised. Very unlike the two of you not to be in perfect sync."

"There was a deviation from how we thought the day would go." The Twin barely moved, patient to wait for his perfect opportunity.

Zosma smiled, almost laughing.. If he was mad at the unfolding events, he hid it well. "Yes, I imagine you didn't see this coming. You realize how weak your House really is. How easily I could come through and take all of you if I wished."

"Yet, you don't. Why is that, I wonder?"

Dee wished she could see the Twin's face to see what look smoldered behind his eyes even as his voice remained calm. Whatever was there brought Zosma forward in a flurry of anger, so easily parried, it was the Twin's turn to laugh. "Careful your anger doesn't ruin this moment for you. Or, is it already ruined since I'm the one with the prize?"

Zosma backed away. "Where will you take her? There's nowhere I won't find her. Not again. Not after all it's taken me to relocate her."

"Which begs the question: Why has it taken so long to find her if she's been yours all along? It's not like you to keep such poor care of what is yours."

Zosma managed control, frowning at Pollux's words. "It is unlike me, isn't it? A gross failing on my part. So long had I gone with poor results that I no longer paid attention. When this ones numbers came back more promising than any other, I raced to find out the details. Little did I know, I'd been lied to by the ones who'd been in charge of that installation. A false identity had been given."

The anger in his face was enough to send a shiver through Dee, and she wondered who it was that had been brave enough to lie to him.

Not dissuaded by Zosma's tale, Pollux mentioned conversationally, posture still set for battle, "Either way, we might just call *finders-keepers.*"

"Finders-keepers?"

Pollux laughed at Zosma's confusion. "Finders-keepers. Whoever finds becomes the keeper."

Zosma's frown deepened. "Not in this. In this, there will be no keeper that is not me."

He pressed forward, this time intent on breaking through to the girl who watched, overwhelmed by this new player and all he claimed. Her mind raced backwards to the night of the fire, willing her brain to give up information that might corroborate what Zosma suggested.

"You did this to me?" Her voice croaked.

Pollux perked his head but didn't turn around. Zosma's eyes found hers behind her guard. His voice softened. "I have sought long and hard for you. We lost much in that fire. We thought you'd been lost, too."

Dee stared at Pollux's back, eyes still not seeing the space around her, only the burning inferno that had taken her friends. "You found me."

"We weren't sure. We were never sure. Hamal's scheming got in the way of too much."

Now, Dee's eyes flashed upwards, meeting the fatherly gaze of the man who was looking at her like she was his long-lost daughter. It wasn't the look she'd expected, and it tempered her anger. "You tried to kill me."

"If you weren't what we thought——"

"——those things would have killed me!" She cut him off, taking a step towards him in her fury. "They almost did. If not for Hamal..." Gritting her teeth, she screamed in her head. She would not break down. She would not lose it right here.

-*At least you're not throwing up in the bushes.*-

Her hands clenched. In her mind, she flew forward, clawing at his face with enraged passion. In reality, she maintained her stance behind Pollux, afraid to let loose her will in fear the Rishis might be forced to kill her.

"I have all the answers you seek. I can show you those things you've forgotten."

Dee looked up, caught by the idea that she might learn the truth, but also stopped by the very same thought. Did she want to know how this was done to her? Did she want to see those last moments of her friends' lives before the fire took them all?

-*He tried to kill you!*-

The voice pushed her to violence.

Instead, she bowed her head under the weight of an impossible decision. "Why didn't you just bring me to you? Why this convoluted game?"

Pollux chuckled, answering for him. "Because he was scared of our reaction. Of all of us. If he'd simply picked you up, everyone's spies would have known, and we'd have been all over him, forcing him to show us what he'd found."

Zosma stepped forward, face snarling. "You would have had no right!"

This time Pollux laughed. "Except you didn't do it. You knew we'd heard the rumor about your science. Your blood experiments that Zibanitu forbade. You knew we'd put you down for it. You knew you'd never survive what would follow."

The end of the corridor erupted in fighting. It was Zosma's men pushing through the Twins' defenses to follow their Master. Castor's voice called, "Zosma, it's over. Surrender to us and avoid this fight."

Zosma turned perpendicular to the Twins. Giving Castor an imperious look, he threw back his head and laughed. The sound belied his attitude over Pollux outing his cowardly schemes. "Surrender? To you? Have you forgotten it was I who elevated you to what you are?"

Castor paced closer, sword in each hand pointing away from his body at the floor. "You may have taught us the art of war, but it was never you who put us here."

Zosma frowned as if reminded of some truth he'd rather forget. "You worked under me. I brought you up. *I* raised you from nothing!"

Dee's eyes widened as the Rishi's rage peaked. A rage masterfully controlled.

She'd taken a step back without realizing it.

Castor continued to force Zosma's attention on him. "Yes, you did teach us. Cared for us. Then, you abandoned us to fend for ourselves when we were blamed for failing to win your war. We owe you nothing!"

This last word was punctuated by the perfect sync of brothers rushing forward.

In her head, Dee clearly heard Pollux's voice command her to run. Without thinking, she did, turning to follow the corridor wherever it might lead.

She ran. The sounds of fighting behind her growing quieter as she moved farther through the darkened corridors of the Twins' secret underground world.

-Why always underground?-

She didn't know how she knew she was underground, but she was sure of it just the same. She'd come a long way from the towering helicopter pad on the top of the skyscraper.

She took random turns as her feet propelled her, not sure where she was going, but even less sure it was safe to stop running.

-You've been running for over four years. Maybe it's time to stop.-

As the words echoed through her mind, her sprint slowed to a run, then a jog until finally, she was still, standing silently in the dark.

She hadn't been running. She'd been avoiding. Avoiding what'd been done to her. Avoiding facing it.

Even before that, it had been the same. Since her father died.

The tingling in her skull pierced through her. She turned, knowing one of them had caught up to her.

The question she couldn't answer was, which one was it?

EPILOGUE

"You're not surprised." Her tone held an edge only someone not used to being taken advantage of could hold.

"We had to draw him out."

"You let him know where we were going?" There was incredulity now, temper flaring. "How did you know it was him and not Han?"

Zibanitu looked away, disgusted by the use of the name that was blasphemous in his House. Composing himself, he turned back to the irate Rishi filling the screen in front of him. "I didn't know. Now I do."

"You risked her. You risked all of us!" Shock overrode her anger. She didn't even try to hide the expression from her face.

Zibanitu allowed an ironic smile to play over his features, voice even. "Risked you how? What could be done to you? Zosma wouldn't dare, even if there was some danger he could serve you."

"But, the girl—"

"The girl is his prize. He wouldn't risk her either, of that I was certain. Now, he will be forced to explain his case to the Council, where we'll hear firsthand what he's been up to." A touch of annoyance that he was forced to explain himself laced his words.

She breathed relief. The slight that he hadn't let her in on his plan overridden by the knowledge that the girl was safe. "So, you know where she is."

"No."

Amalthea was stunned speechless, a feat that hadn't occurred in a thousand years. She sputtered, trying to formulate a cohesive thought.

Zi smiled kindly. "You thought the Twins were in on it? No. Their role I did not anticipate."

Amalthea nodded, thoughtful, long years teaching her how to remain calm in the face of such sudden, unfortunate news. "Pollux was quite taken with her."

Zibanitu raised an eyebrow but didn't ask further after the point. "I had expected Zosma's success in capturing the girl, but this is an even better outcome. They can't stay hidden too long and it makes our bargaining power stronger. Also, it pushes the fighting farther to the future."

"You anticipate fighting for her?"

He gave her a penetrating stare. "Would you have let it go?"

She squared her shoulders. "I would not let it go."

They locked eyes in a look of understanding that reminded Amalthea of why he had become their head. Even in the moments he seemed to act outside of reason, or practicality, or even feeling, he chose the best path for the long game. Only once had he ever failed them, and that couldn't be placed solely at his feet.

He nodded. "When the others hear, I feel they will all want their time with her. A curiosity like this will garner everyone's attention."

I t was dark.

Not complete blackness. He could make out the edges of the door across the room.

He closed his eyes, forcing memory from behind the fog in his head.

There was no recollection of where he was or how he'd gotten there.

He opened his eyes, exploring the space in the hopes that something might spark his memory.

Slowly, he sat up, listening for some sound that anyone was near.

There was only quiet, his body rustling against the stiff sheet draped over him a loud jolt to the deathlike silence.

With precise motion, he slid his feet to the floor, hands pressed into the bed at his sides. He closed his eyes again.

There was nothing. No past before the moment he woke in this space. No name he recalled. No life to think on.

His head lifted as the door opened.

DEE'S ADVENTURE WILL CONTINUE IN:

WE ARE FOREVER

A whirlwind.

It was the only word she could think of to describe the past week. A week of rushing from one place to the next. Hiding in shadow. Avoiding contact with everyone including random strangers and known associates. Her cell phone was miles behind her, atomized by Pollux's foot. All part of some forward direction whose endpoint was never divulged.

If Desiree ever thought life as a fugitive might be romantic, she was long past it. A full nights sleep was a thing of fantasy. Hot food a myth. Jumping at shadows was more than an expression. The palm of her hand was imprinted with the handle of the long knife Pollux had procured for her.

She'd learned not to ask questions. She'd stopped attempting small-talk. There was never answer or response.

So, she'd resigned herself to this scary world where she was hunted. Those days at home, training with Hamal, wondering when the next thing might come was nothing compared to this.

Then, they'd arrived.

All was quiet. All was serene.

After three days, Dee was bored to tears.

This morning of the tenth day, up before dawn, wrapped in a heavy, home-spun blanket, Dee stared out over her new world. Settled close to thirteen-thousand feet above sea level, the view was spectacular.

The wood-planks of the balcony where she stood, red paint clean and fresh, kept her from plunging to the mountain valley below. A year ago, the height might have forced her through an exercise in panic control, but she'd found so many other things to worry about since then.

-Hamal would be proud.-

Dee smiled sardonically at the voice in her head. As awkward as the last encounter with her mentor had been, she couldn't help wonder how he was doing. What he was doing. With too much time to think, she'd struggled to keep her thoughts from slipping to obsession. Her safety in question and her life on the line, she knew Hamal shouldn't occupy any of her thoughts. It was most likely she'd never see him again anyway.

Ignoring the hint that she should think of other things, her eyes lost focus on the surrounding majesty so she might better focus on her reminiscing their time together. He'd taught her so much, all at massive risk to himself.

Unbidden, the kiss they'd, literally, fallen into came to mind. Would things have been different if they'd let their attraction pull them closer? More likely than not, Hamal would be dead.

She ignored the constriction of her throat at the idea, Daniel's words on the matter coming to mind: *His feelings for you. They need to be tempered. If you share his interest, you need to forget it.*

Hamal washed from her thoughts by the only other she'd consider friend, Daniel's presence had helped her more than she'd like to admit during her stay at Amaltheum. That she hadn't been able to say goodbye to either before she'd left for São Paulo weighed more heavily on her than she'd like to admit.

She gripped the banister, using the discomfort of its icy exterior as an anchor to bring her thoughts from their inner-reverie and lifted her eyes to the panorama blossoming under the rising sun. A part of her hoped to never leave this mountain retreat.

It was a third Rishi's House she stood in. As far removed as the Twins' had been from Amalthea, she couldn't get enough of just staring out the windows. There were moments here, full and unhindered, that she forgot her troubles, her mind lost to the majesty of her surroundings.

Nestled into the crevices of the mountainside, Asellus' compound was a marvelous feat of architecture, and the perfect place for Pollux to hide her. Her brain struggled to envision its construction, but the peacefulness of being so removed from others explained why the difficulty was worth the undertaking. Here, Dee had learned to breathe deep and free again.

She leaned forward to better catch the wind in her face.

A bright red awning stretched over the terrace she stood on, its red color matched to the banister she held on to. Below her, marring the perfect view, was the roof of a lower building.

The wind lashed again. Dark hair that had grown to her shoulders over months in pseudo-imprisonment whipped her face so she ducked her head instinctively into the blanket wrapped around her, her thoughts as wide as the view around her.

The Rishis had a weak truce. That much had been explained. But this last attack, the attack that had Pollux scrambling to relocate her across the world, had broken that truce. What that meant for her, she didn't know. What it meant for any of them, they wouldn't tell her.

Asellus, a matronly woman whose kind expression had set Dee right at home here, refused to speak of it, and the Twins had followed suit. Despite the looming threat of an ancient race bent on destroying her, or not, this place allowed Dee to repress her stress. The serenity wrapped a veneer of safety over her eyes. Her simmering rage dampened. The idea that things would be okay, really okay, settled in her thoughts. Even questions of how Zosma had gotten inside the Twins' domain or how the how these Rishis could be so bad at keeping her safe seemed trivial when considered in the shade of this peace.

Her inner-voice, that nagging sidekick who seemed to enjoy pushing the worst of reality into her face, continued to prod her to take her life into her own hands. Not trusting she possessed the facilities to do that, contemplation was as far as that topic ever got. There was still too much she didn't know to risk going off on her own. And what would she do? Try at the normal life her and Mike had talked about? The life he thought she was off starting at this very moment. If he knew what she was really doing…

The banister underneath her hand groaned against the pressure she applied.

Using her mastery of compartmentalization, she blocked how awful she'd been to him, burying it for a future time after she figured out current predicament. *What's done is done*, her father used to say. *Now, what will you do?*

She spun from the scene, chased by guilty thoughts and the rising sun that told her she was late to the day's first meditation session.

The simple room that was her sleeping quarters enveloped her in the warmth thrown off by the refrigerator-sized hearth. Asellus had never bothered to update this place with central air, and whatever system provided the electricity was spotty at best. Dee had learned not to rely on having much light once the sun was hidden behind the looming mountains, or to expect the temperature to be above frigid.

Moving around the room, another compartmentalized thought slipped free, the answer to which might solve all her problems: —-*Or compound them into a suffocating heap.*-— Zosma's claim that he was responsible for what she was. His booming voice in the theatre of the Twins' urban home had triggered nightmares she'd thought long behind her.

The idea that she had been created left her numb. Anger and

286

regret, guilt and sadness warred inside her, negating each other until she was left wrung out. She should be furious at the one who'd claimed her. She should rage against what he'd done to her. Instead, she just wanted an explanation. She was tired of running, tired of the stress of the unknown.

At least the question of who was after her, and why, was answered. That the other Rishis were interested in her was a side-effect of this. Like any siblings, one couldn't have something without the others wanting it as well.

She bristled at this, annoyance quickening her movements so she was throwing clothes as she dressed for the day.

If they were all blood siblings, or if it was just a word they used to streamline conversation, she hadn't braved asking. Based on their dysfunctional relationships, she believed the point to be real.

-*And some of them think you're the newest addition.*-

The idea made her head hurt. With all she'd discovered she could do, with all she now was, learning she was a part of some ancient race of crybabies hadn't been on her radar of possibilities.

All she now was.

Her eyes swept the sparse room as the statement echoed in her head.

All she now was.

Her endurance and speed had matched Pollux's who was one of the most renowned among the renowned.

Before that, she'd sparred with Atkins, another whose prowess on the killing field was only matched by a select few. She'd even killed a couple of the Ophiuchus' Soldiers, another feat that told of her extraordinary abilities. In a matter of months, she'd gone from a spaz throwing up in the bushes to a warrior who could stand toe-to-toe with the best of the best.

A wash of empowerment pulled her posture straighter, damp-ened her negative thoughts of all involved. She hadn't respected Hamal's perspective. She hadn't had the awareness to understand why he pushed her. Too busy hiding, she hadn't been capable of tapping her potential or even understanding what that potential could be.

The calibration of this potential continued to be retooled. Training continued to be the focus.

Pollux, at times energetic and excited about his task of continuing her training, at others, almost fearful of her mortality, hadn't given her a day off. Not that she minded the distractions from too many thoughts that dragged her brain to insanity. She especially didn't mind being honed into someone who could protect herself.

Soon after their arrival in the mountains, Castor had caught up with them. Reunited with his brother, Pollux was pulled from his tendency to stress, though it seemed only because that was Castor's role. His apathetic watchfulness was the balance to Pollux's eager instruction.

Together, they'd showed Dee a laundry list of new tricks.

In direct contrast to her physical training with the Twins, Asellus taught the art of sitting around. At least, that's what Dee first thought. After only a week, she could admit the benefits from calming her mind, from becoming the master of her thoughts rather than a bystander pulled along by the constant directional changes of her psyche.

There was still a long way to go, but her nightmares had calmed, and her ability to let thoughts float away rather than catch her up in their mess was enough to make coming here worth it.

Asellus was a quiet woman. As tall as the Twins, her round face, older than the others, held small features. A busty upper body balanced out her willowy frame and the same motherly demeanor Amalthea had carried shown from her caramel eyes.

Despite her calm, Asellus wasn't patient with Dee's ideas on appropriate sleeping times. Dee's usual late night to late morning schedule was fast obliterated in this place. If Dee didn't show up by dawn, someone would be there to pull her out of bed.

Experience proved the reality of that.

Dressed in thick woolen socks, tight leggings under baggy fish-

288

erman's pants and a dense, coarse wrap-around jacket, Dee made her way to where Asellus would already be in session.

The one-hundred-and-eighty-degree panorama allowed dawn's light to brighten the room. Dee hurried, ignoring this lower level view of what she saw from her bedroom. At least here, the tall windows buffered the sharp wind. Stripping her warm outer layers and throwing them towards hooks set near the door for this purpose, she glanced up. The Rishi's knees hung over the edge of the lofted second floor. If Dee had considered she might not be late, this sight enforced her hope was for naught.

This second story, dedicated solely to contemplation, was where Asellus spent most of her time and where Dee spent each of her mornings. Through Dee's first week, she'd dreaded this exercise in stillness. Her brain didn't understand it. Her body didn't recognize it. Any explanation for what she should be doing, and why, was balked at. Sitting and staring out the window seemed like nothing but a monumental waste of time. Her body pulled her to motion before even half-an-hour had passed. Nervous energy, spawned from ideas she didn't want to face, made it impossible for her to sit still. Compartmentalized thoughts were too eager to slip their cages when faced with nothing but blank time.

On the third day, she hadn't shown up.

When a small, weathered woman had come to collect her, speaking a language Dee had never heard, Dee knew this non-activity activity was non-negotiable. Rather than continue to argue with a woman she couldn't understand, Dee followed with leaden feet, mind stewing in the vat of frustration.

She'd come a long way in the week since then.

Today, with a light tread, she climbed the narrow stairs pressed against the mountain-side wall. With gratitude, and apology, she pushed through the demarcation of quiet, and stepped onto the plank wood of the floor. She wondered if this dense cloud of serenity wasn't some kind of magic spell. Or maybe, it was just some residual projection from the Rishi's constant attendance. Either answer Dee would have believed.

Pollux joined them this morning. He sat with closed eyes, legs folded in lotus position, facing the Eastern window so Dee looked at his right side as she passed enroute to her own spot.

Asellus' position was at the Northern station of the landing, so close to the edge of the railless floor a quick glance might convince she floated at the brink of falling. Dee pinned her eyes to the back of the Rishi's head, knowing the matron's eyes would be open, staring blindly into the sky before her.

Dee hadn't gotten over how creepy this was. She didn't understand how Asellus could be so detached from the world while still conscious of all that went on around her. Dee could barely sit still and concentrate when her eyes were closed.

She smiled, remembering those first days when she would show up with delusions of demanding answers she imagined were rightfully hers. Every morning, these questions would fall away, erased by the peace of the room that overrode her grand plan.

It was this calm Asellus tried to teach, to find it and hold it, even after she walked away from her practice. It was this calm, Asellus explained, that would allow Dee to glimpse the true state of the universe.

Even now, after learning to enjoy these morning sessions, Dee wasn't sure she understood what the Rishi meant by this. She wasn't sure she understood what the Rishi meant by much. Not everything had changed since coming to the mountains.

Dee's smile morphed to a grimace when she thought about the day of her meltdown. It was that third day, the day she'd been dragged from her bed despite arguments for why she wouldn't benefit from whatever this was, that burned with embarrassment.

That morning, volatility was held from boiling over through effort that had her limbs trembling. The soothing nature of the room assisted in keeping her caged anger from exploding, but, like a spiteful toddler, Dee had refused to sit as was required.

Her inner-voice had egged her on, its position that she was long over-due for an explanation compounded by the idea that she should no longer be content to live by the dictums of whatever inner-squabbling was going on with the Rishis. At first, not as confident in her abilities to not die as her ego, she'd held back. But, pressed under the pressure of the Rishis meditative silence, her thoughts had continued to snowball until Dee finally exploded in a geyser of emotion.

Asellus' calm mask turned to watch her rage with sympathetic eyes without interruption or interjection. Pollux, standing from his relaxed repose at Dee's loud words, had remained at the far side of the room, arms crossed over his chest while leaning casually against the wall, eyebrows raised in a mixture of disbelief and mirth.

His amusement at her expense had redirected her rant towards him. A tightening around his eyes as he absorbed her scathing remarks was all there'd been to determine that they'd had any effect while he held Asellus' silent direction.

Their silence had pulled the wind from her tirade. With no feedback to respond to, embarrassment settled over her until it stifled her bluster to oppressed quiet. Deflated, too mortified to walk past the pair whose non-response was more impactful than any words could have been, Dee followed Asellus' gesture to take a seat with minimal hesitation.

Wallowing in the shame of her rage, Dee had found her first moment of detached perspective.

When the Rishi finally spoke, Dee's eyes had been following the soar of a giant bird floating on the wind. She kept her attention on this rather than turn ashamed eyes to Asellus.

"It is more difficult to see oneself as individual in this place. A conducive point for this task."

The kindness of the Rishi's tone had Dee hold back the lashing words that sprang to the tip of her tongue, her tenuous calm overridden by the wash of frustration that forever circled her mood.

-What the hell is she talking about? Just kill them all and be on your way.-

Reigning in the bite of her inner-voice kept Dee distracted from contemplating the possible sense that might lay in Asellus' words.

When the hush continued past comfort, Dee squirmed against the pull to speak. She'd said more than enough. Her ferocious rant still hummed in the air, and she had no idea what to say to such a nonsensical statement.

Asellus spoke again. "It is something even we have forgotten. *Existence* plagues us all."

She pointed a long finger ahead of her, tracking the motion of the bird Dee watched. "The Hornbill does not worry about its place. It simply carries out its duty, knowing in its essence those things it must do to flow with the world around it."

The Rishi lowered her arm and tilted her head as if studying some new curiosity. "Human nature has always acted at direct odds with that innate sense of belonging. A nature that has bled to infect those of us who remain." She sighed and added softly, "So far we have fallen."

Her attention had turned back to Dee, voice pitched like she was giving away some secret. "There was a long time that I was hopeful for our return to who we were. Now, I feel we are too trapped in this construct to ever escape."

These words had brought Dee's attention from the window to Asellus' face, hoping to catch context for what the Rishi spoke of in her expression.

-Is she a little bit mad?-

The idea generated another level of anxiety to settle in Dee's mind. She'd thought there couldn't be more apprehension, but this adventure was teaching her never to construct ceilings for anything. Regarding her emerging powers, this was a good thing to learn. Concerning the crazy surrounding these Beings, not so much.

Dee resisted the urge to glance at Pollux to see if his expression would help her decide how many grains of salt she should add to the words she was hearing. But Pollux wasn't necessarily on her side, so she'd refrained.

A staggering wash of loneliness had threatened her at that moment. Hamal's presence had given her a sense of companionship. With him, she'd no longer had to hide what she'd become. He'd been more familiar with what was going on than she had been.

Then, Daniel had stepped in to buffer her next layer of assimilation. She'd even begun to feel like she might fit in somewhere. While at Amalthea's, Daniel had played a critical part of raising the blinders from Dee's eyes about what she might be.

Things in São Paolo had happened too quickly for her to have time to be lonely.

She was good at being alone. She was an only child. Her mother died so long ago she couldn't even miss her. She was independent. Her introverted nature had kept her removed from the socialite-narcissism that was common of her generation. She'd been close with her father and had found a friend in Mike when she was at the age when true best friends found their roots.

Even so, there was a difference between being introverted and being sequestered. Especially when surrounded by the knowledge that her life was in the hands of these extraordinary Beings who may, or most likely not, have her best interest in mind. It would have been nice to have had someone to look to for support on her level.

"What does your life mean to you?"

Caught off guard, Dee's tongue froze in her mouth.

What did her life mean to her? Was the Rishi asking if she cared if she died? Or was it a question of purpose? Either way, she wasn't sure how to answer.

"I know I don't want to lose it." Dee stammered out a response.

Her answer from that day echoed in her thoughts in the present. She really didn't want to lose it. She didn't want to die, but she also didn't want to live under the thumb of another. She wanted to *live*, rather than hide and run and be protected from constant unknowns.

As she took the half-lotus position that was comfortable to her, she noted the others' hand positions. She mimicked the mudra they'd formed, curious at its use. Fingertips of each hand held together, she laid hers in her lap, rather than attempt to keep them raised at heart level like the Rishis.

There had been a classroom session after her rant day. So much information about mediating, there was little of it she could have recited back. The focus on seeing and feeling the world around her was outside her sphere of understanding. Maybe outside her care to understand.

She did remember the hand positions were called mudras, though she didn't remember what any of their uses were. Connection with the Divine. Connection with the self. Connection with other things she hadn't even tried to retain. At the time, there'd been no sense that she would care about any of this sitting around.

After a few deep breathes, she closed her eyes, changing her breathing pattern so she was holding each breath for a couple of seconds before forcefully exhaling. Feeling as centered as she had learned to be, she switched this pattern to steady in-and-outs, paying close attention to those moments in-between, when the breath ceased as the inhale turned to exhale.

Her mind wandered, thoughts of her journey with Pollux filling the blank slate of her mind.

The farther they'd traveled from São Paulo, the more withdrawn the Twin had gotten. Forced to accept his quiet introspection, wondering if maybe the separation from his brother wasn't causing it, she refused to consider it was regret for saving her that plagued him. Whatever it was, the infatuation he'd held for her at their first meeting was overshadowed by it.

A bell chimed, its echo shattering her thoughts, a reminder to focus her attention on her breath. *Some days will be more comfortable than others,* Asellus had told her. Evidently, this was a day for distraction.

Inhale.
> One.
> Two.
> Three.
> Four.
> Five.
> Pause.
> Exhale.
> One.
> Two.
> Three.
> Four.
> Five.
> Pause.
> Answers.

Dee continued to expect them and continued to be disappointed. Worried about finding out what was going on, she hadn't wasted time considering how to disentangle herself from a web she could barely make out the threads to.

Now that things were more explicit, in their convoluted way, she thought her priorities might have to change.

-Or be created.-

The point from her subconscious was valid. There had been no priorities before, only an apathetic attempt to do as she was told in the hope she'd be freed because it was the right thing to happen.

The bell chimed again and her attention snapped from introspection to breath.

This time, a smile tugged at her mouth that a mere instant had passed before her thoughts fell to distraction.

"The trying is causing your failure. Relax, and let the mind do what it will. When you find yourself drifting, don't judge it, don't be angry about it, don't be humored by it, simply bring your thoughts back to the breath."

Dee didn't open her eyes. Instead, she pictured Asellus' patient manner explaining a thing the Rishis had long mastered. As old as she was, Dee wondered if maybe Asellus hadn't invented the practice.

It was this vastness of time that stretched back to the Rishis origins that Dee's thoughts moved to. She allowed the abstract of the infinite draw her mind to blankness. She let the beat of her heart draw her focus, so she was pulled into a peaceful state as exhilarating as it was calming.

Her heightened hearing made the sound of her heart easy to find, its steady drum anchoring her attention in her chest. She envisioned the circulation of blood the organ drove. This circulation expanded to a sense of a greater connectedness to her surroundings. The movement of the liquid in her system synched with the movement of the wind outside and the water cutting through the mountains and on and on.

The tendrils of oneness crept on her so she barely noticed its genesis, but was reminded of what the Twins' had shown her about their origins.

The image she'd been shown of Sabik Han was of a large, bronze-skinned man whose well-defined physique screamed strength. It hadn't been his perfect form, naked to the world, that drew her attention, but rather, the feeling of what he was trying to do. It hadn't been well explained in the telling, and Dee wondered if the others even knew what the Ophiuchus' goal had been. Whatever it was, it had failed, and the direct result was their immortality.

Tying them to the Earth. She remembered that point distinctly. The point that Sabik Han had thought their technology was taking over what they were and wanted to fix it.

The bell chimed again.

This time Dee was brought back to her focus with no aggravation or laughter to further distract. Her sense of calm remained as her awareness floated on the reverberating sound that faded to silence.

Silence.

Tying them to the Earth.

Breathe in.

Breathe out.

Silence that was akin to darkness, as the warmth of a thick comforter covering one from a cold night fell around her. Darkness, as chased by the light, when the realization that all is well, that all is on its path and no other way could be or has been.

Tied to the Earth.

Golden silence. Teaching silence. Silence connected directly to the source, to that energy that threads the world and its creations as one.

Minutes or hours or decades might have passed, there was no deciphering.

In this time, darkness faded to the brightness of new dawn, hope and the promise of granted dreams.

Breathe in.

Breathe out.

This fading linked directly to her awareness of her physical body seated in this physical place as the sanctuary of her mind let her ego resume its life in her.

Tied to the Earth.

The blankness of her mind conjured an image of the planet as seen from space, the moon's grey sphere just visible near its green and blue parent. Waves of energy were observed, though she couldn't explain what form they took that she was able to perceive the invisible lines that moved around and through the sphere in circular patterns that spawned and vanished at the poles and equator.

Zooming in, pinpricks of illumination, their locations changing, sometimes in line with these energy patterns, sometimes taking their own path, were seen.

As in a dream, Dee understood what she was looking at as some intuitive force inside her awakened. The Rishis were tied to the Earth as literally as a tree was rooted to the ground, or as the oceans pulled their vivacity from the planet's core. This literal connectedness explained their power. Able to pull directly from the vast potency of the world, their power would be infinite, as would their life.

But as powerful as they were, they were far from omniscient and their strength, while impressive, wasn't as scary as this connectedness suggested.

Was this what Asellus had been rambling on about when she said: *our return to who we were.* Had their power waned over their long lives? Had this oneness been lost, setting them adrift from what they'd once been?

The bell chimed.

Dee's thoughts shattered to blissful calm.

Her own connectedness expanded.

As if some exterior layer was cracked, Dee poured outward, tendrils of herself sparking against the ebb and flow of the world around her.

Overwhelmed by the sudden shift, her nerves tingled, and her breath caught, but she refused to let go of whatever it was she'd found.

Except, it was a fleeting thing. Whatever shield she'd cracked reassembled itself and cut her off from this greater macrocosm.

Heart pounding at the strangeness of where her awareness had drifted, Dee accepted its passing, knowing she would search for it again. Knowing she would find it again.

Silence.

Breathe in.

Breathe out.

A VERY SPECIAL THANKS

To my sister, Kim whose enthusiasm for this story kept me going when I'd forgotten it was supposed to be fun.

To Stephanie and Mom, who read it when it wasn't quite ready, but said it was fine all the same.

To my sister, Christina, who showed everyone at work and found me new fans.

For Dad, whose subtle excitement for my work was as loud as the rest.

To Jason, who deals with me at my most crazy, and adapts as needed. He cooks for me too. And of course, designed this fabulous cover.

To Bethany, who gave great feedback and sacrificed much of her own time to help me see what I'd missed.

To Nicola Rose (@nicolaroseauthor), my first real IG partner. Thanks for cheering me on... and of course feedback... and making this creation better.

To Benjamin Kinney, who came into the process late, but made it the best it could be.

NanoWriMo: where I learned how much I could actually get done and that this dream could be a real thing.

To the wonderful #amwriting #writersfollowwriters and

#ishouldbewriting community on Instagram where I find daily inspiration to continue this journey. May your muses continue to sing.

To those on Unsplash who graciously allow us to use their photos for our own creative endeavors.

Of course, to all the readers who took a shot on the unknown by following me on this adventure. If you haven't already, you should grab your travel pass for more free adventures on my website: CMMartens.com

REVIEWS ARE LIKE GOLD TO AUTHORS!

They really do mean so much to us, even if it's only a few words.
Whether you loved or hated this story,
please consider leaving a review on Amazon or Goodreads.
Who knows, you might help someone find their next favorite book.

Much love and appreciation to you!
CMM

Review this book on Amazon and Goodreads
or your favorite book site

LEND IT!

ALL MY BOOKS ARE LENDABLE THROUGH KINDLE.

RECOMMEND IT!

If you think someone else might like this book, please help pass the title along to friends, readers, groups, or discussions.

FIND C.M. MARTENS:

CMMartens.com
IG: author_CMMartens
Twitter: AuthorCMMartens
Goodreads: CMMartens
Amazon: Amazon.com/authors/cmmartens
FB: authorcmmartens

Sign up for a free travel pass to explore C.M. Martens' parallel
worlds and receive first looks, freebies and updates at:
Cmmartens.com

For email updates of new releases,
follow CMMartens on Amazon:
Amazon.com/authors/cmmartens

ABOUT THE AUTHOR

First and foremost, C. M. Martens is a reader. Not having enough books on hand is why she first began to spawn her own tales. Desiree Galen's genesis come from those days, a generation ago, when she had no idea how to form a cohesive story. Long years later, C. M. Martens hopes she's learned a thing or two about that. She will continue to create new realities and adventures and hopes you'll come along for the ride.

Discover more of her parallel worlds at: CMMartens.com

Made in the USA
Middletown, DE
31 August 2025